G000123497

Becoming Catherine Bennet

A Pride and Prejudice Sequel
of Lizzy, Kitty, and
Miss Anne de Bourgh

Joseph P. Garland

DERMODY
HOUSE
PUBLISHING

DermodyHouse.com

Copyright © 2022 Joseph P. Garland
All rights reserved.

The characters and events portrayed in this book are
fictitious. Any similarity to real persons, living (which seems
unlikely since this story is set over 200 years ago) or dead, is
coincidental and not intended by the author. To the extent
characters or places or situations first appeared in Jane
Austen's *Pride and Prejudice*, their inclusion is intentional, as
is one phrase borrowed from Miss Austen's *Persuasion*.

No part of this book may be reproduced, stored in a retrieval
system, used in the development of any type of Artificial
Intelligence, or transmitted in any form or by any means,
electronic, mechanical, photocopying, recording, or otherwise
without the express written permission of the author.

ISBNs:
979-8-9868992-3-7 (ebook)
979-8-9868992-4-4 (paperback)
979-8-9868992-5-1 (hardcover)

The Cover: *Portrait of Mary Sicard David* (1813) by
the American artist Thomas Sully (1783–1872).
Courtesy of the Cleveland Museum of Art.

https://www.clevelandart.org/art/1916.1979.2

Characters[*]

I expect most readers know the main characters in this story. In any case, and perhaps to refresh, here's a list of who they were at the story's commencement.

The Bennets

Mr. Bennet
Mrs. Bennet
Jane Bennet (married to Charles Bingley)
Elizabeth/Lizzy Bennet (married to Fitzwilliam Darcy)
Mary Bennet (married to *Joshua Bowles*, living in a parish in the northeast of England, near the Scottish border)
Kitty/Catherine Bennet
Lydia Bennet Wickham (married to George Wickham)

The Neighbors in Meryton

Sir William Lucas
Lady Lucas
Charlotte Lucas (married to Mr. Collins)
Maria Lucas
Unnamed younger brother Lucas
Mrs. Philips (Mrs. Bennet's sister)

In Cheapside, London

Mr. Gardiner (Mrs. Bennet's brother)
Mrs. Gardiner
Four Gardiner children, two girls then two boys

---

[*] Characters not in *P&P* are italicized.

Netherfield

Charles Bingley (married to Jane Bennet)
Caroline Bingley
Louisa Hurst (sister of the above)
Mr. Hurst
Fitzwilliam Darcy (married to Elizabeth Bennet)
Fitzwilliam Darcy, II (Little Fitz: Mr. and Mrs. Darcy's son)
Georgiana Darcy (married to *Edmund Evans*; Mr.
Darcy's sister)

Rosings/Hunsford

William Collins (heir to Longbourn estate,
married to Charlotte Lucas)
Anne de Bourgh (heir and daughter of Sir Lewis
and Lady Catherine de Bourgh)
Colonel Richard Fitzwilliam (first cousin of
Anne de Bourgh and Mr. Darcy)

New Characters

Frances Elster (widow living in Exeter, Devon, in
the southwest of England)
Teresa Riordan (a maid)
Edwina Jaggers (working woman in Islington, London)
Abigail Johnson (Mrs. Jaggers's sister)

The Lawyers

Quentin Brower (London)
James Drain (London)
William Paters (Sheffield)

Pemberley

Michael Lewis (steward)
Mrs. Reynolds (housekeeper)

The Bennet Family, June 1, 1815

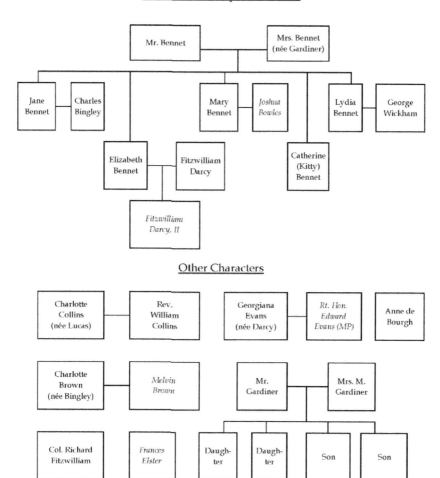

Other Characters

* Characters in Itallics do not appear in *P&P*

Chief Locations*

London

Brook Street (Darcy House)
No. 19, Mount Row (Bingley House)
Russell Square (Anne de Bourgh's house)
Grosvenor Square (Hursts' house)
Gracechurch Street, Cheapside (Gardiners' house)
No. 42, Theberton Street, Islington (Lady Catherine House)

Kent

Hunsford Parsonage (Collinses' house)
Rosings Park (de Bourgh house)

Hertfordshire

Longbourn (Home of the Bennets; entailed to Mr. Collins,
and will go to him upon the death of Mr. Bennet)

Derbyshire

Pemberley (Darcy estate)

Devon

Grove Road (Mrs. Elster's house)

---

* Locations not in *P&P* are italicized.

Here, the pins represent the significant locations, many in London. Rosings/Hunsford is the pin south of London. Longbourn's just north. Pemberley's near Sheffield. One can appreciate the distances involved, including to Exeter.

Contents

Introduction

Although this is perhaps a *Pride and Prejudice* "variation," I consider it more a sequel. I attempt to stay true to Miss Austen's story with the exception of a paragraph in the final chapter. There, Miss Austen, referring to Catherine, writes:

Kitty, to her very material advantage, spent the chief of her time with her two elder sisters. In society so superior to what she had generally known, her improvement was great. She was not of so ungovernable a temper as Lydia, and, removed from the influence of Lydia's example, she became, by proper attention and management, less irritable, less ignorant, and less insipid. From the farther disadvantage of Lydia's society she was of course carefully kept, and though Mrs. Wickham frequently invited her to come and stay with her, with the promise of balls and young men, her father would never consent to her going.

In this telling Kitty/Catherine does go to Newcastle, to Lydia and George Wickham, where she settles in.

I have tried to be faithful to the story, but any errors and any inconsistencies are, of course, mine. In particular, I must note that I am an American lawyer. I have endeavored to get the roles of barristers and solicitors recited properly. Insofar as I have failed, that, too, is on me.

Be assured that while this story is chiefly about Catherine and in large part Anne de Bourgh, Elizabeth Darcy is crucial to the tale and she and her dearest Fitzwilliam will be together at the end as they are at the beginning, an old and happy couple indeed.

*   *   *   *

A Book like this can only be dedicated to one person: Jane Austen. The process of writing this increased my admiration for her writings, not just *Pride* but her other books as well. Be forewarned. An author embarking on a journey as I have can only hope to give the reader some sense of AustenWorld. How well I have done so, if at all, I leave to my readers to decide.

Part I

Chapter 1. The News from Belgium

Mrs. Fitzwilliam Darcy was the first to hear the noise rolling down London's Brook Street early on a Tuesday morning in mid-June of 1815. Her room was still dark, but the shouting made it through the windows, which faced the street and were open slightly to give some relief from the warm night. It was a joyous sound, though she couldn't make out what was being chanted.

She stumbled her way to the windows and opened one wide. Dawn was breaking and she could see the revelers thrusting torches up and pulling them down. "God Save the King"? Yes, that's what it sounded like. She leaned out slightly and the morning air helped rouse her and now it was clear. It was a crowd of all sorts, visible in the first rays of the new, fine day. Servants. Toilers. Even some gentlemen. "God Save the King" and "Hail Wellington." They were marching and laughing and dancing. Probably to Hyde Park with their torches and makeshift banners and a few Union Jacks.

Before she could go to her husband's room, which faced the rear, he himself was through her door without a knock. "You've seen them," he said, with an excitement rare for him.

He stepped up to her, both of them in their nightgowns without a care that they might be seen. Without much of a care in any way, shape, or form.

"It must be news, good news," she told him as she felt his arm encircle her waist and they leaned out and waved randomly at the marchers.

Mrs. Darcy turned to her husband. "I cannot believe it, but we must have won. Surely Bonaparte is done for."

He tightened his grip and pulled her closer. They were both staring out, and he said, "Indeed. Bonaparte is done for once and for all."

It was not long before Bradley—the butler—came through the open door.

"A footman told me, Sir, Ma'am. He went out and they told him of the great victory in Belgium. Do you think it's true, Sir?"

Darcy turned to the servant. "God willing it *is* true, Bradley."

Bradley, suddenly aware of his impertinence, bowed and backed quickly from the room. When the door was closed behind him, Elizabeth and Fitzwilliam threw themselves together.

"Thank God it is over, finally. Thank God," she said, and her husband kissed the top of her head and echoed her words. "Thank God. Peace at last."

"You should speak to the servants," Elizabeth said, her right hand clutching her husband's left as they again looked out over the crowd that seemed to have grown and grown in just the last few minutes as the very day itself brightened.

"I shall," Darcy said. Elizabeth quickly put on a robe and in a moment, the couple stood on the landing overlooking the front foyer. Shouts arose from below and echoed about. The servants hushed when Darcy, with Elizabeth to his right, looked down across the wrought-iron railing.

"I see that you have all heard the news. It is a great day for our country, I think. A great day that will long be viewed as such and, I hope, will lead at long last to peace and prosperity."

"Peace and prosperity!" was hurrahed by the group below three or four times before Darcy's extended arms quieted them.

"Yes, peace and prosperity. Now, I must ask that one or two of you stay behind"—and the butler, cook, and a new maid promised they would and Darcy thanked them—"but for the rest of you, enjoy the day." With that, an eager footman rushed to open the grand front door and he led the rest—save for the three who remained—out into the growing mass of citizens celebrating a great day and, they hoped, a generation of peace and prosperity.

"They will enjoy it," Elizabeth said to her husband as she grasped his hand while they watched the rush to join the crowd surging west to the nearby park.

"Yes, Lizzy. It is as if a cloud were suddenly cleared away to reveal a breathtaking sky."

"There will be rain, you know."

"Yes. But not today, my dearest. Not today."

The Darcys were quickly dressed, and the crowd was gone, to Hyde Park or perhaps the Palace. Little Fitz, all one-and-a-half-years of him, was collected from the nursery and carried for the momentous four block walk to Mount Row and Number 19, the house Charles Bingley bought after marrying Jane Bennet, it being inappropriate that they impose on the Hursts—Mrs. Hurst being Bingley's sister—on Grosvenor Square.

Darcy lifted his son so he could bang the knocker as was his great pleasure and, to him, entitlement, and Bingley himself answered. "Uncle Charles!" was shouted by the child at the unexpected honour. The precious cargo was passed from Darcy to Bingley as Elizabeth rushed into the foyer, where she was met by Jane coming down the stairs.

"We were just coming to see you. Isn't it wonderful?" Jane said.

They had done much the same things some months before, only August 1814 it was, when they were sure Bonaparte was to become an historical footnote, sitting angrily but defanged and helpless on Elba. This time, though, the Allies would surely send him far from Europe and he surely would never return.

While the Bennet women went into the dining parlour where there was coffee and some breakfast—the Darcys having left far too quickly to eat what Cook made for them—the men followed.

"We know nothing other than what we heard from the masses in the street," Bingley said. "I dearly hope it is true."

"How could it not be?"

Bingley smiled at his friend, holding the handle of his cup between several fingers of his right hand. "This is not like you, Darcy, to be so...optimistic. I think it best that we wait for official news."

"You are right, of course. But it is so damned hopeful, do you not think? "

"I *do* think. But let us not count our chickens just yet. Let the others have their fun, but we must be prepared should these turn out to be a hoax and our hopes dashed."

But it was not a hoax and their hopes were not dashed as Wellington's dispatch from the town of Waterloo was circulated far and wide in London after its arrival the next day. However excited everyone was at the *rumour* of victory was nothing compared to what they felt with the *reality* of victory, and it took many days, nearly to the following Monday, for things in London to resume any semblance of normality.

In some places, though, things would never again be normal. A week after the first news arrived from the continent, Mr. Bingley received a letter. It was from Captain George Wickham's regiment late of Newcastle.

June 21, 1815

Mr. Bingley,

I am charged with providing you with sad news concerning the fate of your brother-in-law, Captain George Wickham. He was a brave man and a fine soldier. It was in the latter capacity that he suffered mortal injuries. He led his men in their defense of a crucial spot on the battlefield, until he and too many others were cut down.

His widow, your sister-in-law, is being cared for by her sister Catherine. The Army will do what it can to lessen the blow I fear both sisters, especially the young widow, will never surmount. I ask that you advise your wife and her sister Elizabeth (who I understand lives not far from you in town) at a time and in a manner as you deem most appropriate. A separate letter has been sent to Mrs. George Wickham's parents. I am also taken to understand that your brother-in-law Mr. Darcy may have useful information concerning Captain Wickham's family. If so, I would very much appreciate his passing it on to us so we can make the appropriate notifications.

Again, I am woefully sorry for the loss to your family and to the Royal Army and our proud Nation.

God Save the King.

Sincerely,
Reginald Turner
Colonel, First Foot Guards

Bingley stared at the letter before rereading it. He must see Darcy without delay. Together they'd decide how to tell their wives about their brother-in-law. He refolded the paper and placed it in an inside pocket and left for Brook Street.

Darcy was in but surprised by the early visit. At Bingley's request, they went into the library where, the door closed, Bingley handed the letter to his friend.

"So that is the end of him," was Darcy's immediate response to the news upon finishing the letter, and he would not waver notwithstanding his friend's stare.

"There. I have said it. He is gone, and I will say no more of him. I only wish that his good father and mine were still alive to see that he died a hero. But they are not. That's all I will say. Now we must tell our wives."

With that, he stood, leaving Bingley to stare up at the coldness, however justified in both men's minds.

"Sadly," he added, "I cannot help the Colonel about the family, he being an only child and his parents long gone. I will write to him telling him that."

Jane and Elizabeth would be back soon enough from their regular morning stroll, Darcy said, and after offering Bingley some of the house's refreshments, the two adjourned to the rear garden to await them. To tell them of what had happened to their suddenly widowed sister.

Darcy had not softened when he and Bingley sat with their wives some half-hour later in the drawing-room. After telling the women the news, Jane reminded the husbands that Lydia was with child, based upon a recent letter from Kitty—Lydia, Kitty said, being far too busy to announce the good news herself—and that she prayed that there had been no disruption in the pregnancy. Darcy could not resist adding, chiefly to Elizabeth, "Your sister made a dreadful mistake, but she was young and I shall not hold that mistake against her or against her child, whomever the father."

This struck his wife as most unkind, but Darcy checked her before she could speak.

"I know my dear who the father is. I will not be prejudiced against that innocent and perhaps in time the child will think me a kind uncle."

The rest thought it best to avoid the issue, at least for a time, so Jane and Bingley quickly said their goodbyes and walked back to their home.

All this prepared them for the letter Jane received two days later from Newcastle.

June 22, 1815

Dearest Jane,

I am so excited about joining you in London now that my dear, sweet Wickham is deceased. I will, they assure me, get a generous pension for the rest of my life, and I must take solace in that. They will also transport me and Kitty wherever I wish to go, and of course I said I wished to go to you. I am told that the army can only pay for us to go by post, but I have told the commander that your dear husband will pay the difference in cost for us to take a chaise to London and so we will be with you sooner than you can imagine. Our furnishings, meager as they are, will follow by some conveyance.

I think, however, that London may be too busy for me and my little one (when he comes). I do not dare ask directly, knowing D's unfounded prejudice against my dear Wickham and Lizzy's acceptance of that prejudice, but I should like to live at Pemberley. I am told it is vast and that there is more than enough room for me and my little one.

Perhaps, dearest Jane, you could broach this discreetly. Ideally without even mentioning that I made the request. You can make it sound like your own idea. "I think Lydia and the child will be better off in the country and where better than Pemberley?" Like that. You will think of something more poetic! I am sure, and Lizzy will never know the idea came from me.

You may wonder about my going to Longbourn, but I have lived as a married woman too long from the nest to return to it and believe I have suffered sufficiently to justify being accommodated in a place as heralded as is Pemberley. And, of course, I fear a lingering animosity in Meryton with respect to the debts by dear departed Wickham may have left there even if our dear Papa has resolved most of them.

I must end now and assume you will receive this before you receive me! I cannot tell you how pleased I will be to be with you again and out of the desolation that is the north of England. I will not need a large room when I arrive, but as I am with child, I think it must be larger than what you provide Kitty.

> *Your sister,*
> *Mrs. George Wickham,*
> *Widow of a deceased hero*

P.S. You need not burden yourself with informing dear Mamma and Papa about my misfortune. In addition to what dear Col. Turner has sent them, I have sent a letter. I have asked that they come to see me in your house in London and assured them that your sweet husband will have no hesitancy in paying for a chaise to take them directly.

After rereading portions of the letter and folding it and before seeing Lizzy, though, Jane went to inform her husband. He, upon hearing the news, had her tell the housekeeper to have three rooms prepared for the arrival.

With those arrangements set in motion, Jane walked to Brook Street. As it was plain that Lydia didn't want Jane to show her actual letter to Elizabeth, she merely informed her sister when they next met of what was necessary to be told. That the two youngest Bennets had invited themselves to the Bingleys' house in town—which is how Elizabeth understood what Jane said, though not as Jane actually put it.

Both the houses were already festooned in black draped down from each window. There were celebrations of the great victory everywhere but even in Mayfair there were those houses that had similarly gone into mourning.

Chapter 2. Two Letters

Jane doubted that Lydia, or Kitty, thought to inform their other sister, Mary. She undertook to do so.

By the spring of 1814, after Kitty had joined Lydia in the north and Jane and Elizabeth were long since married off, Mrs. Bennet had tired of Mary's moping about. Without her younger sisters to complain about or her older sisters to rein her in, Mary turned on Mrs. Bennet. Without Lydia to act as a companion, Mrs. Bennet turned on Mary. There were weeks during which the mother and daughter barely spoke—though Mr. Bennet counted these as among the most blessed of his life.

But Mary did find someone of like mind and like temperament on a visit to her aunt and uncle while in London in the spring of 1814. Joshua Bowles was a bachelor vicar with a fine living in Northumberland who happened to be visiting his ailing, and since deceased, mother in Cheapside at the time. He also happened to be carrying the desire to find a woman of a suitably suitable frame of mind who he could marry and with whom he could finally experience the "sins of the flesh" so as to better be able to counsel and perhaps comfort those of his flock who too often were guilty of committing this particular and particularly common sin.

Thus it came to be that Rev. and Mrs. Joshua Bowles were now happily ensconced in a parish not far from the Scottish border.

Happily for them (and sadly for everyone else), the couple reinforced one another in their view of the world and of the people who inhabited it. When Mary wrote to her sisters, which she did infrequently, her letters never strayed far from the sentiments she displayed when they were all living at Longbourn. The others wrote to her only when absolutely necessary.

And now it was absolutely necessary that Jane write to Mary. She gave the news of their brother-in-law's death. She added that she understood if Mary's duties prevented her from coming such a long way to London to see Lydia, though she was of course welcome to stay with her or with Elizabeth. And she asked that Mary and her husband pray for Captain Wickham's soul.

Elizabeth also wrote a letter, though not to Mary. Hers was to Charlotte Collins, who'd become even more of a friend after Elizabeth became Mrs. Darcy and especially after the sudden and untimely (but little mourned) death of Lady Catherine de Bourgh.

They wrote often and in mutual confidence, though once married Elizabeth truly never "polluted" Rosings Park itself until after Lady Catherine's demise. Mr. and Mrs. Collins both were altered after her passing, like flowers allowed to blossom after the removal of an obstacle that prevented the sun from reaching them. In this, Elizabeth was exceedingly pleased that what she once thought impossible—that Charlotte could ever be tolerably happy in the lot that she had chosen—had truly come to pass.

Much as she would have liked Charlotte to come to London, though, Elizabeth asked her to remain in Kent, at least until the initial grief felt by the Bennet family had eased. She promised she would try to visit come autumn, if not sooner.

Her friend's response came almost immediately.

Hunsford Parsonage
July 2, 1815

My Dear Eliza,

Mr. Collins and I are dreadfully sorry to have heard the news about Captain Wickham. Whatever our view of the man, it is sad that he was taken so young. It must be some solace to Lydia and the others in your family that he died in such a heroic manner, for which we must all be grateful.

As to dear Lydia, I pray that she can withstand the storm she is going through and that their child will come and be a healthy remembrance of his father.

Please express our condolences to her and tell her that Mr. Collins and I very much look forward to seeing her when matters have settled.

Your dear friend,
Charlotte

The letter from Mary—"Mrs. Bowles"—to Jane appeared a bit over a week after this. It said she and her Joshua would, of course, pray for the soul of Captain Wickham in the hope that his behaviour since leaving Longbourn so long before and especially the manner of his death would put him in good stead with the Lord. She and her husband (the vicar) opined that it was up to Jane to undertake the correcting of those faults in Lydia—and in Kitty, too—that were inappropriate and that Jane should guide their sisters to a more wholesome and pure life, one as a widow and the other sadly but unavoidably destined to be a spinster.

Mary concluded by saying that of course she and her husband (the vicar) were far too consumed with their mutual duties in his parish to even consider decamping to London for any period of time and that they appreciated Jane's understanding of this reality and anticipated that Jane would adequately explain this to her sisters and, most importantly, to their mother and father to whom she wrote separately to express her condolences and those of her husband (the vicar).

Elizabeth did not share Charlotte's letter with Jane. She merely told her of its contents in broad strokes, Jane did show Mary's to Elizabeth and when Elizabeth finished with it, she merely said, "it is as we expected."

Chapter 3. The Bennets' Arrival in London

At Longbourn, Colonel Turner's letter arrived one day before Lydia's did. Mr. Bennet opened it in the drive immediately after paying the courier. It was much like the colonel's letter to Bingley (and to many others). Mr. Bennet read it twice before folding it and slowly walking into the house to give the news he knew with honesty and some regret would be a much harsher blow to his wife than it was to him.

It was hot, and Mrs. Bennet sat quite unladylike in her favourite parlour chair, which had been moved nearer the window so she might get a touch of any breeze that made an appearance. She heard her husband enter the room but did not turn to him.

"When will this eternal—" she began but the stiffness of his presence stopped her query.

"What is it, Mr. Bennet?" but she was again halted when she saw the official letter dangling from his right fingers.

"At least it is not our girls," he said as he stepped towards her. He held his hand out and let her grab the colonel's letter.

She too read it but could only do it once, and not as deliberately as had her husband. It did hit her far harder. She let the document fall to the floor, and Mr. Bennet bent to pick it up and left his wife to contemplate the news, she being struck dumb by what she read.

The family's housekeeper, Hill, was in the hall waiting to find what happened, and Mr. Bennet told her that his wife's "favourite son-in-law has died a hero" and asked that she get something that might calm Mrs. Bennet's nerves and make sure smelling salts were at hand while he went into his library to meditate on the sad news about his least favourite son-in-law.

He was not there long when he heard a knock.

"Come," he said, and in came his wife.

"I must see my sister," Mrs. Bennet said. "I must see her right away."

"You cannot be serious, my dear. This news has struck you like a thunderbolt. You must calm yourself. Perhaps retire to your room so you can properly absorb what you have just now learnt. I can send someone to fetch her."

"My Mr. Wickham has died a hero, Mr. Bennet, and it would be a grave insult to his memory not to make that fact known far and wide. And I am sure we will be going up to London soon enough to be reunited with my girls and I must ensure that this news gets to my sister and others in Meryton—oh how they thought themselves so superior to my dear Mr. Wickham—without delay.

"If necessary, I will sit with my sister for a minute or two to recover my senses and I shan't be long. But it is my duty and I will fulfill it."

Mr. Bennet stiffened in his chair at this declaration and insisted that he would accompany her.

"No, Sir," his dear wife responded. "This is lady's work and I fear you will be too ready to display your disregard for this hero as you have too often done, especially with those other two."

"Darcy and Bingley?" he asked, with a tinge of annoyance.

"The very ones. Oh, I should like to have seen their faces when they learned that Wickham has forever established his position as greatly their superior without regard to how many estates they have and how many horses they can ride.

"No, Mr. Bennet. I shall go alone. I shall be proud to go alone to share this dreadful news with my sister."

"May I not comfort you?"

"Oh, Mr. Bennet. We both know too well your limitations in that regard. I will see my sister and be comforted by her."

Mrs. Bennet turned and called to Hill as she hit the hall, telling her she must be properly attired for going into Meryton and that Hill must find something black to serve as at least a temporary sign of the mourning she was flinging herself into until she could get the appropriate wardrobe.

And word did spread quickly through Meryton—indeed two or three other families received similar official letters from captains or majors or colonels—about the death of the "hero." Whether it was because of the late-afternoon heat or the weight of the news or a combination, Mrs. Bennet found herself quite unable to rise from her sister's parlour for her return to Longbourn. A message went in her place, asking that things be brought so she could spend the night at the Philipses', Mrs. Philips being Mrs. Bennet's sister.

Mr. Bennet was quite taken aback by the request and hastened to have Hill assemble what was necessary and carried it himself in a single-horse trap to his sister-in-law's. There, immediately upon his arrival, he found himself chastised by his wife for making such a fuss over her though, in truth, she was pleased by the sudden show of consideration (if not affection).

She sent him off though, that she might continue to commiserate with her sister and the two were soon sampling reviving liquor and swinging back and forth between the happy memories they had of Captain George Wickham and the ache of knowing that they would have no new such memories of his and they must be satisfied with Lydia and the child she would be bearing soon enough.

Mrs. Bennet had not yet returned home when (as we said) a different courier appeared. He handed Lydia's letter to Mr. Bennet, who again read it in the drive. It was longer, more detailed, and far less formal than was the Colonel's. Indeed, it repeated much of what Lydia wrote to Jane, with the addition of references to how she hoped her mother would bear up under the news now that her dear Captain Wickham has forever proved his worth and that she was longing to be reunited with her mother at Jane's—"for surely Jane will want us to stay with her"—in London.

The letter's "I can assure you, dear Papa, that Mr. Bingley will surely pay for the hiring of an appropriate coach to convey you and Mamma so that you will be comfortable on your journey" jumped out at Mr. Bennet. *I would not for all the tea in China have myself take further advantage of the kindness of Mr. Bingley and we will pay for our own coach*, he thought before he had retired to his library to again contemplate what had become of his family and what would become of it. Especially the fate of his two youngest and at times silliest of daughters. Perhaps the tragedy would push them into adulthood. He could only hope that it would do so.

But there only so much contemplation that could be done, even for a man such as him, and in two days' time, Mrs. Bennet had returned and was sufficiently recovered that the pair could set off to London to be of comfort to Lydia.

Mr. Bennet insisted that they be as little an imposition on his Bingley son-in-law or, for that matter, his Darcy son-in-law, as possible. It was agreed that they would arrive—in the carriage hired by Mr. Bennet—and stay with Mrs. Bennet's brother (Mr. Gardiner) in Cheapside.

They arrived there in the early afternoon of a rainy London day and had a note advising of this fact promptly dispatched to Jane. The expected response soon appeared, expressing the Bingleys' hope that Jane's parents and her aunt and uncle could come to Mount Row for dinner with the Darcys, where all could commiserate on the great loss the family had suffered as their period of mourning began.

When they were all later assembled in the large drawing room on the first floor at No. 19, Mount Row, once Jane had everyone's attention, she said, "I've received news from the north and Kitty said that she and Lydia should be expected to arrive on this coming Tuesday, in three days, and that they've taken up our offer to stay here."

"Is that all?" Elizabeth asked.

"That's all they say now. They've asked that we make one, or perhaps two, servants available to them while they adjust to London—though I think it is more Lydia who insists that she have her own servant and Kitty would be content to share—and that they do not know what will become of them or how long they will stay or where they will go when they've, as Kitty put it, 'outlived our welcome.'"

"Well, I think we can all agree," Darcy said somewhat thoughtlessly under the circumstances, "that that last bit came from Kitty and not Mrs. George Wickham."

Lizzy shot a look at him while the others looked to the floor.

Darcy lowered his voice so only his wife could hear. "I am sorry, but I will not be a hypocrite."

"Then you best be silent if you must when you are with them."

To this, he could add nothing, and he stepped away and the others resumed their discussion of what exactly needed to be done to prepare for the visit until it was noticed that Mrs. Bennet had drifted off as she sat on a couch off to the side. It was not long after she was gently roused that she and her husband and the Gardiners were on their way back to Cheapside so Mrs. Bennet in particular could recover from what had been a far more taxing and stressful journey than she had expected.

Chapter 4. Kitty and Lydia's Arrival

The two youngest Bennets arrived from Newcastle as planned, on the Tuesday in the Bingley-paid-for chaise. The footman jumped down before it stopped and had the door open as it rolled to a halt. The door to the Bingleys' house opened. The butler, Crawford, stood at the top of the marble steps, watching. The footman held out his hand, and Kitty took it to remove herself. From the pavement, she looked up at the enormity—to her—of the mansion.

She'd been to and even had stayed at the house for a brief period before she joined Lydia in the north but was still awed by it. She stood waiting for Lydia to follow her. And waited. The footman stood himself a statue as he too...waited.

Kitty turned and poked her head through the door.

"Are you coming?"

"Kitty," was the response. "I believe I am at least entitled to have the presence of my family, being the widow of a hero and with child and all, before emerging. Go and see where they are and why they are not here."

Kitty was long and painfully accustomed to this. At each stop along the way south, Lydia made sure everyone they saw knew her mourning was for a hero killed in the recent great battle on the continent.

Now on Mount Row, Kitty left the carriage in her own black dress. She caught the footman's eye and shook her head and walked toward the door. Crawford had not moved. Kitty asked where her sisters and parents were.

He nodded. "Very good, Miss Bennet. We were expecting you. I shall inquire within."

He entered the house. Kitty walked back to the chaise, where the footman was still a statue, holding the door and exchanging smirks with the coachman, who was keeping the two exhausted and steaming horses steady.

Kitty barely said to Lydia that inquiries were being made when Mrs. Bennet herself came bounding awkwardly from the house towards the chaise with Mr. Bennet not too far behind.

They'd come from the Gardiners' in anticipation of the widow's arrival but Mrs. Bennet had tired of staring out and fallen asleep on a sofa in the drawing room about half an hour beforehand. Her husband shook her awake when a footman came looking for them, and the two elder Bennets hurried down the stairs to the foyer and out the door.

When she heard the commotion, Lydia rose from the chaise's bench and, with the aid of the footman, set her foot down on the London pavement and awaited her mother's hug. Said mother swept by her spinster daughter to reach the more valued (and first married) one. Said hug was delivered with a "Oh, my poor dear" and earned "Oh, dear mamma, you cannot know how I have suffered" in response.

Lydia stepped back and patted her stomach. "No one can know what I have been through."

Her mother's arm again encircled her, and Mrs. Bennet whispered into her ear, "I cannot know, but I know you will be strong in these trying times."

The two again separated and turned. Side by side, they prepared to make their appropriate entrance into the Bingley house. They were quickly past Kitty and with the slightest of acknowledgements of its mistress, who had come from the house shortly after their mother had and who stood to the side, they were inside.

Instead of immediately following Lydia and her mother, Kitty turned to Jane. "Thank you so much for having us." She put her arm through her sister's, and they entered the foyer together.

*   *   *   *

WHEN HIS SISTERS-IN-LAW were settled, Charles Bingley allowed his good nature to take over. Lydia treated his house as if it were Longbourn and she were still a girl. After several days of her giving instructions to the house's servants without regard to the fact that she was a mere if honoured guest, even Jane began to chafe at her youngest sister's behaviour.

Elizabeth came each day to visit, and she and Darcy often dined there. It was on one of the latter evenings that things came to a head. When the butler Crawford bowed to those in the dining parlour and said Mrs. Wickham could not join them, Elizabeth stood. She threw her napkin to the side of her soup and was heading to the door when Jane jumped up and stopped her.

"She is a suffering and pregnant widow, Lizzy. You must let her have her moods."

Elizabeth said, for all to hear, that Lydia was also a spoiled brat and always had been and that it was time she rejoined her family, however briefly. Before Elizabeth could enter the foyer, Jane said she'd go. The dining parlour was silent, no one daring to taste any of their soup for a moment, awaiting whatever was going to happen next.

What happened next (if some minutes later) was that Lydia appeared beside her eldest sister, in a quickly donned and simple dress.

The next morning, the house continued as it had long done before the young widow and her sister appeared. Lydia, though, found herself not a part of it. She wondered whether Jane had had the chance to discuss with Elizabeth her going to Pemberley. When they next spoke, Jane confessed that she had not seen an opportune moment to do so but promised she would in the next few days.

For Lydia could not wait to be gone. As a widow and woman-with-a-child, she was greatly limited in what she could do in London (much as she had when she was last there, cloistered with her dear Wickham as he struggled to get his affairs in order and then (upon being discovered by Darcy) with her aunt and uncle and their annoying children before they could be wed). The formality of those visits to the Darcys' house when she made them were also wearing on her.

For her part, the very next afternoon Jane sat with Elizabeth at the Darcys' and repeated Lydia's request. She did not feign, as Lydia asked her to, that it was her own idea. Elizabeth was not such a fool.

"Well," she said, "we will be going there shortly for the season anyway and they'd be coming with us. I'm sure Darcy won't object to their going early, although it will create something of an inconvenience for the servants and we will have to make sure there is a physician there and available to care for Lydia's condition. And Kitty will accompany her. I will speak to Darcy."

Which Elizabeth did some hours later.

"If she is out of our hair, so much the better," he said. "I mean, really, Lizzy, she is such an unwelcome burden on Charles and your sister and on everyone who works at the house. I'd be happy, I'm afraid to say, to see the back of her forever, but this will have to do. I will write to my steward and Mrs. Reynolds. I'll leave them to make arrangements, including as to ensuring the availability of a physician or midwife," Mrs. Reynolds being the Pemberley housekeeper.

Elizabeth wouldn't admit it, but she shared her husband's desire to see Lydia gone, and so she quickly walked to the Bingleys' to give the good news to Jane.

Regarding her parents, they were still staying with the Gardiners but were tiring of London and were anxious about returning to Longbourn and planned to do so when the other members of the family headed down to Pemberley and now that journey would be made sooner.

Chapter 5. Kitty & Elizabeth

The routine at the Bingleys' was quickly established. When Bennets went for strolls, which were rarely long, they were properly attired in black. Jane and Elizabeth had arranged for some simple black frocks in crêpe to be prepared for themselves and their sisters and they were on hand when Kitty and Lydia arrived and within the week more elaborate yet not overly elaborate dresses were delivered to Mount Row.

Plus, plans were made for the young widow and Kitty to go to Pemberley. And on one of the last nights that they were at the Darcys' for dinner, Kitty took Lizzy aside briefly. She asked whether, "in confidence," they might speak the next day about a matter of some importance. She gave no hint of what that matter might be, and Lizzy found the request itself quite disconcerting: She couldn't recall Kitty *ever* speaking with her about anything *in confidence.* But as it was clear Kitty did not want anyone else to know about it, Lizzy did not mention it to Darcy.

The next day broke fine, though it had the feeling that it would grow to be very warm. Late in the morning, Kitty left the Bingleys' for the short walk to see Lizzy, who'd been half-watching for her from the sitting room and was on her as soon as her sister was in the foyer. She dismissed Bradley after she asked him to have refreshments—Kitty was quite warm from her walk—brought to her study, where she quickly led her sister.

"Darcy is out with Bingley prancing around on their horses and will not be back for some hours," she told Kitty in an artificially light-hearted tone as they settled and waited for something to drink and for Kitty to regain her composure.

The two had never been close. If there was an older sister who Kitty'd confide in, it was Jane. Just as was true with Lydia and even (although rarely) Mary. One never need fear being chided or not understood by dear, sympathetic Jane. One could hope but not be sure about Elizabeth. Yet it was Lizzy who Kitty wanted to see and there she was in Elizabeth's study, in one of a pair of armchairs separated by a round table on one side of the room.

They spoke simply as they waited for the refreshments, but as soon as the footman who brought up a curaçao concoction and a plate of biscuits closed the door behind himself, all calm vanished from the younger woman.

"I cannot endure it."

"Endure what?" Lizzy responded stiffly, very much taken aback by the rapid change in Kitty's disposition.

Kitty's eyes were watery.

"Lizzy. I am with child."

Elizabeth said nothing.

"I. Am. With. Child. Lizzy. Say something."

The statement left Lizzy speechless. She'd not been so shocked at news since those letters from Jane telling of Lydia's running off with Wickham. Those horrible letters that made her think she'd lost Darcy just when she'd found him. How long ago that was. And how long it was before she recovered her senses now. She leaned towards Kitty.

"Know that I will always love you no matter what." She grasped Kitty's vibrating hands. Her voice lowered, she added, "Tell me you know that" as she tightened her grip.

Kitty fought the tears but was finally able to say, "I know that. Oh, Lizzy. It's why I came to you and no one else. God knows I need your strength. I have been so weak and so so stupid."

Kitty was sobbing and looking down at her sister's hands and for a moment Lizzy didn't know whether Kitty would ever allow her to release them.

She is such a girl and such a woman, Lizzy thought. When she felt Kitty's hands relax, she pulled hers away to grab a kerchief from her sleeve and give it to Kitty to clear her tears. She then ran a finger across Kitty's cheek before moving her hand to Kitty's chin. That she lifted so their eyes could meet. When they did, Lizzy said with a love she never imagined she could have for this sister, "I am here for you. I will tell no one unless you wish me to. If you have no other friend in the world, you will always have me. Do you understand?"

Kitty nodded, having regained some control of her senses.

Relieved, Lizzy sat back in her chair and Kitty mimicked this.

"Good," Lizzy said. "Now tell me what you wish to tell me."

To Lizzy, all Kitty's youth and naivete and innocence were gone. Kitty, such a childish name, stood and began to pace back and forth. She seemed to be using her arms for balance or to allow herself to keep moving, and she sometimes seemed to be speaking to Elizabeth and sometimes seemed to be speaking to no one. Through it all she kept her voice low.

"I was such a fool. Such a fool. For years there was Lydia with Wickham, always mocking me. She did not mean to. She couldn't help it, and I cannot blame her. She got him first and when I joined her in Newcastle, I hoped to catch the eye of a fellow officer. But none was interested in 'Wickham's cast-off,' as I know some called me. Perhaps some thought he had...had me before he captured Lydia.

"I could hear them, Lizzy. I could hear them when they...when the two of them were having relations in their bed. Always laughing and grunting and I wanted to laugh and grunt like she did. At an officers' ball, Lydia and Wickham were gone early and left me alone and a Captain Johnson came up to me. He was new to the regiment. He asked if I wanted some air. I must have looked desperate. I don't think our absence was noted.

"It was cold and my coat was still inside. He put his tunic over my shoulders and said sweet things to me. Things no officer or any other man had said to me before. They always treated me like a girl, those other officers. It's how they treated Lydia too when Wickham wasn't around. Like the militia officers did in Meryton."

She stopped and glanced at Lizzy, who took it as a signal that Kitty wanted to be sure she was listening. When Elizabeth nodded, there being nothing she could say in the moment, Kitty resumed her back-and-forth pacing.

"It was dark, Lizzy, but he seemed handsome enough. And suddenly he kissed me. I was never kissed, Lizzy, and I fell deeper and deeper into it. It was glorious, like I always dreamt it would be. I pulled him to me. I promise you I pulled him and I felt his hands against—"

She stopped and suddenly returned from that cold place in the north to the Mayfair room where her sister was watching her intently and got back to her pacing.

"I am sorry. I will only say that together we…we had relations, leaning against the building. It hurt and there was some blood, but it was glorious too and I was afraid I was too loud, like Lydia often was. He hurried me back to the ball and as soon as we were through the door he bowed and I curtsied and he went to re-join his fellows and they all shared a laugh and I dared not think of what, or who, it was about.

"I waited a little bit and declined several officers who wished to have a dance with me by saying I felt ill and then one of the nicer ones got my coat and walked me back to our quarters. He bowed to me when we separated but once I was inside, I had to hear the moaning and grunting from Lydia and Wickham, and I fell asleep in my dress."

She stopped her walk with the end of her story and sat back on her chair.

"Tell me I was a fool. I know it."

They both knew it.

"And what of Captain Johnson?"

"Soon he fell right in with the others and treated me as all of the others treated me."

"Never again?"

"Just that one time." She stiffened. "I don't regret it. It was…well, it made me feel like a woman for the first time. But, no, I didn't care for him enough to pursue it, and we were again nothing but strangers and he took to treating me like a little girl. The way the others, even Wickham at times, did."

Elizabeth looked up and down at her sister and realised she was far from a "little girl" now. It greatly saddened her.

"Yes, Lizzy, it was four months ago."

"And Captain Johnson?"

"Dead in Belgium."

No more was said. Kitty stepped to the door. Lizzy jumped to her. She ran her hand across her sister's, which was holding the doorknob. After that slight intimacy, Kitty opened the door and she and then Lizzy went to the hall and down the stairs without another word, even as Bradley hurried to the foyer and opened the door for the house's visitor.

"We will go for a walk," Lizzy said. "It will do us both a world of good."

* * * *

LATE THE NEXT MORNING, Elizabeth went to the Bingleys as usual. Jane and Kitty joined her in the sitting room with tea and cakes. She and Kitty both tried to remain as nonchalant as possible until Jane left to take care of something, and Lizzy hurried to sit by her remaining sister.

"I have thought about what you told me," Lizzy said softly to the shivering girl, though there was no one to overhear, "and I will do everything in my power to help you and I promise you I will tell no one who you do not wish me to tell."

Before Kitty could respond to this happy news, the door swung open and Jane was back.

"What are you two speaking about with me out of the room?" she said teasingly, looking from one to the other.

"Oh," Lizzy said as she moved slightly away from Kitty, "Kitty was just telling me how she was enjoying her brief time in London."

"Yes, Jane," Kitty added. "Sometimes I wish I could stay with you and Lizzy here and not go to the country with Lydia."

Jane, a little surprised by what seemed to be quite a change of heart, said, "We shall be joining the pair of you soon enough." She sat near the others. "And for a fine girl like you, perhaps getting you from the temptations of town is the best course, at least for this season."

"Well, I'll look forward to your eventual arrival at Pemberley," Kitty said. Lizzy got up and suggested the three of them take a turn in the neighbourhood and that is what they did, nodding as appropriate to those they saw and who offered condolences to the three in mourning.

For all of this time, though, Kitty kept her arm through Lizzy's. And the three spoke more about poor Lydia than anything and how she was getting on. And Kitty for a change was glad that the young widow was virtually the entirety of the conversation.

As the Bennets approached Mount Row, Lizzy told Jane that there was something particular she wanted to show to Kitty in her house. This left Jane somewhat suspicious, but she let it pass and bid them *adieu* in front of her house, particularly after what she'd seen back in the sitting room, and watched Lizzy and Kitty continue towards Brook Street.

When they were clear of Jane, Elizabeth spoke, perhaps more harshly than she meant to.

"You must listen to me, Kitty. We must think of what is to happen to you and the child. You know you cannot keep it."

"But why not?" She gave a look of true defiance.

Elizabeth explained that not only would Kitty be ruined, so would the entire family. "You must see that," she said.

"What is it to me to be ruined?" Kitty said, looking down. Elizabeth reached for her sister's arm and stopped her, so they stood facing each other on the pavement.

"We would do what we could, Jane and I, with our husbands' money, but no one in our sphere would know you and I think no one would know us. How far the disease would spread I cannot say. But we are not high enough to be able to withstand the fury and shall all be ruined."

Kitty stepped back from Elizabeth, whose grip had tightened as she spoke. Now angry that her sister would think her so naïve, she said, "I am not as stupid as I once surely was. I understand."

"Please listen to me," Elizabeth said as the two remained off to the side. "I've thought long on it since we spoke. I do not know if it can be done, and I am very doubtful." She reached for her sister's hands, which were given to her. "I think we might get some support from Charlotte."

"Charlotte!? Mrs. Collins?" Kitty said, her voice rising. She pulled her hands away with some violence at the mere suggestion of depending on the horrible Mr. Collins for anything. "I cannot think what help *she* could be."

Elizabeth ignored the tantrum. "You do not know Charlotte as I do. She is a very sweet but practical creature. His patroness is dead and gone—"

"You mean Lady Catherine?"

"The same. She's been dead these two years and Charlotte tells me how different and improved Mr. Collins is since. He fell into a deep melancholia, she says, after the loss but the grief was replaced in time by...freedom. He is secure in his living from her according to her will, and Charlotte says he is a new and better man."

Kitty found this a bit absurd, especially when Lizzy added that she'd actually seen him read a...novel on a rainy day at the Parsonage!

If Mr. and Mrs. William Collins could further her cause, though, she would hear Elizabeth out. They resumed their walk.

"I'll write to her in confidence this afternoon. I assure you of her trustworthiness. She'll be able to tell me whether my scheme has any chance of success."

"Your 'scheme'?" Kitty asked, not unreasonably.

"I thought on it last night before I fell asleep. *If* we can get Mr. Collins to agree, I suggest that he and Charlotte take the child under their wing."

"Adopt it?" It was an outrageous notion. "He would never agree to such a thing, however altered he may be."

"I pray, hope, you are wrong. They—and you must not breathe this to a soul—have been unsuccessful in gaining a child of their own. It is something I believe they both very much want. She has only confided in me about it, I think. I think, though, that it might be a cause of hope for us."

"And me?"

"If they agree, we will arrange for you to continue your confinement with or near them. They would then fulfill their Christian obligations and take on the child as their own, as having been birthed by a woman unfit to care for it or who perhaps died in giving birth. Unlike with anyone else, you would know where the child is and perhaps you could someday meet it."

"If I am somewhere in the area, perhaps only ten miles away, I could see it." Kitty was getting more and more excited with the prospect. "And Lydia need never know."

"Nor would anyone else."

"Not even Jane?"

"Not even Jane unless you wished her to know. Or our mother. I wouldn't tell Darcy of my role. We will find an excuse for your confinement wherever it is and perhaps you can go to the Collinses in Kent until you are fit to return to society."

"Surely, Lydia expects me to be with her before and after her baby is born."

"We must convince her that she will be adequately cared for by others and that *you* deserve to begin to live your own life."

"She will never be convinced. If I am away from her, though, perhaps it will not matter what she thinks."

How they were to go about getting Lydia to agree to this was for another day and not nearly so important as convincing the Collinses. Lizzy would have to start with her letter to her dear friend in Kent and could only hope that he was no longer the man who said in a letter to Mr. Bennet after Lydia had run off with George Wickham that Lizzy had read but Kitty had not, that their sister's "death" "would have been a blessing in comparison" of becoming a kept, unmarried woman.

Chapter 6. Kitty and the Baby

In the autumn of 1813, Lady Catherine de Bourgh had choked on a chicken bone. She was at dinner alone with her daughter Anne, Mrs. Jenkinson (something of a monitor for the then-sickly Anne de Bourgh), and Mr. and Mrs. Collins. A footman and the butler tried valiantly to dislodge the small bone, but Lady Catherine turned blue before the others' eyes, and well before a servant could be sent to fetch a doctor, she was dead.

Now, nearly two years later, Elizabeth was as good as her word. Within a day of her conversation with Kitty, a letter was on its way to Charlotte Collins.

Since that death, Charlotte bore little resemblance to the mouse she'd shrunk into when she moved to Hunsford Parsonage. On her visits after Lady Catherine's death, Elizabeth and Charlotte took long strolls along the paths that the latter enjoyed on her prior trips.

"I know I should never say or even think it, Eliza," Charlotte told her friend on one of them, "but I can breathe this air so much easier now that she is gone. It is, I know, a horrible thing to say but I cannot help saying and thinking it, though only to you."

"And what about Mr. Collins? He seems a different man."

"Oh, he really is. I think his seeming lack of sense and his stupidity were fears of suggesting that he was anything but her loyal supplicant. He fell into it, I believe. He was so grateful to her for promoting him as she had. And how she treated me."

"Treated you?"

"Well, I suppose to someone like you it would seem she ignored me but, in her world, she thought doing anything for the wife of the parson was saintly indeed, and I didn't bother to try to alter that habit."

"I understand," Elizabeth had said as they reached the crest of a hill that offered a wonderful view across the dale. "She was a formidable woman who few dared cross."

"As you once did?" Charlotte could not resist teasing while they looked out.

Elizabeth had smiled and put her arm through her friend's.

"Things were so different then from what they are now. But we must be getting back."

With that, the two turned to return to the Parsonage and Elizabeth thought it one of the finest strolls she ever had with the woman Charlotte had become.

The funeral was well attended and officiated by the Bishop of Kent. Mr. Collins was grateful for the small part he was allowed to have in it. The de Bourgh chapel was far too small for all who wished to attend, so the funeral itself was held at the large church in Caterham some miles away. Afterwards, a long procession followed the hearse to Rosings Park and to the de Bourgh chapel. Her coffin was placed beside that of her late and beloved husband, Sir Lewis, in the family tomb. When the others left, Mr. Collins stayed behind, praying before it, tolerating the pain of the hard marble floor on his knees.

If there ever was a person whose death liberated others it was Lady Catherine de Bourgh. Were she to return a year after her sudden death, she would not have recognised her daughter, her vicar, or her vicar's wife.

It is not known whether Lady Catherine kept her word that she would *never* utter Elizabeth's name should the Bennet girl marry Darcy. One imagines, though, that she at least *thought* of that name after the wedding, and likely with some frequency and much vehemence. Elizabeth never dared visit Charlotte until Lady Catherine was gone, though she got to see Charlotte when her dear friend was going to Lucas Lodge and sometimes in Meryton too. But when Lady Catherine did die, Charlotte wrote to her of a lightness that descended over the Hunsford Parsonage and the whole neighbourhood.

Now, in the early summer of 1815 in a country that itself felt newly liberated, Elizabeth would never have written about Kitty to Charlotte were Lady Catherine alive. But she was not, and as promised to Kitty, the letter was written and dispatched. She told Kitty that it was gone, and the two of them were most anxious about receiving a reply. Lizzy assured her sister that she would immediately come to see her at the Bingleys' the moment it appeared, and Kitty was painfully nervous each day.

Finally, though, there *was* a letter from Hunsford for "Mrs. Fitzwilliam Darcy." The addressee took it to the empty sitting room and when she got there, she scanned it till she knew its tenor. She breathed a sigh of relief, said a slight prayer of thanks to the good Lord, and rushed to her room to change into a dress appropriate for a morning visit. In no time, or nearly no time, without an explanation she was out the door headed to the Bingleys'. When she arrived, she was about to say she wished to see Kitty when that woman herself hurried down the fine front staircase.

"I was watching and saw you hurry up the walk," she told Elizabeth when they were in the sitting room with the door closed. Elizabeth handed the letter to Kitty.

> *Hunsford Parsonage*
> *July 2, 1815*

Dearest Eliza,

> *I confess to being shocked by the contents of your recent letter—which I have destroyed. I admit to having what I believe to be the common view of Kitty when she was a girl and am heartened to hear that she has matured well and grown into a woman.*
>
> *About this other business. I have given it thought—hence the delay in my response—and believe it would be a good solution to have Mr. Collins and myself adopt the child. I am very lonely here since you are so far away and since Lady Catherine's death and its effect on Mr. Collins. It would be wonderful, I think, to bring new life into our small world.*

—Kitty looked up here and saw Lizzy smile before returning to the text—.

> *The obstacles, of course, are Mr. Collins and Kitty. I know of her dislike of him, but I must rely on your ability to convince her that our adoption is not only a good solution, but it is the best solution possible.*
>
> *As to my sweet husband, as I believe you have observed in your too few visits to us, he is wonderfully changed since Lady Catherine's death. I shall endeavour to work my charms*

*on him, slight as they might be, and will report the results.
But I shan't do anything until you advise me that Kitty is at
least receptive to your proposal.*

*Love to you and love to big and little Darcy and the rest of
your family. I so long to again sit and walk with you as we
did so often and so easily too long ago. Know that you are
often in my thoughts and prayers.*

Charlotte

Kitty began to cry at some point during her reading, and her sister rose and sat beside her on the sofa, taking the letter when she was done and placing it in a pocket.

"I hope it's true," Kitty said when she'd calmed, "what Charlotte says. I do not like him. Do you think he's not the fool he was when he appeared at Longbourn?"

"I wouldn't have thought of doing this if I didn't truly believe that having seen it somewhat with mine own eyes and more from what Charlotte says."

"I will always love Charlotte and if what you believe about him is true—and I don't doubt it!—if he becomes the father to my child, I will be happy beyond all measure."

For the first time since Kitty began reading the letter, she had a smile, and Elizabeth matched it, filled with relief.

"You realise that the world can never know," she added softly.

"Oh, Lizzy. If it is my baby and it has a good home, I will be overjoyed. I am not what I was before." She looked down, took a breath, and spoke into her hands. "Do you think I might still have *some* role?"

Elizabeth reached her arm around her sister and pulled her closer.

"We must wait to see what we and especially Charlotte can do with Mr. Collins. But I should think that we, you and I, perhaps may become dear and treasured 'aunts.' I expect no one will pay it a second thought if we are." When Kitty turned to her, again with a smile, though not so bright, Elizabeth said, "and because the baby will be a wonder, no one will doubt why we wish to spend time with it."

Kitty buried her head in Elizabeth's shoulder, and her sister let her have her cry until she was spent.

Elizabeth took the letter from her pocket and handed it to Kitty, who ran her fingers across it and nodded. Elizabeth placed it in her fireplace and lit it. They watched it turn to ash, holding hands. Elizabeth opened the window to remove the smoke, and when the pair left the room, there was no trace of the letter to Mrs. Fitzwilliam Darcy from her great friend Mrs. William Collins. But within a day there was one going the other way that contained thanks and confirmation that Kitty did indeed wish Mrs. Collins to act in the manner suggested.

Chapter 7. Lydia Goes to Pemberley

By the time Charlotte's letter had reached the Darcys on Brook Street, Lydia was anxious to leave the Bingleys on nearby Mount Row. Other than going to services nearby on Sundays or for visits to the Darcys or wandering about the walled-in garden at the rear of the house, she remained indoors.

While members of her George's regiment stopped by for all-too-brief condolence visits, including the inestimable Colonel Forster (with his young wife, who once again proved to be a great source of amusement and diversion) when he got to town, she grew tired of the capital. At least the parades and balls celebrating the famous victory that cut into her heart had run out of steam.

Things got even worse when Kitty's mood brightened for reasons Lydia could not understand. If she didn't know better, she would have thought Kitty was trying to separate herself, especially with how she seemed to be switching her affections to Lizzy (of all people). While the young widow remained confined to the Bingleys' house, Kitty was more and more going for walks with Lizzy (and sometimes with Jane too), abandoning her for it seemed hours at a time.

It was past time for Lydia to take Kitty and head to Derbyshire. Finally, a letter was dispatched to Michael Lewis, Pemberley's steward (who had succeeded the elder Mr. Wickham some years before), to have the house prepared for its guests.

Elizabeth, of course, did regret that Kitty was forced to go. There was no alternative. Within the week, Kitty's and Lydia's things were put in trunks lashed to the back of the hired carriage and sent with the two Bennets on their journey to Pemberley. It would be a long trip even in the comforts of a fine coach, taking at least three days, if the weather held and the inevitable summer storms were brief and caused little disruption to the roads.

"I shall not forget you and you will in any case see me and Jane soon enough," Lizzy had assured Kitty on the eve of the departure. "But I may have news and so you must read any letters I send to you and Lydia with care so I can discreetly pass it on to you."

"Do you think there will be pleasant news?" Kitty asked.

"I've every confidence. You must give Charlotte time to discuss the matter with Mr. Collins."

With that, Lizzy left Kitty to prepare for the trip and the next morning she waited with Jane and Bingley and the Gardiners until it was time to leave and then stood out on Mount Row to bid them farewell, Kitty and Lydia to Pemberley and Mr. and Mrs. Bennet, who had tired of London—Mr. Bennet never able to muster much enthusiasm for the loud and dirty place—and could not wait another moment to be back at Longbourn.

Chapter 8. Reuniting with the Collinses

The carriage to Pemberley and the one to Longbourn were hardly out of London when Elizabeth had a word with Darcy in his library. Because they all would be going to Derbyshire soon, Elizabeth told her husband that she wished to visit the Collinses in Kent. Darcy could not object and since Charlotte was far better Elizabeth's friend, Jane—who was also glad for the quiet she expected with Kitty and Lydia gone—also made no objection.

"And you, of course, can spend particular time with Fitz," Elizabeth finished to her sister, and Jane seemed satisfied. Elizabeth didn't much like leaving her boy, but Jane's nature and availability sharply reduced her anxiousness about it. So, on the Thursday morning next, Elizabeth was off alone in a hired chaise. She'd been to the Parsonage thrice after the elaborate funeral for Lady Catherine yet recognised little she passed until she was upon Hunsford Road itself.

It was a warm day and Elizabeth was glad of the breeze generated by the carriage's movement. She closed her eyes at times thankful that the top was down so she could feel the country air. Memories of her first visit long ago with Sir William Lucas and Maria were brought back, the one during which Darcy *first* proposed to her. The one during which she was such a fool in rejecting him.

The chaise reached the Parsonage early in the afternoon and it stopped at the small gate, which led by a short gravel walk to the house itself. Charlotte had, as it happens, received Elizabeth's letter that she was coming only the day before and after some rushing about here and rushing about there, she and Mr. Collins and two of their servants had the place in quite a pretty condition for their visitor. The hosts were excited when they greeted Mrs. Darcy with the manservant and maid after she stepped from the carriage in the drive.

The Parsonage itself was rather small, as Elizabeth remembered it, but she knew from her prior visits that there would be room enough for Kitty to be made comfortable in her confinement, even with some of the...questionable improvements Lady Catherine had suggested.

As they completed their formal greetings and the chaise and its horses and men were dismissed, Charlotte took Elizabeth aside, to allow her friend to recover slightly from her journey and to speak of what they would do with Mr. Collins, who'd vanished into his garden sanctuary. After fifteen minutes or so, Charlotte called him in and the three settled in the small sitting room. They were all comfortable after their maid prepared tea for them and left. Mr. Collins spoke first, sitting across from his wife and his wife's closest friend.

"It is a bad thing, Mrs. Darcy, as I am sure my dear Charlotte has told you about my loss."

"Yes, Mr. Collins, she has, and I genuinely feel for you and your distress, though it was some time ago and I have seen you since then."

"Indeed, Mrs. Darcy, indeed. You must understand that my displeasure in my current situation should not reflect the slightest desire that your dear father...release his mortal coil, as the poet said. I hope he shall continue to live a long and healthy life. It is in my thoughts and prayers every day. Much as they were for Lady Catherine when she was alive."

"Yes, Mr. Collins, I understand. And that was a great loss."

"A great loss, indeed, Mrs. Darcy. Very great. But Miss Anne, who occupies the great house, does visit my sweet Charlotte regularly and condescends to sit with her in this very parlour, and Charlotte is pleased with the attention from Miss de Bourgh."

"I am very glad of it, Mr. Collins. It is quite the Christian thing for her to do."

"Indeed, it is, my dear Miss Eliz—Mrs. Darcy. She is not yet married, you know."

"I did not know, Mr. Collins," said Elizabeth, who could not have cared less for what became of the solitary issue of the late Lady Catherine. After all, she'd only seen the heiress when she'd deigned to stop in the path and converse with the Collinses and at and after the uncomfortable dinners she endured at Rosings Hall during her long stay years before at the Parsonage. And she did not think highly of her, if she thought of her at all.

Fortunately, though, Mr. Collins changed the subject.

"But I go on too long with my own suffering, slight as it may be. What brings you to speak to me on such intimate terms?"

He leaned towards his cousin with his hands clasped together.

"Well, Mr. Collins—and you must treat this in the most confidential way—my sister is with child."

"Yes, I know. Mrs. Collins has informed me. I do hope my cousin Lydia proceeds well."

"Indeed, she does, Sir. She is at Pemberley for the balance of her confinement. But, no, Mr. Collins. I speak not of Lydia. No. I speak of Kitty."

"Kitty? But I did not know that she was married." He shot back into his chair, his eyes enlarged.

Elizabeth paused. "That is just it, Mr. Collins. She is not married."

"Not married?" Mr. Collins's eyes grew even more and his attention shot from his guest to his wife. Charlotte gave the slightest smile indicating that she was not surprised by this news. Mr. Collins returned his attentions to Mrs. Darcy, much altered in his countenance and tone, though he did recover his practiced condescension.

"I see why you wish my discretion. But, Mrs. Darcy, why are you telling me this?"

"Well, Mr. Collins, the father of the child is dead. He died in the recent war and my sister, of course, expected that he would return and that all would be put to rights. But he did not and he will not. Return. You will understand the scandal to all of us if this becomes widely known."

"Scandal indeed. For us all, I fear."

"Do not fear, Mr. Collins. My being here with you will not cause the taint to affect you and your good name."

"Mrs. Darcy, I am utterly disappointed that you would even *think* I would be concerned with such a thing."

"No, I am sorry, Mr. Collins. That was quite unfair of me."

"Yes." He leaned forward again, his voice lowered. "Although I must admit that it is a relief to no longer be concerned about offending Lady Catherine, who always looked at me with such expectations."

"Yet I know that you, as a man of the cloth, are never one to be concerned with the opinions of others when you are doing the Lord's work."

"Certainly not. Certainly not. Thank you for recognising that, Mrs. Darcy."

"And whatever Kitty's sins, she is your cousin, and she is a member of *our* family after all, and her child will be innocent, an innocent child."

"True. Very true."

"Yet, sadly, it would be impossible for her to keep the child as it would ruin us all."

"That too is very true, Mrs. Darcy."

"Charlotte and I have discussed the possibility of you adopting the baby."

The speed with which Mr. Collins's countenance altered was yet again a wonder to behold. He stiffened in his chair, his hands tightening their grip on its arms.

"Adopt the bas—the baby? Are you mad?"

Charlotte stepped in as her husband fell back again where he sat.

"William, you know I have long pined for a child."

"Yes, but we have not succeeded. It must be God's will."

"Then this, too, must be God's will. That an infant in need of a loving home arrives to a member of your own dear family, to a dear cousin. And who better than us to care for the child? And raise it?"

"But Charlotte," he lowered his voice in the fruitless hope that Elizabeth would not hear it, "it will be the bastard child of who-knows-who. We will be shunned. We may be turned out of our living."

"Your living is secure," his wife said, "Lady Catherine made sure of that. It is yours for your lifetime. And 'shunning'? For doing God's work? It is not *your* bastard child. Whether people know whose it is of no concern of ours.

"Did not Saint Luke say, 'But Jesus called them unto him, and said, Suffer little children to come unto me, and forbid them not: for of such is the kingdom of God.'"

"Oh, Charlotte, you have become a bit of a scholar. So true. Yes, Saint Luke."

She and Elizabeth had memorized the verse for just this purpose and neither thought to make the minor correction that might lessen Mr. Collins's appreciation for his wife's knowledge.

"But it is a grave thing."

Elizabeth jumped in.

"Cousin William. You need not make your decision at this moment. We want you to think on it. Pray on it. As both Charlotte and I have and will continue to."

* * * *

ELIZABETH'S STAY WAS brief. She was back in town two weeks before she, Darcy, and Fitz as well as the Bingleys were to take their annual trip to Pemberley. She wrote a quick note to her sisters who were already there.

So alone in one of the large sitting rooms at Pemberley, one in a corner of the building with the windows to the north and to the east open for the benefit of such air flow as could be found, the heavily-burdened youngest Bennet sat in a chair reading Mrs. Darcy's letter from London and called to Kitty, who was sewing in a nearby chair, anxious after hearing the letter's contents, "Oh my God. Lizzy has become even more boring since she married Darcy. Listen to this."

Kitty feigned complete indifference to what Lydia was going to read from the letter Elizabeth had written to both of them but the younger sister having grabbed it so she could do the first reading of whatever Lizzy had to say.

Dearest Kitty and Lydia,

I so yearn to see you and your progress again when we all arrive at Pemberley for the season.

Shortly after you both left—as well as our mother and father, of course—I traveled to Kent to take the rare opportunity to see Mr. and Mrs. Collins, however briefly. I had quite a successful visit to my dear friend Charlotte and her husband, who I assure you is much changed—and improved—since you last set eyes on him those years ago at Longbourn.

They both directed me to pass on their good wishes for you and the baby and to assure you that you are all in their prayers. I should mention that when I left Hunsford, Mr. Collins was recovering from an illness, but that Charlotte was very optimistic that he would quickly recover. She told me that she expects that he will come around to have visitors who can remain for extended periods if necessary.

Again, we are all waiting anxiously to see you both in Pemberley in the coming weeks.

Your sister
Elizabeth

"Can you believe it?" Lydia asked rhetorically as she flung the letter vaguely towards her sister. Kitty lifted it and began to read as Lydia began to drone on. "As if *anyone* in the world, least of all us, would have any interest in Mr. Collins's health and recovery. Unless, I think, it was being told he was about to die and somehow Longbourn would remain with the Bennets and not with some interloper."

Kitty heard little of this. Elizabeth was far too clever for Lydia to appreciate it, but Kitty understood. She'd heard nothing in so long and now if this were not a glimmer of great hope, she did not know what would be. She was so pleased but pretended to share her younger sister's dismissal of the letter, except for the part about the demise of their cousin which even for Lydia was somewhat beyond the pale.

Chapter 9. "Mr. Tompkins Would Like a Word, Sir."

"What is it, Bradley?"

The butler stood at the open door to his master's library, not daring to speak until he was noticed by Darcy. It was two weeks before everyone was to travel to Pemberley.

"Begging your pardon, Sir. But Mr. Tompkins is here and would like a word."

"Tompkins? Who the blazes is 'Tompkins'?"

"He, Sir, he is the butcher."

"And what does this Tompkins want with me? I have never laid eyes on the man in my life. Can you not take care of it?" Darcy sent a dismissive wave in the butler's direction.

"I asked that, Sir, but he insists that he must speak to you and only to you."

Darcy placed his pen on his desk and stood, adjusting his stifling waistcoat.

"Very well. Show him in."

Bradley stepped into the hall and nodded to the side, and immediately a short, burly man carrying a hat tightly gripped in both hands in front of him entered and bowed.

"Yes, yes. Tompkins, is it? State your business."

"Well, Sir, Mr. Darcy, it seems that, Sir, Mr. Darcy, the bank is refusing to accept the check used to pay your...the house's invoice."

"Refusing to pay? Impossible. Mrs. Darcy handles the house's accounts, and I am certain it is some mistake. Go back to your bank and get it straightened out." He again displayed his particular distant wave. The man's grip on the brim of his hat visibly tightened.

"But, Mr. Darcy, Sir. I have done just what you suggest, Sir, Mr. Darcy, and payment is still refused. Someone said something about a large overdraft in your account."

Darcy stared at the man. Elizabeth would never have erred regarding the house's bills. What's more, what business did this Tompkins have to know the Darcys' affairs?

"Tompkins. I will see to it immediately. I assure you that your bill will be paid."

Tompkins relaxed his shoulders and allowed himself the slightest smile. He again bowed and with yet another "Sir, Mr. Darcy" backed from the room, and Bradley was in it before Darcy could ask for him.

"Damn this. I will just take a cab to the bank and get this taken care of."

"Very good, Sir."

He paused.

"Yes?"

"What if another tradesman appears?"

Darcy stared at his butler.

"If that happens, you will tell him that I am taking care of it. Is that understood?"

"Very good Sir," and after he bowed, the butler stepped to the side to lead the butcher from the house through the servants' stairs and servants' entrance so his master could go down the family's stairs to the family's door and to the street to fetch a cab to take him to his banker to take care of it.

Chapter 10. At the Bank

"I am afraid, Mr. Darcy, that it is true. Wiped out. All gone, and still a fair amount owed on checks that are still out there."

"This is surely a mistake. I shall speak to Stewart about it."

"I am sorry, Mr. Darcy, but you are not the first to say he wished to speak to Mr. Stewart about his account."

The two were in the old banker's office, those mingling about the bank concerning their own affairs being oblivious to the conversation taking place on the other side of the half-glass walls that provided the banker with privacy.

"What do you mean?"

"Well, it seems, Mr. Darcy, that your Mr. Stewart got into a bit of financial difficulty for himself. The word is that he, well, that he bet his clients' money...on Boney."

"Bet his clients' money on Bonaparte?"

"As far as I can tell, that is it exactly. When our grand news reached us, it was the worst possible news for Mr. Stewart. He has not been seen since. In France. In Scotland. Maybe even America, if he could afford the fare which, frankly, I doubt. No one knows, but there are many who would like to find out, I can tell you. Not that it would do them any good. Dry as a stone, I'm sure. Dry as a stone."

"And me?"

The old banker ran his kerchief across his nose.

"I am afraid you, Sir, are dry as a stone as well. Your bonds have all be used as collateral for loans Mr. Stewart took, it appears as a last-ditch effort to gamble himself out of some significant gambling debts."

Getting no response from his client, he forged on with news that was somehow even worse. "And I am also afraid that Pemberley is in serious jeopardy, Sir. Serious jeopardy."

As a frozen Darcy wondered what he and his family would live on without any money, the old banker was certain that his client, soon to be ex-client, would not get far on his charm, and he almost laughed at his mind's observation.

"Anyone else I know?"

"Charles Bingley is, I believe, your brother-in-law?"

"He is married to my wife's older sister."

"Yes, well, 'twas a mistake for the two of you to put your eggs in Mr. Stewart's basket although fortunately for your brother he did not put *all* his there. I am sorry."

Darcy was relieved at least for this last part.

"Oh. And Bingley's sister."

The banker scanned to the bottom of the page.

"Mrs. Melvin Brown now, isn't it?"

Darcy gave a half-hearted "'tis."

"Yes. Here it is. As I...feared. Mr. Brown was not cheated out of the money. No. It appears that he convinced himself and bet—he'll call it an 'investment'—bet virtually everything of his on Bonaparte."

"Caroline's money?"

"Caroline is Bingley's sister? Yes, I would guess, but cannot say for a certainty, that as you know her money became his when they married, thus it too has sunk into the blood of Belgium. Indeed, perhaps some sort of trust should have been set up for her but alas I have heard that that was not what occurred."

The old banker stood, signaling that the interview was over and that he had more important things to do than spend even more time with a pompous man who was no longer rich.

He stepped around his desk and extended his hand. Darcy took the signal and rose, shaking his banker's—now former banker's—hand limply before quickly exiting through the bank's lobby and out into Leman Street where, too, the passersby were oblivious to the dreadful news that just cascaded over him.

It was but four blocks to Stewart's office, and Darcy made quick work of them, speeding up as he went along. He climbed the two flights and rushed into the office without bothering to knock. Stewart's clerk, a nice enough chap from somewhere in the East End, was quickly off his stool.

"Mr. Darcy. We have not seen Mr. Stewart for several days, and you are not the first to seek him out just this morning."

"Where is he?"

"Sir. I don't know. I went to his house yesterday midday, you see, and there was no answer, and the curtains were drawn. Not even a member of staff, Sir. He has gone."

"Of course, he is gone, you fool. With my money."

The clerk was not bothered by the insult, having heard it and worse several times in the past days.

"I fear that this is the case. Sir. Is there anything else I might do for you?"

"Else? You've done *nothing* for me," and again the clerk was unmoved by the bloviation as he bowed to the back of yet another newly-poor victim of Mr. Stewart's loose habits. He resumed looking about the office to see what could be sold to make up for his own salary, that while his were far smaller losses than were Mr. Darcy's, they were of infinitely greater importance to him.

Before the clerk had assembled more than a piece or two, Darcy was on the street. He began to hail a cab but thought it was best to avoid the expense. Bingley's house on Mount Row was within walking distance and a walk would do him good.

It was farther and warmer than Darcy expected, and he was walking fast so when he reached the large door at Number 19, he was breathing heavily with thoughts no clearer than they had been when he left Stewart's. Bingley's butler, Crawford, answered the knock and offered Darcy a drink of water, which Darcy was grateful for when it was delivered in the sitting room where he waited for Bingley.

Chapter 11. In Darcy's Library

"What is it Fitzwilliam? Bradley said it was important."

Elizabeth was just in from walking with Jane and buying things in preparation for the trip to Pemberley when the Darcys' butler said the master wished to see her urgently in his library. He'd been sitting there since he got back from Bingley's.

As she entered his inner sanctum, still in her walking outfit, though Bradley had taken her hat and gloves, she noticed her husband holding a glass of whisky and that it was nearly empty.

"Yes, Lizzy, it *is* important."

"Are you drunk?"

"You will know me if I am drunk, but my news will quickly sober me up. But you perhaps should have some."

"You are frightening me. What is it?"

"Sit."

The couple sat on either end of the leather sofa in the library, he with a whisky and she without.

"Do you remember our dear friend Alex Stewart?"

"Of course. His father managed your father's affairs, and he manages ours. What of it?"

"You are wrong, my dear. He does not manage our affairs. He *managed* them. He is gone and so is our money."

His wife stared at him.

"Our money is gone?"

Darcy made a sound and flipped his hands to the wind and stood for a refill.

"Are you sure?"

She was behind him, now up herself.

"Please, dearest. No more. Talk to me."

"Thank God Georgiana is safely married to Evans."

Elizabeth led her husband back to the sofa, but this time she sat so her hands could reach him.

"Tell me what happened."

"Turns out our Mr. Stewart was something of a republican, at least when it came to betting on Bonaparte."

"Good God. Surely, he did not bet our money on the tyrant?"

"Ours and many more."

"Bingley? Not Bingley."

"Of course, Bingley. Though not so badly. I introduced them, a lapse for which I will always suffer.

"We cannot pay the butcher, Elizabeth. He came to be paid when the check to him did not clear. I told him it must be a misunderstanding at the bank and the banker—who henceforth will likely cross the street when he sees me coming—confirmed this. He named Bingley and said there were others, and that Stewart is much sought after but long gone where he cannot be caught and that if he is he will be unable to provide satisfaction to anyone."

"You cannot think of going there," Elizabeth said.

Darcy smiled in a way she'd never seen before and it, too, frightened her.

"Do not worry on that account at least. Caroline's fool of a husband apparently decided to wager more than he could afford on Bonaparte, too."

"And Pemberley?"

"I have asked Bingley to ride up with me in the morning. We're due to all be there in two weeks, thus it will seem as though we are simply ensuring that everything is ready for us. But I must meet with Lewis, my country steward. That must be done without delay. I do not know the extent to which it has been mortgaged."

"But how?"

Darcy shot up and was on his feet and free of her hands before she could stop him.

"I trusted him as my father trusted his father. He had power of attorney to do what he wished. The accounts he presented at least were always favourable. If he could mortgage Pemberley, he surely has, though with neither my knowledge nor my permission. But if he mortgaged Pemberley, it was surely mortgaged and, and...and I fear it may be lost if he has managed to untie its tail."

And poor Jane. Perhaps Bingley has some reserves. Perhaps Charles's now-married-off sisters would help her, but none of them, especially Caroline, took a liking to Mrs. Fitzwilliam Darcy or to her sister, Mrs. Charles Bingley. And of course, Caroline, according to Darcy, was in a worse financial position than was Jane.

Oh, Darcy thought for a moment, how his Lizzy would gain satisfaction were he ever to tell her of the time shortly after Caroline was married off when she'd approached him as he stood alone on the patio at Pemberley and advised him that whenever he tired of "that country girl" she was available to show him "what a real woman could do to, and for," him. How his blood turned to ice from that point at the very sight of his great friend's sister. He'd never tell this to Elizabeth, of course, but he admitted to himself that he took some inappropriate satisfaction in what had befallen her. *Schadenfreude* the Germans called it.

Elizabeth's thoughts went elsewhere. First to Lydia and Kitty. Lydia, if she learned some frugality, could survive on her dead husband's pension, though Elizabeth knew it was not large. Kitty's situation was infinitely more complex (though only she, Lizzy, and Mr. and Mrs. Collins knew just how complex). Lydia could remove herself to Longbourn to again live with her parents, until their father died, bless her soul, and Mr. Collins moved in. She would simply have to understand and savour her short period living on the Darcys' hospitality before Pemberley was gone.

But Kitty. She was aging rapidly and whatever slim prospects she had with wealthy in-laws were gone forever.

And Mary. Mrs. Bowles. The lectures, and Lizzy dreaded visiting her at the living in Northumberland her husband (the vicar) enjoyed.

These thoughts were shattered when Darcy announced they needed to go to Bingley's.

"Charles assured me he would immediately speak to Jane about it, and we must be with them as soon as we can."

Elizabeth was quickly presentable (with her hat and gloves returned to her by Bradley) if barely recovered from the news, and the Darcys were soon walking to the Bingleys'. They waited in the large sitting room after they were announced. Though their wait was not long as their friends were quick to join them.

"We ride up in the morning to find out what liens are on the property," Darcy said. "But I am not optimistic. If Stewart cleaned out my accounts in the City, no telling how he mortgaged my land. I am just glad," and he nodded towards Bingley, "that you are coming with me."

The four ate quietly together that evening but Elizabeth and Darcy returned to Brook Street immediately after. Then at first light, the two men hired horses for the long ride north. They were both fine horsemen, though Bingley was the superior, and they knew enough not to drive their mounts too hard. Even with a frequent change-of-horses, they would not arrive in Derbyshire until late on the next day. Elizabeth and Fitz would be staying with Jane when the men were in the north.

The two men spoke little while they rode and largely repeated the same conversation each time they changed horses and while they ate and rested on the night they were on the road.

They reached Pemberley itself late on the next afternoon, as they hoped. Darcy had written a note to the steward advising that he was coming on a matter of some importance and that "the widow and her sister" were not to be told beforehand lest they be unduly alarmed. The letter, though, only reached the estate a few hours before Darcy and Bingley themselves did.

Their appearance on the road leading to the house quickly roused the few there, most of the servants being those who tended to the grounds and gardens and were preparing for the families' attendance and seeing to (as well as they could) the requirements of Mrs. Wickham and her more reasonable sister Kitty. The servants had little time, though, to do any but the minimum amount to prepare the house for the master and his guest.

The servants were, it must be said, pleased to see the two. Bingley and his wonderful wife had stayed at Pemberley for an extended stretch of the prior season and were very pleasant. It was after that stay that the Bingleys accepted Darcy's offer that in the future their time in the country be spent at Pemberley and not at some rented estate far away and at least for some time,

Bingley decided to defer his dream of buying a country estate for himself. Though Caroline resented that albeit reasonable decision, since it denied the family's place among landed-gentry society, that slight was now among the least of her concerns.

So Netherfield was given up and an offer was also extended to Mr. and Mrs. Bennet, who were themselves disappointed that Jane was removed from the estate so close to their own Longbourn, to spend extended periods at Pemberley with a large suite of rooms set aside for them.

But all those arrivals were a long way off, and the two men had more urgent matters to discuss with Darcy's steward.

After they arrived, they had a simple dinner prepared for them and shared quietly and somewhat awkwardly with Kitty and Lydia, Darcy and Bingley retired for the evening to Darcy's library rehashing what had been hashed and hashed again between the two for the last days.

They awoke early but Cook already had breakfast for them though neither could make their way much through it, hungry as they were. They were quickly off on a fresh set of the estate's horses for Sheffield.

* * * *

THE DARCY SOLICITOR was on the Sheffield High Street, and he was not yet in when his client and his client's guest arrived. They paced back-and-forth in the small sitting room outside the office while a boy was dispatched to fetch the lawyer. In five or ten minutes, though it seemed far longer to the visitors, William Patters, Esq. hurried in, bowing as he headed to his office and beckoning that the two men join him.

"Mr. Darcy. I must say this is a surprise. But as it is so sudden and as I am your solicitor, I fear it is not a pleasant visit."

"You always were an observant one, Patters."

Patters nodded at his client's sarcasm.

"It is my property. I am here to determine the state of my financial affairs here in Derbyshire and to learn the condition of Pemberley."

He proceeded to tell the story of Mr. Stewart and the empty bank accounts. He said he feared that the disease might have spread to Pemberley.

"Mr. Darcy. You do not own Pemberley. Indeed, your not owing the estate is a very good thing."

Darcy turned to Bingley. "I hoped as much."

"You as good as own it, of course. But in fact, Sir, you have only a life estate in it as did your father though unless you can reestablish it, it will be extinguished when your son inherits it, which of course, we all hope will be many years in the future.

"You have full use of it, but you cannot mortgage it. If what you tell me about this Mr. Stewart is true, he could not use that power of attorney to borrow money against Pemberley. So, it is a good thing."

"You are right, of course. So, I am safe."

"I should not go that far, Mr. Darcy. *Pemberley* is safe. You, I fear, are not. You see, though no one could place a lien on the real property itself, they could put a lien on the income generated by the property. The crops and the rents. We must look but I fear he has significantly, though I hope not fatally, taken the money from Pemberley and you will have to find some other means to...well, to eat. And, of course, I cannot speak of the 4 or 5 per cents you have in the City."

"Sadly," the client informed, "they have been compromised." Darcy, who moments before thought the intricacies of English property law rescued him somewhat as to Pemberley realised that it might be the most pyrrhic of victories.

He and Bingley were soon retracing their ride back to Pemberley. Patters would join them when he was properly dressed and finished his delayed breakfast and his carriage could be brought round.

When they were free of their horses at the estate, the two men headed to the small building that sat just to the west of the stables, on the side opposite the house. It was the steward's house. Each year after the harvest, Darcy sat with him, Michael Lewis, to review the books. He was a good man, and there was never a farthing out of place. While Elizabeth saw to the household's expenses, Darcy oversaw the estate's.

Lewis jumped up when Darcy and Bingley entered the house. Mrs. Lewis asked the visitors whether they would like some refreshments, an offer they politely declined.

"Thank you, Mrs. Lewis," Darcy said. "We have rather urgent business with your husband."

Lewis had been told Darcy was coming so he was prepared to meet him, but he had no idea what it would be about. He waved Darcy and Bingley into the office. Before he sat, Darcy asked Lewis whether he'd been served with any types of legal documents in recent weeks.

"Not as yet, Sir. I would have immediately written to you if I had."

"I understand, Lewis. I am sorry. I know you would have. I wondered if any passed us on our way north."

He looked at Bingley. "I fear they will not be long in coming."

"Sir?"

"Lewis. I have been the victim of a thief in the City. He may have borrowed money for himself to support a bet in favour of Bona—"

"In favour of Boney, Sir?" Lewis was now full awake.

"Indeed. We think it possible that he used my credit and the income from Pemberley to finance his bet, which has, of course, ended very badly for him and—"

"And for Bonaparte."

"Indeed, Lewis, and for Bonaparte. But also, sadly for me and to a lesser extent Bingley here."

Lewis looked at Bingley, who he recognised from the year before, and they nodded to one another.

"I met earlier with Mr. Patters. He assured me that Pemberley itself could not be liened against but that its income could be."

"This is my understanding too, Sir. What am I to do, Sir?"

"For now, I do not know. Mr. Patters will be at the house presently and I will send for you. We will meet in my library to discuss all of this."

With that, he turned and left. Bingley exchanged a further bow to the steward and after a "good day, Mrs. Lewis" called to the stairs followed his friend out.

Mr. Patters was not long in arriving. He declined Darcy's offer of something to eat, and the three adjourned to Darcy's old and well-appointed library, but not before a footman was dispatched to collect Mr. Lewis.

When they were all assembled, Patters told Darcy that he was indeed correct in what he told Lewis. Any liens on Pemberley would hit, if at all, only when Mr. Stewart failed to make a payment on a loan when due. Under the circumstances, it was likely that his lenders knew the nature of his bet by now and would do anything they could to accelerate the payment, each hoping to get what was available before the others did what they were doing.

In the event, it did not matter. The money was already gone when the news from Belgium—the battle was more and more becoming referred to as "Waterloo"—reached London and Mr. Stewart was gone wherever he was gone shortly thereafter.

"It will not be long," Patters said, "before the sheriff appears."

He looked at Darcy. Pale as he was earlier in town, he was paler now. He turned back to Lewis.

"The moment you are served with a paper, you must race to have it sent to me," Patters said. "We will decide how to act, though I do not know yet how that will be. But I must know the instant it happens."

He turned to his client.

"Will you be here, Sir?"

Darcy exchanged a look with Bingley.

"Will it matter if I am in London? With my family? Until we return in under a fortnight's time?"

"No, Sir, it will not. We are in early August. It is some months before any income is generated at Pemberley. We will have time to plan and execute a strategy in response. But if service is made before you are back, I will get this information to you in London as soon as possible."

Darcy rose from behind his desk. He extended his hand to Patters.

"Thank you, Patters. I know I am in good hands."

They shook and his solicitor and his steward left the others alone.

"This is very bad, Bingley. I think we must return to London as quickly as we came."

Chapter 12. The News from Charlotte

While Darcy and Bingley were trying to learn the truth about Stewart at Pemberley, Elizabeth received from Charlotte the letter she'd prayed for. She went to her own house each day to check on things generally and to see if Charlotte had sent her letter.

And one day it was there, in the foyer awaiting her. After "much prayer and further discussion," her friend wrote, Mr. Collins agreed to the plan for the child. It was his Christian duty and, he admitted, the prospect of having a child to raise and teach (and spoil) was something he suddenly had a hankering for.

The letter was sufficiently precise that Elizabeth did not dare have anyone see it so after she digested its contents, she would like to have burnt it. It had just turned into August, though, and there was no convenient fire for the purpose. Instead, she tore it into as many pieces as she could and before returning to Mount Row, she would deposit the scraps in waste bins set up along the path as she went.

Before that, though, she would write to Lydia and Kitty. With a sheet of stationery, she sat at the small desk by the window in her study and wrote:

Brook-street
August 1, 1815

My dearest sisters,

By the time you receive this, you may have heard of the difficulties that have arisen regarding my family directly or indirectly from Darcy and Bingley on their unexpected trip to Pemberley. We will discuss these matters further when we all arrive shortly.

Though it will scarcely counter that news, I am certain you will both be pleased to hear that Mr. Collins has fully recovered from his recent illness. According to a letter I received from Charlotte this very morning, he has expressed the desire to have visitors, even long-term visitors, sooner rather than later.

Again, this will not be of great interest to you, but I felt it best if I included in this letter some glimmer of good news even if it is only concerning Mr. Collins.

We will speak further when we all arrive. In the meantime, please understand how excited I am about our impending reunion.

Elizabeth

That sent and with nothing to do about the financial difficulties Darcy and Bingley were examining, Elizabeth thought of how the plan with Kitty would be effected.

And Lydia, upon reading the above, was completely at a loss about receiving more useless information about her awful cousin.

Kitty, though, understood and was quite pleased. Quite pleased, indeed.

Chapter 13. The Return Flight to London

Darcy and Bingley stayed at Pemberley just for the night, and not long after dawn on Friday morning, the fourth of August, they were already heading south to London, reversing the journey they took just days before.

They were well clear of the estate by the time Lydia dragged herself from her plush bed, though Kitty as usual in recent months was up near the dawn. She sat, as had become her custom, in the window seat in her room with its east visage and where she could watch the new day begin and, on that day in early August of 1815, saw her brothers-in-law hurry away for reasons she could not understand but which troubled her. It seemed more than they said it was. Plainly more than simply ensuring that preparations for the families' arrivals were well in hand. She didn't mention it to Lydia.

Darcy and Bingley did not speak except when they changed horses or ate at the inns along the way back to town. As before, their talk was circular. Neither man knew what was to become of Fitzwilliam Darcy even if Pemberley was safe from creditors. His liquid assets were long since compromised.

Perhaps it was the shock, but while their husbands were gone, Elizabeth was (especially after receiving Charlotte's letter) far calmer than Jane expected her to be. Jane would sit with her on the sofa in the sitting room on Mount Row, with the door closed. Or the two took extended but comfortably silent walks in Hyde Park when the weather allowed till they felt a pleasant numbness from near exhaustion from their many steps, stopping at one of the kiosks that offered sandwiches and ales and had small tables and chairs for ladies and gentlemen to use to eat at midday.

It was at one of those tables the day before their husbands returned to London that Elizabeth spoke of something that had been bothering her for some time.

"Jane, do you not find this life tiresome?"

"Of course. But what shall you or I do?"

Neither had an answer to this question that each long harboured and they could do nothing but rise and slowly head back to Mount Row to await word from their husbands.

Word and their husbands reached London on Tuesday afternoon after a very hard ride. When rid of their horses, they immediately went to Bingley's, where they found Jane and Elizabeth, who'd spent each night there, with Fitz.

Darcy said that "thank God Pemberley is safe" but that its income was heavily liened and that matters were very bad, far more severe than were the Bingleys'. Charles assured Jane that they at least were solvent.

"'Solvent'? You assure me that we are 'solvent'? And they are not. What happened?"

Darcy then explained what he and Bingley were told by his solicitor and steward and that while he and Bingley had spoken about it, they had not reached a conclusion of just what had to done now. "It is very complicated," he said. "I fear it will take some maneuvering to make it through this test."

Even Elizabeth was having difficulty fully understanding what her husband was saying.

On the next afternoon, the two couples sat for a small dinner at the Bingleys'. The servants were dismissed after they'd set the food and drink along the mahogany server that presided over the short wall of the room. The four prepared their own plates, with Elizabeth venturing to suggest, half-in-jest, that it was something they might need to practice doing for the future.

"The reality is," Darcy said, "that things will have to change, and they will have to change somewhat dramatically."

"Yes," Elizabeth said, "Jane and I spoke of it after you first left. Do we really need all of this, Darcy? Do we *really*?"

"Surely there will be enough to live quite well on when we are through this," Jane added, showing that she and her husband had rehearsed what they would say.

The couples sat opposite one another. The Darcys' view was out to Mount Row and the Bingleys' across to their friends and to the large country landscape that dominated the long wall opposite the window.

Elizabeth said. "And from what you say, I gather that we may not have much of a choice."

"Do not worry there." Bingley said. "I expect I have enough to keep you lot fed at least."

Darcy attempted not to take this as an insult. It was meant as things were always meant by Bingley, kindly. But Darcy was a proud man. He'd never dreamt that he would someday become reliant on anyone else's kindness (it not signifying that his very existence was built on his inherited wealth since such randomness was the way of the world). He took much comfort, though, in what his friend had said.

"You are a good man, Bingley. A truly good man."

Bingley gave his friend an awkward nod before Elizabeth interrupted. "What shall we tell the others?"

What would be said to the Bennets, parents and daughters, had hardly been given a thought.

"Well," Darcy said, "before we get to that I must speak to the banks. Let us not tell anyone until we know more of what is in store for us. Your sisters may suspect something from our sudden appearance at and disappearance from Pemberley. But I doubt either of them much cares at the moment beyond making sure they are properly taken care of, as I assure you they are.

"In the morning, I will seek out the chief creditors. It does them no good to act hastily in foreclosing. I should be able to buy us at least some leeway. Bingley will be with me."

"Yes," that gentleman agreed. "We hope to meet with the banks and see if an arrangement can be made."

"So, I think we need to keep quiet about it," although secrecy was long lost among the servants at the Darcy house—and letters had been dispatched by servants to Pemberley with the news—since the butcher (and thank goodness not another tradesman, yet) appeared with a complaint about not having been paid.

By this point, the four had cleaned their plates. Bingley got up and rang, and when Crawford came in, Bingley said they were all adjourning to the sitting room and asked that port and coffee be brought there.

"It is smaller than the drawing room and larger than my library. We can be comfortable and left undisturbed there."

When they sat with the noise and some bugs of the summer air intruding through the windows that opened out to Mount Row, the conversation turned more intense.

Bingley told the women, "Darcy and I spoke about Pemberley. It is, well, it is far too expensive to keep without significant cuts in what is spent there."

Darcy said, "It is of course far too late to seek a tenant for this season."

"'Tenant'?" Elizabeth was horrified at the reality of the word. Her father, of course, was a "tenant" at Longbourn, with a life tenancy, but she never thought of it that way. Though she was fully aware and constantly reminded (by her mother) that Mr. Collins would take over the estate and they could and assuredly would be forced out the very moment her father died.

But *Pemberley*. The idea that the Darcys would be required to lease it out to another family and that her husband would be the first Darcy to have to do so was like a slap of how desperate things had suddenly become thanks to the thievery of a scoundrel. Jane was struggling to understand as well.

"Thank God we are still not leasing Netherfield," Bingley added. "That money will go to you instead, Darcy."

"But," Darcy said, taken aback at the suggestion, "You will again be our *guests*. I could not imagine taking a farthing from you."

"Darcy. Don't be daft, man. We are in the end in this together. Our families are bound by blood and friendship. We are not just *anyone*. We are with you through thick and thin. We can afford to pay you for using your property this season and, frankly, you cannot afford not to take it. We will sort out matters later."

"But what of your losses?" Darcy asked.

"They are not nearly so large as yours," was the answer. "Darcy, it wasn't your fault."

"Of course, it was my fault. Trusting that scoundrel. I should have known."

"But, how, Darcy? How could you have known?"

"He's right, Fitzwilliam," Elizabeth said before her husband could contradict her brother-in-law. "You could not have known."

He again looked across the street. *Could he have or couldn't he have.* It did not matter. The money was gone, and they were at the earliest stage of understanding what that meant to their lives. Bingley was right. He did have the resources, however reduced, to pay for using Pemberley as he once paid for using Netherfield. More than enough. Darcy hated to acknowledge it and he could barely accept it, but it was the reality and he had no choice.

Even that addressed only the most immediate issue, though. They could get through the season in Derbyshire with at least the trappings of wealth. But far more significant decisions would have to be made. And quickly.

"This is the *Darcy* family's money," Darcy observed. "Pemberley itself might be entailed and thus out of the reach of creditors, but not whatever else we do—or do not—possess. It is *my* failure. To Little Fitz most of all."

"Fitzwilliam," Elizabeth quickly said to this self-pitying. "You have never treated me as my father treated my poor mother."

Yes, Darcy thought, *but at least Mr. Bennet did not squander what money he obtained from his father and his father's father.*

She glared at him, but it quickly ebbed as he looked at her.

"I am sorry, my dear. We are equals. As Jane and Charles are. And you both shall be treated as such. Correct, Bingley?"

Bingley endorsed what his friend said.

Elizabeth said, "Stewart stole the money. From you. How can the banks look to you to pay anything, after they've stripped you of...Pemberley?"

"They will say, Lizzy, that they lent to my authorized agent and that I stand in Stewart's damn shoes, that's how they can."

"It does not make sense to me."

"Lizzy. It is my fault—"

He stood and moved towards a window.

"Yes, but only in part," Elizabeth called to him. "Stewart took the money."

"That is true, but as between me and the banks, I must take the loss because I authorized him to act for me."

"Why on earth did you do that, dearest? Why?"

"I trusted him as my father trusted his father. I had no reason to doubt him or his honesty or his skill with money."

"You were such a—"

Elizabeth stopped, aware of the futility and the cruelty of what she nearly said in her frustration. It had been building inside her and she'd promised herself she would not say it and was glad that she stopped before she said more than she did. She rose to stand next to her husband. The other two, sitting on the sofa, merely watched. They were affected. But not as Mr. and Mrs. Darcy were.

"So, Fitzwilliam, it is up to us." Elizabeth turned to look at her brother-in-law and her sister. "All of us."

"Yes, Darcy," Bingley said. "We will do all we can."

"But he stole from you as well."

"Yes. But not as much as he stole from you. I will have enough even if we must do without some of the frivolities we have become accustomed to."

"Well, Bingley, I am sure we will not need to dress as often as we have. No one will invite us to their balls and parties, and none would come to ours. The news will soon spread, and we will cease being known around town and wherever else we might be."

The four did not have much more to discuss. The situation was dire, even if the details were as yet uncertain. The options were limited, though if Bingley did not exist, they would have been far more so.

With the cash gone, Darcy's sole source of direct income was the harvests and the rents on the fields that made up the Pemberley estate. Mr. Stewart pledged that income to secure loans and since he would be unable to repay those loans, let alone any others, it was only a matter of time before the lenders seized the estate's income.

Darcy hoped to be able to buy some time in negotiations, but time itself could never solve the problem.

"What about the lease here in town?"

"It has fifteen years to run. But, yes, it is far and away our greatest expense, next to those who work at Pemberley itself."

"I think you must give it up," Bingley said.

"What? Give up this house," Elizabeth said.

"It cannot be avoided, my dear," Darcy told his wife. "We cannot pay for the lease here and the servants here and still be able to pay for the servants in Derbyshire. It simply cannot be done."

"I know, Fitzwilliam. I just was not prepared when I said we couldn't afford some things anymore that it meant...that it meant we could not live here."

"Perhaps you can find more reasonable accommodations," Jane said, with her husband quickly adding, "Or consider this house as yours as often as you'd like."

"Again, Bingley, I appreciate your offer, but I will not treat your house like an inn. I will not."

Darcy again sat.

"But we are running far ahead of ourselves, I think. Let me speak to the banks first. That is the first thing. Then we can think about—"

"And discuss," Elizabeth interrupted.

"Yes, and 'discuss' what we, the four of us, will be able to do and what we will be able to afford."

With that, Elizabeth rose and told her husband it was time for them to go home and after bidding the others good night on the house's front steps, the pair headed back to Brook Street, not sure what, if any, true progress was made on this evening.

Chapter 14. Mr. Brown "Travels" to America

At one point as they rode north, Bingley had asked Darcy about his sister Caroline.

"Has there been any further news about her debts?"

Darcy said he knew nothing beyond what his banker had said.

It was not long after they were back in town that they knew significantly more. A mere two days later, in fact. That is when Caroline herself appeared at Mount Row. It was still morning. She insisted she speak with her brother, but he was out riding with Darcy as was their usual form of exercise. After a moment, she took a breath and asked to speak with her dear friend Jane.

Crawford directed her to the sitting room while he went to see whether his mistress was available. *She had better damn well be,* Caroline thought, never long able to hide from herself the inner disdain she cradled for the pretty Bennet daughter (who had long since forgiven Caroline for her (ultimately futile) duplicity from years before). Though she had only recently finished breakfasting and was planning to go for a stroll with Elizabeth, the weather being quite favourable, Jane told the butler, Crawford, she would be pleased to sit with her sister-in-law and would be down shortly.

It seemed a long period for Caroline but soon Jane knocked on the sitting room door and entered.

"Caroline, it is always so good to see you," Jane said with a well-practiced air after the women exchanged curtseys.

"I must see my brother immediately," Caroline said without any nicety.

"But he is out riding with Darcy," Jane said.

"So I've been told. Can someone be sent to fetch him?"

Very surprised at this unusual demand, needs must, and Jane rang and asked Crawford to have a footman jog over to the bridle path in Hyde Park to get Mr. Bingley to return as soon as possible. The two women attempted to converse with little success until refreshments were brought and Crawford was dismissed.

Caroline declined the offer of tea. Instead, she paced back and forth before the windows, saying little beyond periodically asking "how long is it?" and "how long will it be?" to which Jane, sitting in a comfortable chair watching the other intensely, said she was sure he would be here as quickly as possible.

The clock in the foyer was just striking half-eleven when Caroline saw Bingley *finally* rushing up the house's walk. It was just a moment later that he was in the room with his sister and his wife. Caroline asked Jane to leave and after Bingley gave her a slight nod, Jane stepped out with an exchange of curtsies.

She waited on the first-floor landing until the sitting room door flew open, and then stepped back so as not to be seen. Caroline was rushing out as the butler opened the front door, and Bingley stood staring at her wake.

When he did, Jane hurried down. She followed him into the sitting room, where he closed the door.

Before they could sit, he said, "He is gone."

He must have meant Caroline's husband. Jane did not move.

"When she came down after breakfast this morning, their butler handed her a letter. He'd been instructed not to give it to her before eleven, and it was a bit after when she appeared dressed to go out. The letter said he was gone. Gone to America."

Jane was shaken by this news.

"He left yesterday."

The two sat and Bingley continued. "She thought he'd stayed late at his club. Instead, he'd long since taken a stage south and will be catching a ship to New York or Philadelphia or somewhere he never intends to leave."

At that moment, Elizabeth was announced and after Bingley said, "she will know soon enough," Jane directed Crawford to show her in. She gave her sister the gist of what Bingley had told her.

To Elizabeth's own (if less sympathetic) astonishment, Jane said, "Lizzy, I do hope you are not harboring ill will towards her for her attempts to snare Darcy. She did, after all, do more damage to me with her dear brother than she did you. I have forgiven her that so surely you must as well."

Elizabeth smiled. Whatever could be said about their little skirmishes, she'd won the war. So, Mrs. Fitzwilliam Darcy promised Mrs. Charles Bingley that she had forgiven Mrs. Melvin Brown and hoped that she was still able to "dine at your wonderful house countless times in the future."

But she'd not be more than a guest. Once the tenancy on the Brown house she and her husband occupied was inevitably terminated for non-payment, Caroline would do as was expected. Move in with her sister. Caroline did not particularly like Mr. Hurst but that did not signify as she and her sister could together ignore him to their hearts' content. And he them.

Two things to note about the great differences between the two husbands that the Bingley sisters married.

First, Mr. Hurst. Though he was fashionable, he was not rich until he married. But he did well with the money Bingley's eldest sister, Louisa, t to the alliance and was careful in what he did with it. In particular, he did not entrust his assets to anyone but himself. Like all of society London, he saw the comings and goings of the speculators. Real estate. Cotton. Railways. Grain. Slaves. Anything.

All this speculation was disturbing to solid men like Mr. Hurst, who kept *his* money in 4 per cents. He gloated internally with each wave that washed away the rickety riches that temporarily enchanted certain parts of the City, even if his in-laws were among those swept away in this one.

His pride seeped into his dear wife's own marrow so when Caroline Bingley sought aid and comfort—more of the former than the latter as it happens—from Mrs. Hurst, the answer was: "My dear Caroline. Much as I would like to assist you, we do not have the ready capital to provide even a farthing to you. I am so sorry." The least she could do—and it was surely that—was allow her sister to occupy a room where she could sleep and provide food to her so she could eat.

As to Mr. Brown, after his letter was delivered, during the course of this story's telling, no one in England is known to have received any communication from him, even of whether he safely arrived in America. Which is the second (and final) thing to be said about that.

Chapter 15. The Banks

Even his detractors, of which there were many, considered Fitzwilliam Darcy a man of integrity and action. He would face the financial difficulties straight on and straight away. Perhaps all could have been avoided if one of London's major banks—such as the one that was (or had until recently been) Darcy's—had been involved. Then an officer would have contacted Darcy to confirm the legitimacy of the loan request. Which would have defeated Stewart's purpose. Which was why it was not done.

Instead, the thief Stewart went to several less respectable banks thrilled with the prospect of doing business with Mr. Darcy of Pemberley. Stewart brought more than sufficient evidence that he was acting for his client, including quite good forgeries, which were relatively easy to pass since they knew little of the actual signature other than what was in the powers-of-attorney.

Darcy realised that shouting at the incompetencies of these bankers would be more likely to expedite the speed at which their banks foreclosed. He controlled his temper and exercised his diplomatic best as Bingley waited on the street for news of his interactions.

After each stop, Darcy reported that the bank agreed to withhold action for sixty days but only if each of the other exposed banks did the same.

As one banker said, "If any of us makes a move to snatch a piece of Pemberley, we shall be right on its heels." The first gave Darcy a document.

August —, 1815

—————— *Bank hereby agrees not to take any action with respect to its lien on the property known as Pemberley in Derbyshire or on any personal property contained thereon or any crops grown in its fields or rent paid for the use of its fields until the earlier of the sixty-first day hereafter or the day on which any other entity holding a lien on said Property or any portion thereof takes a step to enforce its rights as to said Property.*

While Darcy waited at the first bank, five copies of the agreement were drawn up. The first banker signed, as did Darcy. Darcy repeated the process with each of the other three banks. When the last one signed, its banker had a boy deliver three fully signed and notarized copies to the other banks and dividing the other two between himself and Mr. Darcy.

The agreement to refrain from taking any action was not much from the banks' perspective. By mid-August, very little could be accomplished in the court system since all the judges and virtually all the solicitors and barristers would be off to an estate they owned or to which they were invited.

The cream of London's legal establishment was scattered as if by the wind to the four corners of Britain and even to Ireland and the continent. No, holding off for sixty days was surrendering nothing, and so bank officer after bank officer signed without hesitation.

Now it was up to Darcy, and Bingley, to figure how to extract Darcy from the depths into which his finances had sunk.

Chapter 16. Quentin Brower, Esq.

One of the bankers with whom Darcy met gave him the name of Quentin Brower, Esq. Brower was widely regarded as the preeminent authority in the country on issues related to insolvency and bankruptcy, who'd have expertise that Darcy's own solicitors lacked.

Darcy wrote to him on the very afternoon of his meeting with the banks and received an invitation to meet two days later.

"You are fortunate in one respect, Mr. Darcy. I am to head into the country for a month on Sunday and I should not be available for you had I left. We must consider your timing a good omen," the solicitor began.

Darcy was in no mood to speak of good omens, but he saw it was a way for Brower to lighten things up. The chambers were on the first floor of one of the buildings that lined a small park. It was well appointed but seemed to have more scrolls and other papers than it did furniture.

"Pay it no mind, Sir. Please be seated," and Darcy lowered himself to a leather chair that faced across the large desk, on the other side of which sat Quentin Brower.

"Well, Mr. Fitzwilliam Darcy. I know very little of your matter except that you are among the four or five gentlemen who have been...been left short by the malfeasance of one," and he lifted a paper and lowered his spectacles to read from it, "Francis Stewart." He removed the glasses and replaced the paper on his desk. "Is that about the nub of it?"

"Yes, it is. And not only did he take my money, but he left me in debt to his creditors."

"Yes, I understand that too. Mortgaged your bonds and estate using the power of attorney you gave him. Yes, yes. You, Sir, are not the first and I fear you will not be the last. Though I admit that it is very good for my business, Sir. Very good indeed."

Darcy did not like this characterization, and he had half a mind to leave the solicitor then and there.

"Do not take offence at my observation, Sir. I say such a thing," and his voice turned serious, "to tell my clients, or potential clients, that I am expensive. If you do not understand that and are not agreeable to my fees, I will be forced to decline representing you and can perhaps find another solicitor for you. Do you understand?"

"I do. I was told that you are the man to see for this, and my friend Charles Bingley agrees to guarantee that your fees will be paid."

"Very good. I assume he has the money?"

"He does."

"Good. We will say no more of it. I will have my clerk draw up an agreement setting forth my terms."

"But are you not going away?"

"Indeed, I am Sir. This Sunday. As I said. But I will be in Derbyshire not too far from your Pemberley and you will be able to consult with me if need be. But very little happens in August in the courts."

"The courts?"

"I will be clear to you, Mr. Darcy. If we cannot resolve this matter through prompt negotiations, you will have to seek protection from the courts."

"You mean, bankruptcy."

"That is precisely what I mean."

"But the shame. I will not do it."

"If you hire me, Mr. Darcy, I can do no more than follow my instructions from you. My job is to make recommendations about the courses of action I believe you are to consider and to execute your decisions. But you must understand that I have seen this before and I expect that we will have to discuss the prospect of your bankruptcy long and hard unless you are able to locate a source of funds to pay off your lenders."

"But they did not lend the money to *me*."

"Again, I understand. But the law will still hold you liable. So, we must find another way, or you will, I fear, have to declare yourself and your family bankrupt and rely on the courts to protect you."

The solicitor sat back in his chair. "Cheer up, man. That is down the road. I see that you have obtained two months of peace from the creditors." Darcy had included this observation in his request for a meeting with Brower. "We must use that time to search high and search low for any other sources of funds."

The two discussed, with some degree of cold-bloodedness in Darcy's view, any possible ways for him to get money. He knew Bingley would do what he could, but what he could do was significantly less than what it once was given what Stewart took from him.

Bingley walked in the park outside Brower's office while Darcy met with his solicitor and rushed up to his friend as soon as he saw him leaving the building. Darcy said he did not like the man.

"He was too cavalier about my money and too concerned about his own."

"But his advice, Darcy. What of his advice?"

"Advice? All he had to offer was that if I did not find money elsewhere, I would surely be forced to file bankruptcy. I did not need him to tell me that, Bingley."

"I told you I would take care of his fee."

"On that. He wants that in writing. Your agreement. He does not trust the word of a gentleman. It is another reason I do not like the man."

"I am happy to sign anything. You know that."

Darcy knew that and knew he needed the solicitor and knew he had to accept the conduct of a tradesman, as he deemed Quentin Brower, Esq. to be. That he had to deal with the man did not make him any happier about it. But he accepted the solicitor's suggestion that an immediate proceeding short of a formal bankruptcy filing be brought to protect his assets in the event one of his creditors sought to grab them, notwithstanding his agreements with the banks.

He and Bingley walked to a tavern on a side street off the Strand. It was nearly empty, which suited the men just fine, and they spoke of little other than the fact that each tankard of ale they drank seemed better than the last until Bingley had sense enough to get them out of the place and into a cab so they might be tolerably sober by the time they had their dinners.

Chapter 17. A Return to Pemberley

With Darcy having done all he could do in London for the moment, his family and Charles Bingley's made their journey to Derbyshire and the grand house at Pemberley. It was only the year before that Charles and Jane Bingley decided it was foolish to spend money on renting an estate anywhere else since they most enjoyed being with the Darcys as the Darcys most enjoyed being with them.

For her part, Kitty was most anxious to see Elizabeth again but they both took pains to make their meetings as seemingly random as possible. On the very first morning after everyone was there, with the newcomers barely settled in, Kitty *happened* to pass a small nook off the estate's main eastern garden where Elizabeth *happened* to be reading a tract she picked up shortly before leaving London. To any observer, it looked to be a coincidence that the two sisters *happened* to run into each other and that the older one carried a pamphlet that was of the greatest interest to the younger.

When they spoke, after satisfying themselves that no one was within earshot, the sisters were careful to use the pamphlet as a kind of prop, passing it back and forth with Elizabeth pointing—or so a viewer from afar might surmise—to a sentence or a paragraph of particular consequence.

Of course, the document could have been in Chinese and upside down for all they cared. This was the first chance they had to speak properly and at length and what they spoke of was Kitty's willingness to go to the Collinses and how soon Kitty's expansion would be too noticeable to allow her to delay her trip to Hunsford.

Kitty allowed Elizabeth to very discreetly run her hand along her stomach.

"It will not be long now when you must leave," she said. Which confirmed Kitty's own view.

Elizabeth immediately dispatched a letter expressing Kitty's consent to Charlotte. Her letter also proposed how it should be done.

And the pair waited and waited for news.

The days passed pleasantly and when the weather was fine, the Bennet sisters, often without Lydia, who remained in her room more and more, walked the grounds while the men were doing their fishing or riding or shooting. On one such day, just over a week since the Londoners arrived, Jane found a letter waiting for her on the silver tray kept on a small table in the front foyer.

"It's from...Charlotte Collins," Jane told the others with surprise, and they followed her into the sitting room to the right after the butler said he would fetch them some refreshments. Lydia was not with them that day, and Elizabeth and Kitty were glad of that as they stared at Jane while she read.

"Charlotte is asking about...Kitty," Jane said, stopping to look up. Elizabeth reached for Kitty's hand as Kitty tried to keep her resolve.

When Jane finished, she said, "I didn't know that Charlotte had anything to do with Kitty even when we were at Longbourn. Here, Kitty. What do you think?" she added as she handed the letter to that sister. Elizabeth tried to read it as well, but it was made difficult by Kitty's hands, which shook at first but eased as she went.

My Dearest Jane,

I must ask your advice on a matter concerning your sister Kitty. Do not be alarmed, I pray. I would like to have her come visit me, perhaps as something of a companion for some time. As I'm sure Eliza has told you, pleasant as things are in some respects, there are periods when I am exceedingly lonely, particularly when Mr. Collins is so dedicated to his work in the parish. As to my sister Maria, I do not believe my mother could spare her from Lucas Lodge.

When Eliza visited last, I spoke to her vaguely about this. Indeed, I feel lonelier after she leaves me. She, of course, has her family and her Fitzy and I cannot long impose on her. She suggested that perhaps Kitty would be an appropriate companion for me. I have given that suggestion extended thought and I believe she may be correct.

I write to you to solicit your opinion on the matter. I know that Lydia has certain expectations about her sister, but I cannot help but feel that she asks too much of Kitty. I do not know her well of course, but Eliza reports that she is more mature than I expected her to be after her period in the north with the Wickhams.

It may well be that Kitty cannot bring herself to leave her sister but, frankly, I think she should be given that choice as I feel she too often—and Eliza agrees with me on this—is led by Lydia and loses the opportunity to become her own woman.

Still, I think it is for Kitty to decide. Thus, I ask that, if you agree, you speak to Kitty about this. Tell her that I would be very pleased for her to move to Kent for a period. I truly would like the companionship of a Bennet and to have the chance to discover this one.

I write directly to you and not Eliza because I think she would be biased in favour of my request, and I truly wish someone to whom I am not so close to advise. Mr. Collins and I await her answer. As Eliza can assure her, there is more than enough space in our little Parsonage so that she will have a room of her own.

With best regards to you and yours,

I am, your friend,
Charlotte

Kitty pretended to be completely surprised by what she read, and she handed the letter to Elizabeth, who quickly scanned it to fully take in its contents. When that was done, Jane said, "It is a generous offer and it gives you the opportunity, I hate to say it, to come out from Lydia's shadow. What do you think, Lizzy?"

Elizabeth acted as if deep in thought for a moment. "Well, Jane. I think you are right there." She turned to Kitty. "I have long thought you are...stifled with Lydia. I truly have. Charlotte is the most wonderful of women and I think she could be the most wonderful of friends for you. I am inclined to agree with Jane. And, you know, Lydia and her baby will not be abandoned. She will have the rest of her family. She will not like it, of course. But I think Jane and I can assure her that it is for your good, Kitty, and that she and her baby will be in capable hands even without you."

Elizabeth proved right, though no one doubted she would be. Lydia was very, *very* unhappy but she was ultimately prevailed upon by references to how much it was in her character to think first of others and how it was best for Kitty to explore herself away from her dearest and youngest sister.

Darcy and Bingley could not fathom just what had gotten into their wives in their dealings with both Lydia and Kitty. But as it seemed to keep the peace, they were quite happy about it.

Chapter 18. An Empty Bed

Elizabeth awoke with a start in the night. The bed was empty beside her. While they each had their own bedrooms, Darcy usually remained in hers and in her bed on those evenings when they were intimate. They both came to relish the closeness as they drifted off and when they awoke (and particularly when things happened soon *after* they awoke).

On this night, they had been together, and she was taken aback that he'd left her. At first, she thought he must have gone to his own room as he sometimes did. She sensed, though, that he was more troubled than usual and that she should be with him whether he wanted her to be or not. She lit a candle and after confirming that his bedroom was empty, walked down one flight and a long hallway to his library. When she opened its door, the room was black and only her candle gave enough light for her to see her husband asleep in his nightshirt, draped across his desk, his arms splayed across its top. A candle had long since burned out and a group of papers was scattered beneath and around him.

Darcy's breath was quiet and rhythmic. She approached to get a better view of his countenance. As always when she watched him sleep, she was taken by how, stripped of all pretense, peaceful he seemed and was reminded of how much a fool she was for not seeing it sooner than she did and how happy she was that her pride—wounded by her having chanced to overhear him tell Bingley that she was no more than tolerable on the evening they met years earlier—had been overcome by affection and love.

She knew as he slept that at whatever hour it was, he was sad and lonely and lost but that his mask would return with the dawn.

Not long after she took this vision in, with her own candle running short of time, she awakened him. He shuddered but his senses were quickly regained. The couple returned to their shared bed where he fell into a sleep promptly upon hitting the mattress. It was then Elizabeth's turn to be sad and lost as she looked into the dark of their room wondering what would become of her family.

In the morning, the Darcys decided to go for a walk with Fitzy after breakfasting. Elizabeth said that the thoughts that she struggled with when she was trying to sleep had crystallized when she awoke.

"We will fight it," she told her husband. "And we will find a way, my dearest."

Darcy could say nothing to this beyond once again that whatever came, they would conquer it together.

As the Darcys approached the house, Jane came across the drive to meet them and asked Elizabeth to take a short turn with her over towards the lake. With Darcy taking charge of Fitzy, the sisters began their stroll.

"Lizzy, do you recall that time when I was in London with our aunt and uncle."

"How could I forget?"

"Well, I recall one gentleman who visited with us several times. I think our aunt hoped there might be some attraction but there was not."

"There was none on *your side*, I daresay. But I venture that there was more than a little attraction on his. But do go on."

"Lizzy you are incorrigible. We must be serious."

"Jane, I am being serious. There surely is not a man alive who is not attracted to you."

"Except of course that horrible Mr. Darcy," a sentiment she punctuated with a mocking shake of the head.

"Now, Jane. It is you who must be serious." Lizzy gave a loving tug to her sister. "Please tell me about this man."

"His name was James something. Our aunt will know. He was just finishing his law studies. He was with us several nights and he played cards with us four or five times. I thought him quite intelligent and ambitious. The sort of person I would feel comfortable speaking with and confiding with and sure that he would act in my best interest."

"Well, it certainly is worth considering, given how Darcy reacted to the old solicitor everyone told him to hire. But can you get his information from our aunt without arousing suspicion? You cannot confess to having a personal interest in him."

"I know. Help me figure it out."

By this point, though, the Gardiners knew generally about the misfortunes of the Darcys and the Bingleys. Lydia had written to her dear mamma shortly after that brief visit by the two men to Pemberley in early August. "I don't know what it is," she wrote, "but it looks as if the great Mr. Darcy may be falling on hard times. I cannot be sure, and you must tell no one, but he and Mr. Bingley came very suddenly and neither was in a fine mood, I can tell you. Not even Bingley! After meeting with the estate steward *and the solicitor*, they were gone as suddenly as they had come. Even the servants are talking, wondering whether they'll be put out."

Upon reading this, Mrs. Bennet of course hurried to her sister (Mrs. Philips) to discuss "the calamity Elizabeth has fallen into/I never did trust that man/oh to be with poor George Wickham."

To her credit, Mrs. Bennet displayed a rare and, for her, remarkable forbearance in not writing to Jane or to Elizabeth to express her great sympathy and to offer her maternal comfort. Mostly this was simply because she did not wish to yet again run afoul of her son-in-law, the proud, moody one, particularly once she realised that if the rumours were true, she soon might lose the ability to enjoy the comforts of his estate at Pemberley that she'd come to enjoy.

Still, Mrs. Bennet did dispatch a letter to her sister-in-law in London along the same lines as she spoke to her sister in Meryton.

Though Mrs. Gardiner quickly wrote back to Mrs. Bennet, she declined the invitation to spread those "details" of the calamity she knew lest they be spread though Meryton as they were already washing through London society. She was not the sort to "carry a bone." Still, when she got a letter from her sweet niece Jane inquiring about the identity of that lawyer from years before, the aunt had no doubt as to why a City barrister was suddenly needed for Mr. Darcy.

It did not take Mrs. Gardiner long to identify the "James" from those years before as James Drain. He was a young (and now married) barrister at Gray's Inn, and when she had this information, she forwarded it to Jane.

On the afternoon after Jane received Mrs. Gardiner's letter, the weather was neither too hot nor too wet, and so the two couples went for an afternoon stroll. When they were not too distant from the house itself, Jane told the others what she'd learnt about the young barrister.

After a moment's thought, Darcy recovered himself. "Dear Jane. This is, I think, frightfully good news. I so feared being bound to that Brower fellow. He is young and clever you say?"

"Indeed, he is," Jane confirmed. "I know little of these matters, but I do think if there is anyone who can be of help, it is him."

When Darcy looked at his wife, Lizzy said, "she will deny it, but I do believe Jane is quite a good judge of character," and Bingley added, "notwithstanding her horribly mistaken judgment about me, for which she must suffer for the rest of her days, I have to agree with Lizzy."

They turned back to the house, increasing their pace from their normal leisurely stroll. Inside, Darcy rushed to his library with an excitement that astonished the others. They'd not seen him so enthusiastic in many days. Within the hour, he'd written a letter to this James Drain, Esq., begging that he consider acting as his barrister in appearing in court instead of whomever Brower proposed. Within eight days Darcy received the response.

September 14, 1815

Dear Mr. Darcy,

It is perhaps well that you wrote when you did as I was forced to return to town just two days before your letter arrived and will have left again by the time this reaches you.

It can be a delicate thing to have a barrister appear for a solicitor when there is no prior relationship, especially with an esteemed solicitor such as Mr. Brower, but, frankly, I sympathize with the reason you give for wishing me to speak for you in court. I of course know Mr. Brower. He is widely respected. I fear, as I understand you do, that he might be too ready to concede points regarding your situation in order to expedite its closure.

I am generally aware of that situation and am acting for another who had the misfortune of entrusting money with Mr. Stewart (who, I note, has still not been heard from). I will be pleased to act as your barrister in this matter in lieu of who Mr. Brower has selected, who I am sure is quite competent in his own right. I ask that you promptly write to Mr. Brower advising him of this. I will then communicate directly with him to discuss the appropriate matters.

I will be back in town on the first Thursday of next month. That is October 5. If possible, I would like to meet with you and Mr. Brower or someone from his Chambers on the following day.

I have endeavoured to obtain the court calendar in the matter in which a petition has been filed on your behalf to protect your assets. I have learned that there is a hearing set on Thursday, October 19, though I do not expect anything of substance will then occur.

In any case, I look forward to representing you in this matter and extend my good wishes to you and yours and especially to your sister-in-law Jane, who (sadly, at least to your humble servant) had thoughts of someone other than me when we first met.

Very truly yours, &c., &c.
James Drain, Esq.
Gray's Inn

Chapter 19. Kitty's Journey to Kent

The normal leisurely pace at Pemberley was evaporating on two fronts. First was Darcy's having Brower arrange to have Drain act for him in the Chancery Court. He himself wrote to Brower as soon as he decided that he wished Drain to act as his barrister and thinking of what would take place at the October hearing.

Everyone knew about that. No one but Elizabeth and Kitty, though, knew about the other. Which was Kitty herself. She'd been able to hide her condition thanks to the formless dresses that were so popular (and comfortable) but that could not be true for much longer.

As to this latter front, with the agreed-upon date for Kitty's leaving Pemberley nearing, Lydia's initial altruism began to fade. "You cannot go," Lydia said to her time and time again when she was alone with her sister. "You *mustn't* go."

But of course, "go" Kitty must. Lydia's angry and petulant pleas fell on deaf ears. While Jane was non-committal and evasive, Elizabeth was downright hostile to the suggestion of Kitty remaining and had no hesitancy in expressing it directly to the young widow whenever it was brought up. Of course, as she'd learnt long ago, Lydia knew better than to bring up subjects that brought out Elizabeth's dark side, Lydia largely limited her petitions to Kitty herself.

The arrangements thus were made. Lydia, though, was herself too heavy to go to Derby with Kitty for the first part of her journey. Jane and Elizabeth went instead in one of the Pemberley coaches. They shopped in the city after seeing Kitty off. From there, Kitty caught the Derby to London post for the long trip. Although Bingley naturally and kindly offered to hire a carriage to take her all the way to Kent, Kitty had declined, having come to understand the need for less extravagance and appreciating, as Lizzy long had, the importance of the expense of travel for one without a fortune. Also, there was much to be said for the benefits of anonymity.

After two nights at inns along the road, Kitty would stay at the Bingleys' for the night when she got to London—she feared exposing her condition to the too-observant Gardiners—and then continue by post to Hunsford as Charlotte Collins's companion. There she'd hire a carriage for the remaining miles to the Parsonage.

The trip went to plan. When she finally arrived at the Collinses', she was quite exhausted. Mr. and especially Mrs. Collins were very excited about their visitor. Kitty was slightly showing (if one cared to look), but soon would be beyond being able to hide it from anyone. The room Lizzy had used during her stays was prepared for her. It was small but well furnished, somewhere between the grandness of Pemberley and the Spartan nature of the army's facility in Newcastle. It looked out the rear of the Parsonage. Instead of seeing the church, Kitty had a view of a small wood that stood between the Parsonage and the fields that were goldening with wheat.

Kitty thought it perfect. More tired from her trip than she realised. Once alone in her room she fell into a deep slumber and slept more soundly than she had...well, since she had in she knew not how long.

Charlotte went to awaken her with a plate of food soon after the sun was down. They were never close, Charlotte and Kitty. Indeed, *distant* would be the accurate way to describe them. Largely this was because of the age gap between them, nearly a decade, combined with their quite different natures and Kitty nearly always being with Lydia.

On that first evening, with the tray, Charlotte placed it and her candle on the small table beside the bed and sat on a small, wooden chair. The candle shed some flickering light on the girl. She watched Kitty's breathing and the angelic look that defined her countenance. It was a pleasant face, somewhere between Jane's and Elizabeth's. She expected her child, whomever the father might be, would be pleasant looking.

A shudder swept over Charlotte. For the first time, she realised, *truly realised,* that the child in this girl's belly would soon forever be her responsibility. That she, Mrs. William Collins, would be this child's mother. She was afraid she'd awaken Kitty with her sudden sobbing and controlled it but could not resist reaching over and running the tips of her fingers across Kitty's cheek, rising up and down with her breathing.

Charlotte only knew what Elizabeth told her about how Kitty ended up as she ended up. She knew she should not be overly sympathetic to her after the sinfulness of what she did. In a thousand thousand years Charlotte would not have done such a thing. Nor would Elizabeth or Jane or any of Charlotte's few other friends (though she feared that her sister Maria just might make such a mistake).

Sitting there, though, staring at the innocent face and knowing enough about Kitty and how she was with Lydia and thinking of the child growing in her, Charlotte Collins promised herself she would do everything within her powers for the woman and her child. Then she woke Kitty up and gave her the small meal she'd carried upstairs.

Chapter 20. In Court

With Kitty gone from Pemberley, thoughts in Derbyshire turned to that other topic: The unpleasant business about the damage wrought by Stewart. Darcy showed Elizabeth a letter from his solicitor. It confirmed the hearing in his matter in mid-October and that Darcy would need to meet with Drain and his solicitor beforehand. "Drain does not expect much of consequence to occur at this appearance," Brower wrote, "but one must be prepared."

Since all of them were increasingly anxious already, they agreed to leave so as to be back in town by the first week of October. Because Lydia was getting closer and closer, a letter was sent to Longbourn requesting the presence of Mr. and Mrs. Bennet. When they arrived at Pemberley, Jane remained while the Darcys and Charles Bingley headed south. In a Pemberley carriage, they were off to town.

Some days later, Darcy looked at Bingley. They were in a dark, paneled courtroom on the first floor of an ancient stone courthouse whose front faced the Strand.

"This is intolerable," Darcy said, beneath his breath.

Bingley put his hand on Darcy's thigh and leaned over.

"You must remain calm in the face of this."

"'Calm in the face of this'? I think not," and before Bingley could stop him, Darcy was on his legs, shouting, "My Lord, My Lord," as his words echoed about the cavernous room.

All eyes in the courtroom turned to him. Most anxiously his barrister's, who whispered loudly, "Darcy for God's sake, sit down." Darcy's solicitor, Mr. Brower, remained stoical in the face of the ridiculousness of his client.

"I cannot. I will not remain seated while this fool runs off his mouth," Darcy said, quite loudly himself.

He made a hand gesture towards the bench, but no one was in doubt as to who he considered a fool.

"Sir," the Most Honourable Thomas Kincaid said, "Who are you?"

He asked this with a practiced calm and predator's smile.

"I am a gentleman, Sir. I am Fitzwilliam Darcy, and I will not stand for being spoken to and spoken about as I hear in your courtroom right now."

All eyes shifted from the debtor to the judge and all but the barristers were surprised when he smiled and said, "Ah, yes. Mr. Darcy. Well, Mr. Darcy, in the court's eyes and in the eyes of the law, you are no gentleman. You are merely a debtor. You are the fool in this courtroom. Who allowed someone to take advantage of him and take all of his money and then some.

"No, Mr. Darcy, you, Sir, are the fool in this room and it is up to me and to your barrister, Mr. Drain here, to try to correct the stupidity in which you and some of your fellows have engaged. I will hear no more from you. You have a fine barrister. He will speak far better in your interest than you ever could."

"Better? He is nothing but a hired man, retained to do *my* work, to do *my* bidding, and I will speak, Sir, when I decide it is appropriate for me to speak and I will not be silenced by someone as arrogant and prejudiced as you are."

"Let me be clear Mr. Darcy." What began quietly was now bursting for yet another of the idiots who appeared before him day after day. "In this courtroom, you are a party. No more. No less. Whether you entered this courtroom as a gentleman or as royalty or as a pauper, the law treats you all the same."

From his perch, he waved his extended arm across the room as if he were Lear gazing about his estates.

"In this courtroom, Mr. Darcy, you are nothing but a supplicant seeking to have the court resolve disputes in which you find yourself. I will not tolerate insolence from you as pretending to be any more than a party to this unfortunate business and, Sir, if I hear one more word from you, you will be taken down for the contempt of the court that you so plainly hold.

"Your barrister, should you deign to listen to him, will tell you that I will not hesitate to do it, Sir, and I promise you that I will not. Do I make myself clear?"

Darcy paused, his fists tightening at his sides. Bingley tried the impossible task of supporting his friend while making himself invisible.

"Perfectly," Darcy said through his teeth.

"Good." The Hon. Thomas Kincaid sat back in his tall chair. "But I assure you, Sir, that in this courtroom justice is blind, and I will not be swayed for good or ill by your outburst. I will decide the matter fairly and as the law requires me to. For now, I suggest, Sir, very much that you defer to the guidance and leadership of your counsel. He is a fine if young barrister. He will serve you better than you possibly could.

"This matter is adjourned for four weeks, at ten o'clock."

With that, the judge hurried from the bench, and the courtroom was silent until the door to his chambers was closed. Then, the entirety of the courtroom, barristers, solicitors, and clients alike, burst into excitement about the dressing down they'd just witnessed, except for Darcy, Bingley, Brower, and James Drain, Esq.

In the hallway, Drain assured Darcy that he, Darcy, had done quite well all in all. To Darcy's, and Bingley's, confusion, he said, "I have seen him treat debtors far worse than he treated you, Mr. Darcy. I assure you. Sometimes he is in a difficult mood and is simply waiting to speak to someone as he spoke to you, establishing his primacy in his courtroom. But as long as you do not repeat what you did, it will not signify that you did it the once. He is a fair judge and will not hold against you the fact that you are a gentleman who trusted the wrong man with his money.

"No, Mr. Darcy, it was not nearly as bad as it looked. But you will damage your case if you repeat your outburst. So as the Most Honourable Mr. Justice Kincaid said, you must trust *me* in this matter. We will set it to rights. I promise you. We will set it to rights."

"I believe this is true, Sir," Mr. Brower said in the silence, and he looked somewhat crossly at the barrister who he felt bore some of the blame for their client's very poor behaviour.

"What a horrible, horrible man." This was Elizabeth just as she reached her husband, Bingley, and Darcy's lawyers. She'd watched the proceedings from the gallery above that largely encircled the large courtroom. "Horrible, horrible," she repeated. She was still shaking from her fury. "He is a pompous ass, and I would like to give him a piece of my mind," and she would have done just that if he came down the hallway at that moment. But he did not and Drain smiled at her.

"Mrs. Darcy. Please pay it no mind. As I just told your husband, judges like to establish their authority in their courtrooms, and there is often a debtor who rises and takes the court's abuse so that everyone in the courtroom understands who is the judge and who is not."

"A stalking horse?"

"Precisely, Ma'am. But as I assured your husband, if he refrains from repeating what he did just now, he will be treated fairly by this judge, and it is my job to ensure that that is the case."

Elizabeth seemed to relax in the barrister's words. She was glad they had retained him.

"We must continue," he said, "to focus on getting this business resolved in a positive way and that is what we are going to do. I promise you." He looked at both Darcys in turn as well as to Bingley. When he finished, as he lifted his pile of papers close to his chest and removed his wig, he repeated it. "I promise you all."

With a bow, he turned and headed from them as did Brower, after his own bow, the lawyers' footsteps echoing loudly on the marble floor until they mixed with the clamor of all the lawyers and parties mingling, their voices echoing about the mosaic tiles that defined the arched hallway, with each of the parties being quite happy that he was not the once-rich fool who'd jumped to his feet.

Chapter 21. Elizabeth Goes to Kent

The matter was adjourned for the four weeks, during which Darcy's barrister assured his client that he would be working to lessen the impact of the proceedings.

More immediately for everyone, then, was that Lydia's delivery was imminent. It was agreed that they should all be in attendance when that happened. Jane had stayed behind with her and been joined by Mr. and Mrs. Bennet.

At Pemberley, Lydia savoured being the center of attention. She went into labor less than two days after Elizabeth and the others returned from London. She was young and strong, and it was not long before a new baby's cries echoed through the manor and Lydia insisted that one and all come to praise little Georgie Wickham, which was promptly and dutifully done (except by Little Fitz, who Lydia barred out of fear that he might infect her infant).

It was not long after that blessed event that Elizabeth received a letter from Charlotte. It was not a particularly long letter and did little more than report on the goings-on in Rosings.

Hunsford Parsonage
October 20, 1815

Dearest Eliza,

The weather has been quite warm at times, but I believe or at least hope that the worst of it is over. I know you are anxious for news about your sister Catherine—who has expressed a preference for that name since she arrived. She has proved invaluable to the needs of Mr. Collins and myself. She spends much of her days wandering around the paths that you are so familiar with.

I would dearly love to see you again, as would Catherine. We hope Lydia progresses well and that if her child has come that they are both healthy and that the child provides your sister the opportunity to renew life after the tragic death of her dear Wickham.

As always,
Charlotte

Indeed, Georgie had appeared and was well and since Lydia preferred Jane's company to hers as she always had and even better had their dear mother with her, Elizabeth would be able to head through London to Kent ten days after little Georgie joined the world, Darcy and Bingley having already returned to town.

The night before she was to leave Derbyshire and was settling in for the night in anticipation of the trip, she heard a knocking on her door.

"Come in," she called, and in came Jane, also ready for bed.

"I shall miss you, Lizzy. But I must tell you something. It is early days, I think, but I am quite beside myself because, you see, I am with child."

Lizzy, who was sitting at a small table brushing out her hair, overturned her chair and lost track of her brush as she rushed to the widely and wildly smiling sister.

In their hug, she whispered in Jane's ear, "Oh I am so happy for the both of you. Do you know how long?"

"I do not but—" She stepped back and lifted her sister's hand to run across her belly. "It is several months I think."

"I mustn't go."

"Don't be silly. You are the first one I've told. Not even Charles. He was gone before I was confident in my condition."

Lizzy noticed an envelope in her sister's hand, and Jane lifted it.

"I therefore charge you with a most important task. You are to deliver this to my dearest husband. In it, I tell him to tell this news to your dear husband, so I ask that you refrain from doing so."

"Of course, I will not."

"Or anyone else. It is only for the four of us, plus the apothecary, to know, and I think it is the proper thing that the father be the one to tell Darcy."

"Oh, Jane. I agree completely."

There was a pause during which the two sisters found themselves sitting on Lizzy's bed.

"Lizzy," Jane said. "Please tell me you are happy for me."

"Oh, Jane, I could not be more joyful about anything else in the world."

So, at Jane's insistence, the secret left Pemberley in the morning as Lizzy began her trip to Kent, over enthused by what her sister told her the night before.

Though she knew Darcy would have insisted she hire a carriage for the trip, she had not permitted it. "The reality is, Jane, that we may well be taking public stages with some frequency when we can afford to travel so I might as well try to become accustomed to it," she said. "And it is not as if I didn't take one long ago after my first visit to Hunsford."

After a final, extended hug with her dearest sister, Lizzy got aboard one of Pemberley's chaises. It carried her as far as Derby where she boarded a post for the trip to London much as Kitty did a few months before. After two nights at inns along the way, she got to Brook Street early on an afternoon. She promptly fulfilled her duty and handed Jane's letter to the waiting Bingley in the front sitting room when Darcy had left them alone briefly and then left the two men when he returned.

It was not ten minutes later that the pair burst into the foyer and rushed up the stairs to find Lizzy anticipating their "intrusion" in her study and her brother-in-law could not control his glee at the news and Darcy was not far behind in his own enthusiasm.

It was not long before contentment and anticipation filled the room and was only dissipated when the three sat down for their dinner, enjoyed quietly in the dining parlour that overlooked the street.

The next morning, Mrs. Darcy would take another stage to Hunsford where she'd hire a chaise to take her to the Parsonage itself. It did take some effort on her part, though, to convince the two men that she would be quite all right traveling "in a manner all sorts of people have been taking for many years." Darcy would, of course, accompany her to the post station.

The following morning, though, a carriage appeared outside the house on Brook Street shortly before Elizabeth finished her slight and happy breakfast with Darcy and Bingley in the dining parlour.

The footman who was the house's *de facto* butler while Bradley remained at Pemberley announced that "a carriage was sent to take Mrs. Darcy to the Hunsford Parsonage and it is waiting out front."

"Carriage?" she asked, quite surprised.

"Yes, Ma'am. Quite a fine one if I do say so meself," said the young servant before he recalled his place. "Beg your pardon, Ma'am. The coachman just said he'd been sent by his mistress—"

"'Mistress' you say?"

"Aye, Ma'am. That's what he said. 'My mistress hopes that your mistress'—that'd be you, Ma'am—'would do her the honour of riding in her carriage so as to make it easier and quicker for you to get to Hunsford.' That's what the footman said, Ma'am."

Bingley got up and looked out to Brook Street.

"Indeed. There is a fine one waiting. A landau with four."

The others joined him. It *was* a fine one, in dark green with a maroon trim and gold piping with a crest that could not quite be made out. Its horses were handsome and could have been brothers, all sharing a deep, dark brown and white strips across their snouts.

Darcy turned to the footman. "Tell him that Mrs. Darcy will be out when she is ready."

"Who could it be, Fitzwilliam?" Elizabeth asked when the servant had gone.

"I will enquire while you get yourself prepared."

While his wife was upstairs, he went to the carriage, and he was waiting for her when she came down some minutes later. He'd directed two footmen to carry her bags to the landau and have them loaded.

"It is from my cousin," he said as she reached the lower steps of the staircase.

"Your cousin?"

"It seems that for reasons I do not understand, Anne de Bourgh is aware of your journey and is wanting to facilitate it."

Elizabeth was at a loss as well.

"Anne de Bourgh? I've not spoken to her since that first trip there, and as you know I barely spoke four words to her then. Are you sure?"

"That's what her man said, and it is the de Bourgh crest. It must be true."

Bingley—who, we should note, had already penned and dispatched a brief letter to his bride—stood with them, and the three walked to the curb where the landau's door was held open by the de Bourgh footman. When Elizabeth was safely inside, she promised her husband that she would let him know what Anne de Bourgh had to do with anything as soon as she herself learned it.

With that, Darcy gave a "drive on" to the coachman and they were off, though the footman moved to sit beside the coachman shortly after they crossed the Thames and began the passage through the countryside.

The de Bourgh carriage pulled up to the Parsonage in the early afternoon.

The Collinses must have heard its approach since Charlotte and Mr. Collins and Kitty were standing by their gate when it pulled up. Mr. Collins reached the carriage door before the footman could. He opened it and helped Elizabeth disembark. Charlotte was soon on her dear friend. Kitty stood off to the side slightly, and her condition was clear. Elizabeth stepped to her, and hugged her and both women cried, although just slightly, before they were led into the Parsonage by Mr. Collins, and Elizabeth was able to sit in the window seat in the kitchen so she could catch her breath as they heard the carriage-and-four return to the Rosings Park stables.

Chapter 22. The Rumours

As soon as she had her wits about her, Elizabeth asked about the carriage.

"I must take the credit for that, my dear cousin," Mr. Collins said. "When Miss de Bourgh was passing by several days ago, she stopped when she got to our door, as she is often so kind about doing. I told her we were to expect a visit from you and that you were coming to see your sister. We'd just received your letter telling us when you would be arriving and without a thought, she told me that she would have a carriage sent to London to bring you down.

"'I cannot have your cousin suffer in a post,' she said. She is so good that way. And yesterday afternoon we saw her best carriage-and-four drive past and we knew it must be to collect you, so we were ready when you finally appeared."

With that bit of intelligence and none of them knowing *why* Miss de Bourgh had gotten involved beyond wishing to do a good deed for her parson, they prepared for dinner.

When that was over, the four adjourned into the Collinses' parlour. Elizabeth immediately saw when she arrived that Kitty could not remain much longer. Word of her condition would quickly circulate, making it difficult for their plan to succeed and significantly compromising Mr. Collins's integrity and position.

He'd sent discreet inquiries to a number of parsons in the county, and two or three responded that there might be a place where Kitty could be adequately cared for in the last months of her confinement. To each, Mr. Collins wrote, telling them that he would stop to visit them when he did a circuit of the county.

His cousin Elizabeth naturally insisted that she accompany him, which the other two ladies agreed to.

"They will be day trips, Mr. Collins. If your wife does not object, I cannot see how anyone else could. And we will never be alone," Elizabeth argued.

It was an argument with which Mr. Collins found little to dispute and given the delicacy of the task, he could not see how any of the vicars they met with could object to the subject's sister being part of the matter. After a prayer, it was settled. The first visit would be in two days' time.

The next morning before the others were up and after penning a note to Darcy saying she'd arrived quite well but still did not know why Anne de Bourgh sent her carriage, Elizabeth decided to walk. She was well familiar with the paths around the Parsonage from her first visit there, when she met with Darcy and also with his cousin Colonel Richard Fitzwilliam.

She had reacquainted herself in her prior visits with what became her favourite walk from the Parsonage, through a gate in the pales opposite. It was a nice, sheltered path that meandered along the open grove that edged that side of the park. There was a slight brook that paralleled it, and the sound of its water passing over stones had long been a comfort to those who passed near it.

Now she returned to this path. The air, slightly but distinctly different from what it was at Pemberley and worlds apart from London's, would serve as a wonderful tonic after her trip and in anticipation of what could be a difficult series of journeys to come.

She tired more quickly than she expected. After perhaps only a quarter of an hour or twenty minutes, she decided to turn back to the Parsonage but not before resting briefly on a large tree bench that was in the shade off to the side. The tree fell in a storm some years before and it and a number of others were sprinkled along the path, their tops—their sides before they had fallen—shaved slightly to create a comfortable resting seat just to the side.

Elizabeth was sitting for only a minute or so, attempting to summon the energy to begin her journey back when she heard and then saw a light carriage. It was a two-wheeled gig with a single white horse. It was not going very fast and had a pair of occupants. The fairer of them climbed out, leaving a footman holding the reins. It was, much to Elizabeth's astonishment, Miss Anne de Bourgh herself.

That woman directed the servant to return to the house, and after dusting herself off, exchanged curtsies with Elizabeth.

It in fact had taken a moment for Elizabeth to recognise her unexpected visitor. She was still a small woman but hardly the sickly and cross creature Elizabeth thought her to be when she first saw her, on this very path, stopping in front of the Parsonage on Elizabeth's first trip to Hunsford. While her skin was light in tone it was far from being pale and was well set off by her black hair which she'd allowed to flow down below her shoulders. Her appearance was so altered from those long ago visits to Rosings Park when Lady Catherine presided that Elizabeth might not have recognised her had they passed one another on Meryton's high street.

"Might I have a word, Mrs. Darcy?"

To Elizabeth it was reminiscent of this woman's mother asking nearly the same question at Longbourn in those rough days before she became Mrs. Fitzwilliam Darcy. Notwithstanding the kind things said about Anne by Charlotte, and also (if less credibly) by Mr. Collins, she feared Lady Catherine's blood ran too deep in Anne de Bourgh's veins. She prepared to be treated with the same disdain and that it would have serious consequences for Kitty and all the plans made with the Collinses. *Surely, she could not know of those plans. Surely, she would not destroy them.*

These thoughts flashed through Elizabeth as she stood and for a moment she could not move.

When the gig was turned around and heading back whence it came, the two women began to walk back to the Parsonage. Elizabeth was wearing a comfortable dress and comfortable shoes—the types the Bingley sisters so enjoyed mocking. Anne was dressed in much the same manner, a pair of country girls bearing scant resemblance to the society ladies they in fact were.

"Thank you for sending your carriage for me," Elizabeth said.

"It was my pleasure when Mr. Collins told me of your plans." Anne paused in her speech. "I normally would ride out on my own on a fine morning like this, but I wished to walk with you. I am glad we can be alone. I happened to see you leave the Parsonage for your early walk and I rushed to make myself tolerably presentable and roused one of my footmen and he roused one of the horses so I could be with you."

The women's arms were intertwined and soon the dust disturbed by the small carriage was back in the path and the only sounds were of the birds and insects in the wood.

"You must know that I regret what my mother did to you so long ago. I believe she went to her grave thinking she might have precipitated your marriage to my cousin instead of preventing it."

"I cannot say that is the case. At most she might have *expedited* something that I like to think would have occurred anyway."

"I assure you, Mrs. Darcy, I did not suffer long the loss of Fitzwilliam as a husband. I very much doubt we would have been suitable for one another, and I do know that you are far more suitable for him than I ever could be."

There was nothing to say to that, so they continued in silence.

"There is a matter of more immediate concern, which is why I am glad I saw you this morning," Miss Anne de Bourgh said.

"Tell me about your family, Mrs. Darcy."

"*My family?* Surely you cannot care about my family," Elizabeth said, taken aback by the peculiar question.

"I may surprise you as to what I find of interest. I understand that your father has been blessed, or cursed in some respects, to have only had daughters. That the estate—"

"Longbourn."

"Yes. That Longbourn is entailed and will go to our Mr. Collins when your father dies, which I hope will be a long time off. I know of you and your oldest sister, who married Charles Bingley, and of course the one who ran off with the soldier."

"My youngest sister, Lydia. They were married and he joined the regulars but was killed at Waterloo."

"So I have been told. Mr. Wickham. It is very sad. And she is with child, according to Mrs. Collins."

"Indeed, Miss de Bourgh, the child is born and healthy and named Georgie after his father."

They stopped at Miss de Bourgh's insistence.

"I do not like that," she said. She pulled her arm from Elizabeth's with some force.

"'Miss de Bourgh' indeed. No one calls me by my Christian name, and I would like for you to do it in return for you allowing me to call you "Elizabeth.'"

Elizabeth blushed a bit, said she would like that, and had Miss de Bourgh reinsert her hand through her own.

"I will call you Elizabeth. You seem more an 'Elizabeth' I think than a 'Lizzy' or 'Eliza.' May I do that?"

"Of course, Miss...Anne."

"It will be our little secret," and the lady of the manor was quite pleased by this little intimacy.

"I have only learned recently about another sister. She is the one staying with Mrs. Collins."

"Indeed. I thought it would benefit them both for Kitty to move to the Parsonage here."

"I have seen her strolling, but she seems rather nervous, your sister. I've asked that she join the Collinses for dinner at the house, but Mrs. Collins always makes her apologies and says she has one ailment or another. I sometimes fear your sister is being held as some sort of prisoner."

Elizabeth held her breath in, but Anne had quickly moved on.

"Is that it then? I mean as to your sisters."

"Indeed not. My middle sister is Mary. She married a clergyman whose living is in Northumberland."

"Well, that is quite far, to be sure. Do you ever see her? Perhaps at your parents'?"

Elizabeth hesitated. The flow of conversation required her honesty.

"None of us gets along particularly with Mary. She can be...sanctimonious and is I believe as glad not to deal with us except in letters from a distance as we are to deal with her in that manner."

"Ah, the woes of multiple siblings. I have none, but I will defer to you regarding how you treat one another."

They were silent for a time as their stroll continued, the only sounds coming from the various birds flying among the trees and now and then bouncing along the path itself and from the stream's gurgling. Elizabeth, then, was startled when Anne spoke.

"I believe I know the reason for your journey here and why your sister is here. Servants *will* talk. You are right to be concerned about gossip, as I am sure you are. I am here to mention a possible resolution to you.

"It is my understanding, to be clear, that Catherine is pregnant."

"'Catherine'?"

"'Kitty' as it was. She is too old and in no condition to be called 'Kitty,' don't you think?"

"Mrs. Collins expressed Kitty's wish to be known as Catherine."

"There you have it then. We are all in agreement so far. I further understand that in the end the Collinses hope to care for the child and raise it as their own. I know my mother was forever encouraging poor Mrs. Collins to 'be fertile and multiply' and I expect they have endeavoured to do that without success."

There was nothing Elizabeth could say to this, of course.

"You must know, Elizabeth Darcy," Anne continued, "that I fully support the efforts regarding the baby and that I will do whatever is in my power to ensure he or she is well cared for and I hope well loved. And I will rely on you to be my intermediary. I cannot let my involvement be known *to anyone*. Is that understood? Other than absolutely necessary. Which means only Catherine and Mr. and Mrs. Collins. But no one else must know."

Anne de Bourgh stopped as she said this last, and Elizabeth turned so they faced one another.

"Understood."

Elizabeth did not quite look at Anne before this. She was a small woman, as Elizabeth remembered from their meetings at what was then Lady Catherine's years earlier.

"Devon," Anne said.

"Devon?"

"It's far away from here or London or Pemberley for that matter. I have made arrangements, if Catherine agrees, for her to go there and complete her confinement in what is a small but sufficiently sized and sufficiently anonymous house occupied by a widow, though not aged by any means, who is one of my not-so-distant cousins. Her connection to me will remain a secret."

They came upon another of those tree benches that appeared along the path. Anne directed Elizabeth to it.

"Catherine must realise that her only chance in our sphere is for no one to know. If she is in the southwest, no one who matters in our world will know, I promise you. In this parish, it will be accepted when it arrives at the Parsonage that the child's mother is not one of this parish or anyone they know. We will fashion a story. Perhaps a waif from London's East End.

"But no one can suspect Catherine. If she agrees, our remaining difficulty is explaining to those who know her where she has gone while she is in Devon. I need you to think on that. But of course, that has always been something that needed to be considered."

Anne stood, and Elizabeth did the same.

"How do you think Catherine will react? Being sent so far?"

It was such a strange suggestion. Elizabeth had been pondering the question of where Kitty would go just as the Collinses had with Mr. Collins's letters to the parsons he knew. In many respects his solution was better as Elizabeth at least might be able to visit her sister discreetly. There was much to be said, though, that the farther away Kitty was the better and that if Anne de Bourgh suggested it, Elizabeth was confident that Kitty would be well cared for.

With Mr. Collins due to leave the next morning, they'd have to take the decision that day.

To Anne de Bourgh's question, Elizabeth said, "I truly believe her only concerns will be the baby. She has grown so much with what is in her belly. If she knows it will not be an undue imposition on this cousin of yours, she may agree to do it. I think she is in any case resigned to be largely alone. It will not be for too long, though, and it may make things easier for everyone if she is far away until the baby comes."

"Please let me know when you can."

Elizabeth nodded and the two resumed their stroll, both silent till they reached the Parsonage.

"Whatever happens, Elizabeth, I want to think of me as your friend. I have few, and I would like you to be one of them."

Elizabeth nodded and repeated, "I should like that. Anne." Then she went into the Parsonage where Kitty was waiting to pounce on her when she saw her sister appear with Miss de Bourgh and was desperate to learn what they spoke about.

And Anne de Bourgh walked to her mansion, satisfied that her mission had gone as well as she could have hoped.

Chapter 23. The Lady's Companion

Kitty—we have arrived at a point in this narrative where this one woman is referred to by different names by different people, but we will continue as we tell the tale to refer to her as "Kitty" for as long as possible aware that some but by no means all of the others consider her to be Catherine Bennet (not least that lady herself)—quickly decided that she'd prefer to live far away in the southwest for some months than in a Kentish Parsonage—"I do not mean to offend you, Mr. Collins"—so as the two Bennet girls sat with the Collinses after dinner it was agreed.

"I've given a fair amount of thought," Elizabeth said, "to how it can be done without raising undue suspicion."

She would explain to everyone in the family that given the recent financial restraints on the Darcys and the Bingleys and adding Kitty's desire to become independent, she would remain with Charlotte in Kent but would visit when the Collinses came through town on the way to seeing Charlotte's family in Meryton. Of course, when that time came, Kitty would be reported to be suffering an ailment that prevented her from traveling, but that would be for later.

"Lydia will not like it," Kitty said.

"You must be going away. Lydia will like *nothing* we do. I think this may be our best chance."

"I'd like *someone* to visit."

Elizabeth smiled. "I would if I could, but it will be impossible at the time of year."

"I know. But you will write?"

"Of course. Discreetly."

"As will I," added Charlotte, and this seemed to satisfy Kitty who, after all, had no options.

That night, Mr. Collins wrote notes to the parsons he planned on visiting explaining that circumstances had changed and that he would not be able to see them as planned but hoped to at least during Christmastime. He rode into Hunsford early the next morning to dispatch them.

While he was doing that, Kitty and Elizabeth walked to Rosings Hall. They found Anne de Bourgh taking a turn in the garden to the side. It was the garden visitors would pass before reaching the house. When she saw the two Bennets, she called them to join her. There was a small gazebo in a corner of the garden surrounded by a pebbled walk with two small benches within.

The garden had lost most of its colour as it prepared for the coming winter, but several sturdy late-blooming flowers offered some tinting. Anne led the others up the steps to the gazebo itself. It was not large, so when Elizabeth and Kitty sat on one bench and Anne on the other, they were close enough to converse without any strain.

Kitty was very nervous, but Elizabeth had told her as they walked that Anne was a kind woman and nothing compared to the woman—her mother—who appeared at Longbourn those years before and who Kitty saw only briefly when Lady Catherine came to berate Elizabeth before disappearing as suddenly as she'd come.

Kitty had seen Anne de Bourgh several times when the lady rode past the Parsonage and had greeted her once or twice when she stopped to speak briefly with the Collinses. But when she was invited to go with the Collinses at Rosings Hall, Charlotte always had made her excuses. There was no more putting it off, though, now that her secret was out.

Kitty was surprised at how sweet and gentle Anne was, always calling her "Catherine." However small she was in stature, Kitty thought her dark but somehow shiny eyes framed by superb dark hair and below thick eyebrows rendered her uncommonly intelligent and perhaps even...beautiful.

All of this confirmed Kitty in her decision. "I have decided," she said when announcing her choice, "to take advantage of your offer. Lizzy suggests that people be told I am remaining here as Mrs. Collins's companion."

Anne looked at the older Bennet. "I knew you'd come up with something and that is quite a good idea."

Elizabeth nodded and said, "I know nothing of the circumstances of your cousin."

"She is a widow, not too old but with few prospects in a small house who wishes to have a companion so it will hardly raise concerns there. No, it is a fine solution."

She asked Kitty to stand and after a "May I?" and a nod she ran her hand across Kitty's belly.

"It won't be long now, I think. We must make final arrangements promptly. I'm afraid that it may be too late to have her visit her family on the way, assuming they do not know."

"No one knows except for the three of us and Mr. and Mrs. Collins."

"Not even Mrs. Bingley?"

Elizabeth looked to Kitty, who answered, "Someday she may know, but I don't wish word to be spread too far and I hope she'll forgive me for not including her. I fear she won't be as careful with the information as I know Lizzy is, though I do not mean that she would reveal anything intentionally. Just that it might slip. I had to tell someone, and I decided it was better that it be Lizzy."

They separated soon thereafter, with Anne promising to expedite the arrangements with a letter to Exeter where her widowed cousin—a Mrs. Elster—was to confirm everything and ask that Kitty be allowed to come as soon as possible, now that Anne saw how far along she was.

As the Bennet girls reached the path and were nearly to the Parsonage, Kitty hadn't said a word since leaving Anne. Elizabeth finally asked, "Out with it, Kitty. I know you too well not to know there is something you are afraid to say."

Kitty stopped, and Elizabeth turned to her.

"Lizzy, I know you have not told anyone my secret. But I must confess something to you. There is no Captain Johnson."

Elizabeth was not as shocked by this revelation as perhaps she should have been.

"I made him up and that he died at Waterloo."

"Wickham?"

Kitty nodded. She might have fallen had not Elizabeth quickly placed her hands around her sister's waist.

"They were going to battle. He couldn't lie with Lydia. Oh, Lizzy, I am so miserable. It must be him. He was the only one."

"Oh God, Kitty," which may not have been heard as the other woman was awash in her own tears.

Elizabeth pushed slightly away, which frightened Kitty until she used a finger to lift Kitty's chin. She saw the welling up in Kitty's eyes and tightened her own hands' grip.

"I told you I would be with you whatever. Do you remember?"

Kitty nodded.

"This does not change that. He is gone. Right now, we must deal with the baby who is coming. Not with the man who is not."

Elizabeth tightened her grip around Kitty's waist.

"It is alright. We will survive this. We *will* get through this."

With that, the interview ended, and they resumed their stroll. Whether Kitty got any sleep Elizabeth could not know. She only knew that she did not.

Chapter 24. Dinner with Anne

Anne de Bourgh insisted that those at the Parsonage join her for dinner the next evening. It was rainy, so she sent her carriage for them, and they were happy to get in, shielded by an umbrella held by a servant. The Collinses were sporadic visitors to the house now that Lady Catherine had met her maker, though few others came by.

Anne did little entertaining. Even at the very fine house her mother bought on London's Russell Square in Bloomsbury she rarely hosted traditional dinners. Her preference was to invite musicians—singers and players—for small groups of suitably appreciative friends and acquaintances.

As far as the Collinses knew, she rarely had guests for dinner at Rosings. They felt honoured about being asked this night, and it proved to be a delightful meal, excepting the secret that Lizzy and Kitty kept in their breasts.

Anne more than anything focused on Mr. Collins of all people and drew from him parts of his history that not even Charlotte knew and some things that helped the Bennets to better understand what unpleasantness separated their father from Mr. Collins's.

It was still raining when it was time to depart and the four returning to the Parsonage were all enthused at the good time they had.

Elizabeth went for a walk early the next morning. This time, though, she turned towards the manor house. She was unsure after the horrible thing she'd learnt from Kitty and perhaps without realising it hoped to come upon Anne's kind face.

As she neared the house, then, she was pleased to see Anne in the gazebo with a book in her lap, sitting at such an angle that she would see someone approaching and Elizabeth understood that her being there was no accident.

"Come, Elizabeth, let's take a turn," Anne said as she placed her novel on the bench she'd vacated. They headed to the path and continued to the north, away from the Parsonage. They were not far when Elizabeth asked whether Anne heard of her cousin's financial misfortune.

"Even here, word of that has traveled. It must be very hard on him."

"He feels he betrayed his family more than anything and that he is forcing me and our boy to undergo hardship."

"And are you?"

"It is early days, but I was not born into luxury or society and will be happy enough with him and Little Fitzy in a little hovel somewhere."

There was a brief silence beyond the sound of their feet slapping the packed dirt on the path.

"You must be his rock. He will be lost without you."

"I know that. It sometimes frightens me."

"Why?"

"He was so very independent when we met. I could see him living a life as a bachelor. He would make a fine monk if he didn't enjoy the company of others so much. But I fear he will lose that company now that we may be poor."

"You do not know whether you will be 'poor'?"

"Matters were being resolved or at least considered when I came here. I expect to hear word shortly about where things stand. But I fear it is very bad and that he will blame himself for it all when it was not his fault that he trusted the wrong man."

Anne pulled Elizabeth closer.

"Because I would not have made him a good wife does not mean that I cannot make him a good friend. If you will allow me."

"*Me?* What am I to do with it?"

"Were you born into society you would know. A man and a woman who are friends and no more is practically unheard of. A man with a woman of good or young appearance must be in want of something more than friendship is society's common understanding."

"You cannot mean people think that about my friendship with Charles Bingley."

"I can mean that. You are clever but naïve, I think. To your credit you don't notice it, but I'm sure people are wagging their tongues about it because they live to wag their tongues about others."

"Especially when others come from the country."

"Maybe you are not so naïve as I thought."

Anne smiled, and Elizabeth saw it.

"I assure you, I will be nothing but a friend to your husband."

Chapter 25. Return to London

In two days' time, Elizabeth and Kitty would travel to London together. They'd spend a night at a hotel in town. Kitty would continue on to Devon, and Lizzy would head to Pemberley to see Lydia and Jane and the others. Darcy and Bingley had already returned there. Kitty's fleeting passing through must be a secret.

Things changed, though, when Elizabeth received a letter from London. *From Darcy himself!*

Pemberley
October 27, 1815

My Dearest Elizabeth,

I am afraid that I must tell you that matters are coming to a head more quickly than I anticipated. If you can pull yourself away from Charlotte promptly, I will be forever grateful. It would be a great comfort to me to see and be with you. I am too lost without you and will surely need as much of you as I can get in the trying times ahead.

By the time you read this, I—with Bingley—shall have returned to town. I will be on Brook Street awaiting you with the greatest anticipation and expectation.

Be assured that I leave everyone in good health and hope that we can again join them without a great delay.

Fitzwilliam

The letter arrived just as she'd come in from her afternoon's stroll, something she generally did alone when the weather was fair and, on occasion, when there was a bit of a wind and a slight drizzle for she had long enjoyed taking solitary walks, dating back to her days at Longbourn.

It was, though, a quite fine day and though the paths she took were not so nice as those at Pemberley, she'd come to relish the peace she found here in Kent on these walks. She would miss them. But now she sat in the small front parlour at the Parsonage and twice read what Darcy wrote. The group planned to go to Rosings Park for a final evening with Anne de Bourgh.

"What is it, Eliza?" Charlotte asked as she came into the room to do her needlepoint with her dear friend.

"It is nothing to do with health. It is just that Darcy has returned early from Pemberley to address some lingering matters and has asked that I join him as soon as I can. It is well that we were planning on leaving already. I will not be going to Pemberley after all."

"But everyone is fine?" Charlotte asked.

"It's a brief note but he does assure me that they are."

"Will this alter your plans about leaving us?"

"I can't see how other than me not continuing up to Pemberley after parting with Kitty and I'm afraid our plan for Kitty and me to spend a night together in London cannot be realised. It cannot be helped."

When news of Elizabeth's need to immediately return to London was shared at the house that evening, Anne insisted that she would join the others on the trip to town. Hence, shortly after Elizabeth and Kitty finished breakfasting at the Parsonage in the morning, Anne's carriage-and-four rolled to a stop at the front door. After the exchange of farewells far exceeding what any of the parties were accustomed to, the two Bennets and one de Bourgh were heading to London and to they knew not what.

Before reaching Brook Street, the three parted. Kitty got out at a station in time to catch the first of a series of posts that would carry her through Reading and Salisbury and that would in some days' time get her to Exeter. Anne had sent a letter alerting the cousin to the expected arrival time.

After Elizabeth and Anne were back in the carriage following the farewells, Anne said, "Your Catherine has quite impressed me, and I confess that she has touched me in a particular way. You and she and the Collinses have comported yourselves extremely well, and I am quite impressed by all of you, though I confess that I am not surprised as to you."

"Me?"

"Do not be so modest, Elizabeth. You won *the* Fitzwilliam Darcy and that was no mean accomplishment. You are a very clever woman, and I am glad to have finally made your acquaintance."

"We *had* met before."

"Aye, we had indeed. But never on such terms as we have now done, and I at least am very glad of that."

Before Elizabeth could respond, they were approaching the Darcy house.

"I will tell you," Anne said as the carriage slowed, "I told you that I do not have many friends. I know you will be one of them."

At that moment, one footman had the door open and a second was removing Elizabeth's trunk from the roof and before any of them reached the door, it opened, and Darcy and Bingley were there and quickly to the pavement, and Elizabeth was quickly with them.

The carriage and its remaining occupant waited until the Darcys exchanged their emotional reunion. Darcy approached while Bingley greeted Elizabeth.

"Thank you, cousin, for your kindness to Elizabeth. We are forever in your debt. Won't you come in?" He was standing looking into the carriage through its open door.

"I promise to visit but am tired now." She lowered her voice. "As I'm sure you know, she is a rare gem and I told her I would like to be her friend."

"As indeed do I."

"You should know, Fitzwilliam," she added, after leaning closer to him, "that while she broached no inappropriate confidences to me, I am too aware of the general nature of your recent reversals. I told her, and I am telling you, that I will do what it is in my power to provide assistance."

She sat back and her voice rose.

"I've always been somewhat fond of you, cousin, as you know. But I am now quite fond of your wife."

Darcy stepped back and closed the door.

"Tomorrow," his cousin said. "I shall be pleased to visit both of you in the afternoon and we can speak more about what we shall all do while we are in town."

He nodded.

"And I assume that is the famous Mr. Bingley," who was indeed conversing and laughing with Elizabeth some feet away, "and you shall make sure he is with you so that we may be properly introduced."

"I will make sure of it," Darcy said as Anne called her goodbyes to Elizabeth, and she was soon off to Russell Square.

Chapter 26. The Banker's Office

When he entered the banker's office several days later, Darcy was disoriented by the person sitting at the banker's desk.

"Surprised, Darcy?"

He looked around.

"Close the door."

He did and turned back to the woman sitting before him.

"I was told the man holding my chit was meeting with me."

"'Man.' Or 'person'?"

"It might have been the latter but that hardly matters. What are you doing here?"

"Come, come, Fitzwilliam. You can figure it out."

"You? You hold my chit?"

"I prefer to think of it as me holding you." Anne de Bourgh reached her open hand across the desk. "In the palm of my hand. Sit."

"Now that I have gotten over the shock, I am truly glad to see you. I thought this 'person' would be some horrid man from the City. I don't know how I can repay you for saving me."

He sat back in the stiff leather chair, his shoulders and stomach relaxing for the first time since he received the summons.

She smiled, herself sitting back in the banker's chair. She shook her head.

"You're my cousin so I owe you something on that score," Anne said. "But I have learnt, I do not say how, of the generosity and indeed kindness that you extended to the Bennet family related to that awful business with the late George Wickham."

"I did it for selfish reasons."

She leaned forward. "So I am to understand. You did it for the woman you loved, even though no one in the universe at the time, perhaps excepting Elizabeth Bennet by then, could have thought you capable of love. Surely my mother didn't, though, frankly she knew quite a bit about *respect* with my father, but I do not think it was ever 'affection.'

"But that is neither here nor there. You did and do love her very much and I will assure you, lest you need any assurance, that she came to love you without as it were Pemberley."

"She told you that?"

"Not in so many words, cousin, but a woman, even one as kept from society as I have been, could recognise it in her."

He sat back a bit deeper into his chair as just such a woman across the desk continued. "I've become quite fond of your wife and her sister Catherine—as I'm sure Elizabeth has told you she prefers to be known—"

"I've barely met her, Catherine or Kitty or whatever, and she always seemed attached to Lydia. Indeed, I was quite surprised when she agreed to go to be some sort of companion with Mrs. Collins."

"I of course stumbled on her with the Collinses and came to enjoy her company and, frankly, Fitzwilliam, I do think her being with your Elizabeth has helped her immeasurably.

"But as I say, I am extending a kindness to you as my cousin and nearest relation and as Elizabeth's husband. As you did with regard to buying off George Wickham for Elizabeth, I have acquired your debts for her and for her younger sister.

"You should not breathe too easily, Darcy. While you threw that money away on Wickham's picadilloes, I intend to earn my money back at a tidy profit."

Darcy's body stiffened as the sudden, uncomfortable turn of events.

"Do not fear, Fitzwilliam. I will not be seeking my pound of flesh from you, or I must add any part of you." He noticed a slight smile cross her lips at her slight tease, which was quite unexpected. "And I know you'd never take this any other way. No, I expect that over time you will be able to pay off these debts which are now *your* debts to *me*. I bought them at a sizeable discount from those who did not have such faith and did not expect to get many pennies on the pound were the court to enter a verdict in your matter.

"I will not, though, be charging more than a nominal interest rate and I will grant you much time to resolve these obligations. I should tell you that I've done the same with Charles Bingley's debts, which are so small in relation to yours. While I abhor what I have learnt about his obsequious and scheming sisters, I think him a man of very fine character from his reputation and the brief dealings I have had with him since I came to town. And I know he will do what he can for his sisters."

"He already has," Darcy said.

"I expected as much based on what I have heard of him. And as he too is married to a Bennet of some renown and much respect, I very much look forward to being introduced to her."

"Jane is an angel and—"

"So, she would not have suited you, cousin?"

"You know me too well," Darcy responded with an encroaching fondness for Anne and an increasingly relaxed mood.

"To be sure, Fitzwilliam, I am completely and immovably convinced that the only woman in the universe for you is the one you have snared—"

"I cannot say who did the 'snaring,'" the banter continued, "but I am sure you are right in that respect."

"Believe me, Darcy, it is true. As I said, I have become quite fond of that Bennet girl as well.

"But back to you. Be assured that I am not doing anything out of charity. I know you too well to know you would never accept it if I offered it so I will insult neither of us by offering it. But if you need any justification for the favourable terms on offer, think of it as an unforeseen benefit to what you did those years ago about Wickham and what you did with Elizabeth when a man of a lesser quality would have fled her without as much as a 'by your leave.'"

Darcy had barely moved during this speech except for jousts but Anne saw how much more comfortable he was in contrast to the desperate soul who entered the office not ten minutes before.

Anne smiled. "You are a very good man, Fitzwilliam, much as you pretend not to be. I do not think my mother appreciated that in you nor, frankly, do I think my mother appreciated much about me or about so many others, including your wife and the Collinses.

"My mother, I fear, proved to be a very poor judge of character and God forgive me for saying it, but I think that many of us have prospered from being out of her long shadow."

Darcy did not know how to respond to this fountain of glad tidings, not only about his debts but about the things his clever cousin said about his beautiful wife. Anne rescued him. She stood and reached across the desk with her hand, which he shook properly.

"My solicitor will forward the appropriate documents to your solicitor and to Mr. Bingley's. I must ask you, though, as I believe you asked Elizabeth those years ago, that you say nothing to *anyone*, including your wife and Bingley, about my role in this. As you had your own reasons for doing what you did, I have mine, though in my case, I assure you, I hope to make a tidy profit thanks to the bankers who didn't believe in your ability to rise from the ashes caused by your Mr. Stewart."

She smiled. "I can see all of this comes as something of a shock to you. Very well. I will give you until sundown tomorrow to accept or reject my proposal. I am at the house on Russell Square. I will rearrange things just so I can be there to see you. But, again, no one can know of my role in any of this. Now or ever."

"I will be there."

She smiled as she walked around the desk and after the slightest pause, she pressed herself against him and he found his arms encircling her.

She stepped back. "Oh, Fitzwilliam. How good it is to see you again. I do hope to see you again very soon. In any case, whatever your answer, the three of you must come to dinner on Russell Square tomorrow. Agreed?"

"Agreed." He rushed to open the door for her. He watched her nod to his banker—he was waiting and pretending to be busy in the hallway—when she passed him as she proceeded directly to the door and out to the Strand. The moment she was gone, the banker returned.

"I am sorry, Mr. Darcy. She insisted that I not...*warn* you it was she. She said she thought it likely that you would be able to work something out as to your debts. As she is your cousin and you go way back especially with her mother, I was glad it was her and I am certain things will at last end well for you, Sir. You should be very happy, Sir."

He reached for Darcy's hand, which Darcy took.

"Indeed. I am overjoyed at my good fortune."

The banker leaned in and whispered, "Word is she spent an absolute fortune to buy it up, though she can, of course, well afford it. Received quite the discount, I'm told, but still a princely sum. But as the Bard put it, 'all's well that ends well,' eh?"

With Darcy gone, his former banker had again become his current banker, a banker much pleased to be able to be of some slight service to Fitzwilliam Darcy of Pemberley.

*   *   *   *

AT DINNER LATER ON Brook Street, during a lull after the soup, Darcy told the others, "Thank goodness for Jane and that lawyer she put me onto. An absolute genius, and we will benefit from it. He has somehow arranged for a schedule for the full repayment of my debts at virtually no interest and for a period that is eminently achievable so Elizabeth and I and you, Charles, and, of course, Jane, will in time be free of Stewart's stain."

Bingley was not taken by surprise by this since Darcy told him when he got back that he was told that Bingley's solicitors were preparing the necessary papers for him too. And Darcy signed his set the next afternoon at Anne's house, where her solicitor graciously prepared and supervised the execution of the documents that confirmed that he was in his cousin's debt, for not too long financially but forever otherwise.

Chapter 27. Leaving Pemberley

Anne de Bourgh's kindness eased some of the pressure on the Darcys. So did completing the unsavoury but necessary business of surrendering the house on Brook Street. The Darcys would move at the new year.

Back in town, Elizabeth received her regular dispatches about Kitty on her regular visits to Russell Square. She continued to report to the others about how well Kitty was doing "in Hunsford." If anyone harbored suspicions about why Elizabeth didn't visit or suggest others visit with her, they kept them to themselves. The truth was that things were too busy in London with preparations for the move and that satisfied such curiosity as the others had in this lesser of the Bennet sisters.

By this point, Pemberley had been closed down. Elizabeth did not journey there once she was back in town, but Darcy and Bingley rode up shortly after their financial situation stabilized (thanks (as one knew and the other did not) to Miss de Bourgh). Darcy took care of a number of matters with his steward and returned to London while Bingley remained at Darcy's Estate with Jane and Lydia (and little Georgie) until he and Jane would come south to town in late October and Lydia and Georgie (with a nurse) would divert to Longbourn, where they were (or at least Lydia was) confident that they would receive the level of attention that was their due.

The reunion between Jane and Lizzy was not as joyous as expected, though. Shortly after the Bingleys were settled, Darcy and Lizzy came to celebrate the return. Jane took Lizzy up to her study and Bingley did the same with Darcy to his study.

As to the sisters, when the door was closed and they sat beside each other, Jane spoke.

"I know you are anxious about me and my condition, but I must tell you that whatever we hoped would happen will not."

Elizabeth sat back to get the measure of her sister.

"I don't understand."

Jane lost such composure as she'd managed to maintain.

"Oh, Lizzy. The baby. I have lost the baby."

Lizzy was immediately at the front of her sister's chair, reaching for Jane, who was well chortling by then.

"I do not wish to speak of it and the apothecary confirms I am recovered but it came in the night a week ago. Thank God Charles was there. If he wasn't, I don't know how I could have made it through. I recovered enough to have made this trip.

"Before you ask, no one but the four of us and the apothecary knew, though I daresay Mrs. Reynolds might have suspected. I'm sure Lydia never did, and I don't want anyone else to know. Charles and I need to recover and will just have to begin again. That's all."

At the end of this, Lizzy was up and standing behind Jane, her arms dangling over the older woman's shoulders. "Oh, sweet Jane. I am so sorry. But I'm sure you will have many more chances."

"I do hope so. But I cannot speak about it now. I know Charles is saying the same to Darcy so please let us leave it at that."

Lizzy tightened her grip. "Know that when you are ready, I am here."

"Lizzy, I've always known that. It is why I love you so."

"Now that I have no money?"

"I loved you before you had money, as you well know."

"Yes, since you didn't have any money then either."

There was a pause and the two remained together in their own thoughts. Finally, Jane shook.

"I think we must join our husbands now," and Lizzy replied, "I think we must," and no more was said but much was thought about Jane and Charles's great loss.

*   *   *   *

SOME TWENTY-FIVE MILES AWAY, though, the young widow was well greeted at Longbourn, with the Philipses and the Lucases coming to the house right after they heard that she and Georgie were there. She settled comfortably in the large bedroom once shared by Jane and Elizabeth.

And word of her ever-improving condition and that of her child was sent regularly to town by Mrs. Bennet, though Lydia did not deign to send any herself other than a brief "thank you for your kind consideration" when she received something from either of her sisters.

Elizabeth was not surprised, though, when Anne handed her a letter from Lydia. Anne had received it at Russell Square. The envelope was addressed thusly:

Miss Catherine Bennet
C/o Mrs. William Collins
Hunsford Parsonage
Kent

The conspirators had agreed that Charlotte would forward any letters that Kitty "received" at the Parsonage—unopened—to Russell Square, where they would be held for Elizabeth. Though Lydia was the one most likely to send such a letter, Mrs. Bennet might do so as well and having them sent off to Devon directly from Kent would have taken far too long. Elizabeth would promptly send whatever was received to Exeter.

November 11, 1815

My dearest sister,

Oh, how I miss you. I care not for whatever slight need <u>Mrs. Collins</u> has of you as mine is infinitely greater and my rights to you infinitely superior to hers! Mamma is good enough and tries to be of help to me, but she has no idea about my needs and those of my Georgie. She may have experience with little baby girls—and quite a great deal I should think!—but as to a baby BOY, she is all confusion and anxiety.

And papa? He spends his time in his library and in brief walks on the paths around the house. Some days he walks into Meryton on some excuse or another and might come back with a package of something he took a fancy to in town—a book more likely than not though he has so many that he has never opened!—and returns to his library.

The only relief I have is Maria Lucas. Oh how different she is from Charlotte, much as I do truly love that old married woman. But you must acknowledge, Kitty, that Charlotte is a rather cold creature.

It is...it can never be enough though. I need you to come to Longbourn. Think of it as me rescuing you from the <u>boredom</u> you are surely suffering in Hunsford.

Oh, Kitty, please write and promise me you shall be here by Christmas! I am sure our parents will be likewise pleased by your appearance as I am sure you will not be missed by <u>anyone</u> in Hunsford.

I promise you, Kitty. Should you not promptly respond positively to my plea, I shall be forced to extend an invitation to Mary, and you shall forever be weighed down by the guilt of having compelled me to take such a drastic step!

> *I am your great friend and*
> *best sister,*
> *L*

PS. Do not fret yourself. I will never actually invite Mary. But please come to me and to my Georgie!

Neither Elizabeth, nor Anne when see read it at Elizabeth's invitation (and pursuant to permission given by Kitty), were, as noted, surprised. Its contents and tone were as expected, and they had prepared for it. Within the hour, Kitty's (undated) response was *en route* to the Parsonage. From there, it would be dispatched by Charlotte to Longbourn, with Lydia's letter similarly being off for Devon.

My sweet sister,

Oh, how I do miss you. I am sorry for your loneliness, but I am afraid I cannot come to see you as yet. I find that our dear Charlotte not nearly so well as I expected, and you can understand that the presence of our cousin (Mr. Collins) does very little to soothe her.

Much as I regret it, I cannot leave her as yet, even to see you and Georgie. I have every expectation, however, of accompanying Charlotte to Meryton for the holiday and you can expect me to spend much of my time with you and my dearest nephew.

Until I can again set eyes on you, I remain.

> *With my best to you and your angel,*
> *I am,*
> *Kitty*

The vagueness of Kitty's plea did not stop both Mrs. Bennet and Lydia from then writing pleading notes to Jane and Elizabeth begging that they make Kitty "see sense," but neither of the older Bennet girls varied from insisting on the importance of Kitty remaining where she was, particularly since she was expected in Meryton shortly anyway.

In fairness, Jane didn't actually know where Kitty was and was in any case far from being of a mind to cater to whatever it was Lydia wanted. But Elizabeth convinced Jane that it was better *for all concerned* that Kitty remain away from Lydia so that she could "flower into her own woman," as Elizabeth put it more than once.

It was helped, too, that among the things they anticipated was the coming holiday season. Charlotte and Kitty would be expected to make the trip to Lucas Lodge shortly before Christmas, with Mr. Collins for at least a part of that time. He would be returning in order to be in Hunsford for Christmas itself. How to explain Kitty's absence, especially to Lydia and the Bennets?

This was handled by a brusque letter cleverly written by Elizabeth and Kitty. It explained that Kitty came down with some sort of fever that prevented her from leaving Kent for some time. It wasn't contagious, she said, and Miss de Bourgh insisted on her being seen by her own physician, who pronounced—the letter said—that Kitty should fully recover as long as she avoided excess excitement and travel. This meant, the Collinses regretted saying when they got to Meryton, that Charlotte would have to leave with her husband sooner than expected but they expected to all be able to visit come spring.

It will suffice to say that neither Lydia nor her parents much regretted that Charlotte left early with Mr. Collins who, on one of his visits to Longbourn, sought to assure Mrs. Bennet that he hoped Mr. Bennet enjoyed a long and healthy life.

For Lydia, she was glad to see Charlotte leave so she could resume the increasing adoration she bathed in from Charlotte's much younger sister, Maria. As well, one might expect, increasingly from Charlotte's eldest and well-developing brother.

Chapter 28. Alterations Abound

Things could never return to what they'd been.

For his part, Darcy was much altered in his behaviour towards others. He had never been a particularly easy man with strangers but the first months after the incident with Stewart had made him downright taciturn to them and only a fool would venture to deal with him if it could be avoided. His conduct in these days shocked his wife, and there were stretches when his civility only extended to her, to Jane, and to Bingley.

Slowly, though, beginning with his initial, optimistic meetings with his barrister James Drain (and his solicitor Brower) and plainly after what his cousin did at his banker's, he again was the man who displayed such unbridled joy when Elizabeth accepted him and when he first heard the cries of Fitzwilliam.

Bingley had been somewhat repressed in the same period, but both his losses and his character were such as to not throw him into the depths that sometimes threatened to envelop his friend. All that was enhanced by what had just happened to Jane.

Unlike their wives, Bingley and Darcy did sometimes speak of this while they went for a morning's ride. It didn't and couldn't accomplish very much but the ability of Bingley to express his disappointment to his great friend and that friend's reassurance that when the time came, "As indeed I am sure it will," Charles would make a fine father and Jane a very fine mother.

But of the family, it had become established that Kitty would never revert to being Lydia's lesser companion. She'd long suffered in that role and long since outgrown it, less irritable, less ignorant, and less insipid than she had been, even without the pregnancy. The family's understanding was that she'd gone to Hunsford to be a companion of sorts to Charlotte Collins, and the four of them—Kitty, Charlotte, Elizabeth, and Anne—were careful to prolong this illusion after Kitty went to Devon.

On a chilled Thursday afternoon, Elizabeth and Anne were sharing tea on Russell Square. It had become their custom. Early in this particular conversation, Anne said, "I have given it much thought and I think she should stay with me."

Elizabeth looked over. "You? We could not impose."

"Here and at Rosings. I've plenty of room. Acres of room. I do like her very much and it would be pleasant to have the companionship of someone I like. With Russell Square, she will enjoy seeing you and Jane and the others in town. It is decided, Elizabeth," she said as she loudly placed her cup and saucer on the small table that stood between them. "I shall have her if she wishes to come."

"Oh, I believe we can surely say she will wish to come."

"Then it is settled. I will write to her and invite her and that will be that."

And it was "that," as Kitty made clear in her response to Anne, which came just over a week after this conversation and which Anne was pleased to show to Elizabeth.

Everyone knew by this point that Elizabeth and Anne de Bourgh had become great friends. When in town, they took to walking even in the cold, sometimes with a fully recovered Jane, on pleasant early afternoons. They ventured together to dress-fittings and for visits to friends of one or both.

It was during one of the walks with just the two of them that they dove into what was to be done with Kitty and the baby. Not the long term, for that was already decided and agreed upon. The more immediate question of how the baby would get from Devon to Hunsford and just where Kitty would be.

"When it's time," Anne said, "I will make the arrangements for them to go to Hunsford. There is a small inn in Islington not two miles from Russell Square where Kitty can spend the night with the baby and the nurse who will be traveling with them. No one will see or notice them there and I will join them in the morning in my own carriage for the drive to Hunsford."

"What of me coming?"

"I think the fewer involved the easier it will be for everyone to settle in. Catherine will stay with me at Rosings after the baby and nurse are at the Parsonage. There will be time, but for this period, I think it best that your sister and I make the trip alone. You will have more than enough chances to visit with Charlotte and the baby once we enjoy the arrival of spring, I promise you."

They were nearing Brook Street, and both were tiring.

"You must trust me, Elizabeth. As must Catherine. We will see this through, I promise you. I believe in you and Mrs. Collins and especially in our Catherine. We will see this through."

Elizabeth asked Anne to come into the house for at least something to warm her up, but Anne declined.

"I will warm up best, I think, before my own fire," she said, "and the fastest way to be at my home is for me to find a cab."

She said her farewells to Mrs. Darcy and waited only a moment for an empty cab to come by, which she got into quickly and in which she found a blanket to cover herself and she was in fact warm in her house very, very quickly after leaving her great friend.

Chapter 29. Kitty's Baby

Much was done to continue the illusion that Kitty was in Hunsford when she was in fact being well cared for by the widowed Mrs. Arnold Elster at her small house on Grove Road in Exeter. Mrs. Elster was a childless widow nearing thirty and had had some difficulties since the death of her (it must be said) cruel husband and her elder brother's insistence that it was that dead husband and not her live brother who bore any financial responsibility for her.

She was born Frances Weathers and survived by a mix of sewing and needlework and the kind intervention of an unknown benefactor some two years previous, an intervention that was enough for her to have that small house to herself, not too distant from the River Exe.

She was quite excited about the company suggested by her cousin and in her little house Kitty—though she was known to Mrs. Elster as "Miss Nancy Wilson"—could remain undisturbed and (largely) unobserved. Anne arranged the discreet services of a somewhat renowned physician to tend to Kitty, and very late in the evening of Friday, December 15, 1815, a seven pound/eight ounce bundle took its first breath and was handed into the arms of Miss Catherine Bennet.

At about ten o'clock in the morning five days later, a footman arrived at the Darcys' with a message for Mrs. Fitzwilliam Darcy. Within twenty minutes of his appearance, Elizabeth was on Brook Street *en route* to Russell Square.

In the event, she was at Anne's almost as quickly as she would have been had she taken a cab. She went so hard that she was sweating under the coat and scarf she'd put on at her house. When her foot hit the first of the marble steps where she'd become a familiar presence in the last month or so, the house's front door opened and the butler Taylor directed her to Anne's study, the way to which Elizabeth well knew.

"It is a boy, and it is healthy so far as they can tell. As is Catherine."

Elizabeth was still somewhat out of breath from the race to the house and the rush up the stairs. She took the letter Anne held out to her. It was in an unfamiliar hand and not long.

Grove-road, Exeter
December 16, 1815

My Dear Cousin,

It gives me the greatest pleasure to inform you that your friend has given birth to a boy of average size who, the doctor says, appears to be quite healthy. The mother is recovering from her ordeal quite well. She wished me specifically to tell you that she is the luckiest woman in the world and asks that you tell her dear sister that she loves her and looks forward to their being introduced to one another in the new year.

Mrs. Arnold Elster

The two sat in the armchairs that had become so familiar, and Elizabeth could not suppress a smile as she read the letter from Mrs. Arnold Elster a third or fourth time.

"I am quite fond of this sister of yours," Anne said, "and I am very relieved and happy and pray that they both shall remain healthy."

"A nephew. A nephew."

Elizabeth looked at her friend whose hand was lying gracefully but loosely on the round table that separated them and she took it.

"Three boys. My mother will be so jealous," Elizabeth said.

"But she shan't know."

"Aye. Perhaps someday in time. Perhaps someday."

"You must write to Mrs. Collins."

Anne rose and went to her desk. She opened a drawer and removed a sheet of stationery, a quill pen, and a brass inkwell. These she placed on the desktop. Elizabeth took Anne's normal chair and with Anne sitting back in the armchair watching with a surprising degree of contentment for what had happened to Kitty, Elizabeth wrote a brief note to Charlotte repeating the joyous news from Mrs. Elster and saying she would advise of the arrangements that would be made for allowing the Collinses to welcome the child into their home.

Thus, it was done. Then both wrote letters to be sent to Mrs. Elster for Kitty saying how grateful they were and pleased they were about the new boy and saying arrangements were being made to take him to Kent when they were able to.

In her letter to Kitty, Elizabeth had written,

My Dearest Sister,

Now that there is this very welcome addition to our family, I believe there are two people who must know about it. I will leave it for you to speak to Jane, but I think I must advise my dear husband as well. He is, I promise you, the soul of discretion and I do not like keeping any sort of secret— even if it is not truly my secret—from him for a moment more than is necessary.

I will not press you on this. I know you will tell me when you are ready for me to speak to him about it, and about your captain friend. And I await the day when I have your leave to do so.

Your most happy sister

Permission arrived in Kitty's next letter (including expressly the request that "Captain Johnson"'s existence be excluded) some two weeks after the foregoing. On the very night she received it, Elizabeth revealed the situation when she and her husband were in bed. They lay in a post-coital bliss, with his left arm wrapped around her and with her grasping his left hand to her stomach.

"I must tell you a secret," she said as she looked away from him.

He kissed the back of her head. "A *secret*? You never keep secrets from me."

"It was not something for me to share. I know you will understand."

Before he could respond, she spun around so she could look at him and he, as he always did, ran the fingers of his left hand across her cheek.

"It is Kitty. She's had a child. It is a boy, and he is healthy and he is to be taken in by the Collinses."

If Darcy was surprised by anything in his life, even the news about his fortune, it was nothing compared to this. While there surely was a time in which his reaction to such news would be abhorrence and revulsion, those prejudices had been softened by his more understanding wife, especially insofar as they touched on the Bennets. He tightened his grip on her.

"You will tell me what you think is best for me to know. Of that I am certain."

They remained quiet for a time.

"Do you...do you know who the father is?"

"I do. He is dead, and only Kitty—who prefers going by 'Catherine' now—and I know. Not even your cousin Anne."

"Anne?" His head shot up. "What's she got to do with it?"

"She has been a saviour. If it weren't for her, I do not know what could have been done. That is all I can, and will, say about it. That she has been a saviour. But she does not wish it to be known and you must say nothing about it."

"That explains the sudden friendship that has arisen between the two of you."

"In part it began with that, when Anne had her suspicion about why Kitty was visiting the Collinses in the first place. But I've truly become quite fond of your cousin and she, I believe, of me."

"As she has said. I'm glad of it," he said.

"Don't worry, Fitzwilliam. She has assured me that she harbors no jealous feelings towards me for having been the one fortunate enough to have married you."

"Fortunate? Other than the money—which is largely gone—what did you get from me?"

They often spoke like this, in a manner so comfortable to the two of them that no outsider would believe it unless they were to witness it themselves.

"You mean other than Little Fitz?"

And they both smiled, lying beside each other and returned to their thoughts until Darcy spoke.

"It happened while she and Lydia were in Newcastle, I assume."

"Indeed. She confided in me when she came to town with Lydia after Wickham's death. I then spoke to Charlotte about it and visited Charlotte to try to convince Mr. Collins—"

"And are you saying *he* agreed to this? I cannot imagine how you did that."

Her fingers unconsciously drew beneath his nightshirt and played with the hairs below his navel.

"I snared you, didn't I?" she said with a smile. "As to Mr. Collins, he is quite a different man since the death of your aunt. Anne even more so."

"Well, I have witnessed it with her. But I cannot imagine that *he* would be much changed by it, beyond being devastated by the loss of his patroness."

She pushed away to look at him.

"You sometimes still allow your prejudices get the better of you. Have I not told you that?"

"More times than I care to count."

They shared this smile, and she fell onto her back. She explained what happened and how Anne arranged for Kitty's going to Devon for her confinement. How the Collinses would explain that they were doing Christ's work by taking in the "unfortunate child of an unknown parishioner."

And he said he understood why he could tell no one.

Chapter 30. Christmas in London

Christmas itself passed quite enjoyably, all things considered, in London. It was stressful to all, given the Darcys' impending move to Mount Row as all agreed was the best if not happy option to save money.

Life was even more stressful for Elizabeth, given the news from Devon, which she could only speak of freely when she was alone with her husband or at Russell Square, where Mrs. Elster directed letters reporting on Kitty's and the baby's condition (though she knew Kitty as "Nancy Wilson") at least weekly. She wrote in one letter that Kitty while well was having difficulty assembling her thoughts and begged to be forgiven for not herself sending a letter to her "dearest friends" but that she, Mrs. Elster, was faithful in conveying Kitty's thoughts.

The days before and after the holiday were beyond hectic as arrangements were made to move the Darcys. Fortunately, they agreed to sell their furniture to the owner of their house—what would soon be their former house. This not only raised some needed cash, but also did away with the task of moving it somewhere other than to No. 19, Mount Row.

For the servants, though, the Christmas season was not such a happy one in the Darcy house. They were given enough notice that most, Bradley included, were able to find new positions, and though some left as soon as they found those positions, others waited until the Darcy house was abandoned before doing so.

Two or three were able to retain their positions at the house. Edward Hastings graduated from footman to butler for the new tenants. They were not up to Darcy's social standing, or at least the social standing he had while he still had money. More to the point. *They* did have money, albeit newly-acquired-in-trade (the master was some kind of importer).

The Darcys were as generous as they could be on Boxing Day and it was quite a sad occasion all round, so different from what it had been six months before.

With no option, once the move was completed and the family members were adjusted to their rooms, they all settled in for the cold days to come.

Chapter 31. What's to Become of Kitty?

Those who knew of Kitty's situation agreed that when she could actually travel turned on the views of her physician in Exeter. At least for the first month, with the cold of January, it was out of the question. It was well into February when the trip was permitted. After being delayed by two days by a raking storm, it was not too cold and on February 14, 1816, it began in the fine carriage Miss de Bourgh hired for the long trip. The roads were not in good condition for much of the journey, though, and it took nearly a full week before Kitty and her baby reached Islington on the outskirts of London.

It was early afternoon when they did, though there would be only a little of the day's light remaining for them. Soon after the group arrived for the single night before the final stretch of the journey to Kent, Kitty scrawled a note that was promptly dispatched.

Miss de Bourgh,

> *We have arrived safely. As my stay will be brief and we depart in the morning, I beg that if at all possible, you visit me with both my sisters so I can see and speak to you all before finishing my journey.*

> *Your faithful servant,*
> *Miss Catherine Bennet*

The receipt of this promptly prompted Anne to have a footman deliver a similarly brief note to Elizabeth saying they must fly to Islington to see the new mother "and that Catherine expressly requests that both of her sisters come to see her. If Jane is up to it, please have her prepared to join you with no hesitation when my carriage reaches her door."

With little time to spare, Elizabeth told Darcy what was happening. She assured him that it was likely that Kitty would allow Jane to tell Bingley the news but that it was best if Darcy could distract his friend so that she and Jane could go to Kitty without having to address possibly uncomfortable questions.

With that, the two men were quickly off to a favourite tavern several blocks away and just behind them went a footman to Russell Square with a note saying that Mrs. Bingley and Mrs. Darcy would be pleased to venture out with Miss de Bourgh at her earliest convenience.

That convenience, in the form of a de Bourgh carriage, quickly arrived at Mount Row.

* * * *

THINGS WERE HAPPENING very quickly now. Jane was initially shocked at what Kitty told her and hurt that she'd not been told sooner. That Kitty had a child and she did not could have crippled a woman not as eternally optimistic as Jane, but her own hurt quickly turned to happiness for her long absent sister.

And it was no surprise that Mr. Bingley himself took joy in hearing of the boy—Kitty allowing Jane to tell him—though he and Jane did speak quietly about it and what they had so recently gone through before retiring for the night. He, too, gave his word as a gentleman that he would not breathe a word of it.

In any case, early the next morning, Anne was taken in her carriage to the inn in Islington. After the luggage was safely latched to the rear, she and Kitty, the baby, and the nurse began the concluding leg of Kitty's very long journey. They would head directly to Rosings Park with the briefest of pauses when they reached the Parsonage. The Collinses would be invited to dine at the house to see the baby. After several more days at the house, he'd move to the Parsonage to begin his new life.

Worse by far was Kitty. She nearly rebelled at the thought of being separated from her baby, but she'd long come to accept the necessity of it. That Anne had agreed to have her nearby and in quite luxurious surroundings were perhaps the only things that could have been tolerated without Kitty falling into a den of misery.

Chapter 32. Will Meets the Collinses

It was cold but not wet. Mr. Collins burst through the door so he could gain sight of the carriage at the earliest opportunity, and when it came around a corner, he called out that he could see it, and the others were up and joined him at the gate to await its arrival.

It stopped for only several minutes because of the cold and after both Collinses had a peek at the slumbering infant, the carriage continued to the house.

Mr. and Mrs. Collins quickly got bundled up for the walk across to the house, where they were welcomed and directed to the sitting room not half-an-hour after Anne and the others had arrived. Ten minutes later, they all went up to what would be the baby's nursery for the next several days. The small room was next to what had been and would again be Kitty's and fires were already burning in both. The child—who Charlotte immediately (if as yet unofficially) christened "Will"—had been covered in a blanket and was delicately placed into a yellow crib.

Since Anne de Bourgh was mostly in London at this time of year, the staff was slight. Many rooms were closed off, and as she had but only recently arrived, the house was in general quite cold outside of where fires had been lit.

Kitty found it hard to recover from the trip, unable to remove her eyes from her baby and several tears emerged from them. Anne put her arm around the mother and pulled her closer. She was very cold from the trip, and she shook from that and from what she was seeing and doing.

She would not leave Will to the care of the nurse, though, until Anne prevailed, and the group went down to the smokey sitting room, which a fine fire had warmed and where an array of refreshments had been set out.

"Ah, Cousin Catherine, you cannot know how impatient we were for your arrival," Mr. Collins said when they all were seated, none of them straying too far from the fire.

"Thank you, Sir," she said somewhat stiffly. All this did not take long, but it did take long enough so that Meadows, the country butler—Taylor remained in town—had the chance to prepare and bring in a tray of tea and cakes and told the others that Cook made soup that was intended for dinner but would bring bowls of it to Miss Bennet as soon as he could to warm her innards.

* * * *

TWO WEEKS AFTER SHE arrived, Kitty left Kent for London with Anne but not with her baby.

The roads were rough but generally clear, and it was not horribly cold. The pair was bundled close to one another beneath several blankets until they reached Anne's house. Given the tightness in the Bingleys' and her own personal inclinations, Kitty would stay on Russell Square, still suffering terribly from having left Will with the Collinses. Indeed, on the first night on Russell Square in her new home, Anne fell asleep in a chair in Kitty's room keeping a vigil over the new mother. It was not a comfortable sleep, and Kitty was embarrassed when she woke in the night and heard the sleeping breath of her guardian angel.

If there was a moment when the relationship between the two was confirmed, it was this one. Though, of course, neither of them knew it at the time.

When Elizabeth arrived as intended early the next afternoon, Kitty was sufficiently recovered—though not *completely* recovered—to visit the others. So late on that chilled mid-February afternoon, the de Bourgh carriage pulled up to No. 19, Mount Row (Anne did not come), Kitty was helped from it and greeted everyone in the foyer before adjourning to the sitting room for the more complete reunion with what had become the London part of her family.

* * * *

IT HAD BEEN VERY LONG since Kitty had seen her parents or a (still livid) Lydia so when she was recovered enough, Anne arranged for her to venture north to Longbourn to visit.

Kitty still suffered from the physical effects of her ordeal with Will, but she'd learnt to conceal them. She discovered, though with no small disappointment if not surprise, that the lack of interest in her among her mother, her father, and her youngest sister did not require much subterfuge on her part.

It was a warmish day, for March, and after paying appropriate tribute to Georgie, Kitty and Lydia strolled into Meryton. It was far, far different from when they'd last done it. Kitty was a different person than the girl she had been. All signs of the militia had long since disappeared and the flood of sympathy showered on Lydia about her dear Wickham's death had long since dried up. Indeed, without any sisters and without the diversion or attentions of the officers, Lydia rarely went into town anymore except to accompany her mother to her aunt's or to visit with Maria Lucas (and perhaps seeing her brother in the process) or in seeking out some frivolity for herself or her Georgie.

In any case, Kitty was soon anxious to return to London. Not only for Anne's company, which she missed more than she could have imagined, but also for the pleasures of living a pampered life in the great metropolis (and far better to get news from Hunsford). And, sadly, she'd soon tired of her mother and constant display of the favouritism towards her youngest daughter and her constant insistence that Kitty was being selfish and lazy in not seeking out her own husband and having her own children.

"Were you *finally* to have a child, it would never be as sweet as Georgie, of course," Mrs. Bennet said more than once, "but I am sure it will be sweet enough for you, Kitty."

"Yes, Kitty," Lydia also said (and more than once), "it would never be Georgie or anything like my Wickham's baby, but it will be enough for you should you finally get around to having one."

But after a week, the Longbourn residents agreed to Kitty's suggestion that they join her on a trip to London. They clustered in a carriage hired by Mr. Bennet and the four of them—six counting Georgie and the nurse—were soon entering the capital, depositing the elder pair at the Gardiners' in Cheapside and the three (and Georgie) to Russell Square, where a note from Kitty had alerted the hostess that they were coming.

Kitty had prepared Anne for the test that Lydia's presence would likely put her to, but Mrs. Wickham proved uncharacteristically sedate in the de Bourgh home. She quickly, though, became disenchanted. She was not receiving the attention there Lydia knew she merited, a disaster she seethingly attributed to the ill manners that Anne de Bourgh displayed, not surprisingly since she was the daughter of the horrible Lady Catherine.

When word got around that the young widow was on Russell Square, more and more of Wickham's former colleagues in the regulars and the militia appeared to pay their respects, and Wickham's great friend Denny did so more than once—leading more than one to express concern that the boundaries of appropriate mourning behaviour were being pushed.

Even with such pleasant diversions, though, Lydia found the restrictions she did abide by suffocating and her parents needed no convincing and in less than a fortnight, she and they and Georgie and the nurse were happily heading back to Longbourn.

We should note here that Mr. Bennet himself was doing quite well notwithstanding the irksomeness of London. He showed no sign of hastening the date on which Mr. Collins would gain title to the estate. If there was anything that gave him comfort it was his correspondence with Elizabeth when they were separated. That began in earnest sometime after the news about Darcy's financial difficulties reached Longbourn. In those days, Mrs. Bennet became nearly impossible with her tirades about the uselessness of Darcy, particularly in contrast to Lydia's late Mr. Wickham.

There was always the gross inequality between Mr. Bennet and the woman to whom he was disastrously married. The contrast with Elizabeth and her spouse was telling, and when Mr. Bennet offered heartfelt sympathy for what the Darcy family were going through, it was the impetus for Elizabeth to open herself up to her dear father and he to her.

She was, of course, largely a force of reason and contentment even if some of her letters slipped into banality. He found unexpected pleasure in one thing Lizzy wrote to him regularly. The changes she saw in Kitty, who they both increasingly referred to by her true Christian name. Mr. Bennet was pleased beyond measure in confirming Lizzy's observations with his own at Longbourn and in London and about being wrong at least about that daughter.

Chapter 33. In Hunsford

Will's early days at the Parsonage—he was officially William Collins, Jr.—passed quickly if hectically (though it is safe to say that he at least did not particularly notice). But whatever was going on around him, Mr. Collins was completely lost to the boy from first sight. It affected him in his role in his parish as well.

In several of his sermons in the weeks preceding the arrival, he had extolled the virtues of children and of *charity*. He often used the quotation from Saint Luke his wife shared with him. In his visits through the parish, he again and again remarked how blessed the mothers were to have been given the opportunity to raise children in the image of our Lord. He reminded one and all of Christ's message to care for and open one's heart to the less fortunate, especially the sinner who has found the true way and sought redemption.

More tellingly, on that first Sunday *after* Will's arrival, he said, "My friends in Christ. In these dark days of winter, I must share with you some rays of joy. A child has come to our village. A child born through no fault of his own but for whom my dear wife and I have found room in our hearts, and I hope you will find room in yours.

"I can say no more but that through the wonder of our Lord, Mrs. Collins and I have been blessed with the arrival of one William Collins, Jr. He is a most precious gift and will, I pray and I hope you will too, grow into a fine man.

"It is, of course, far too cold to take him out but I hope that when it is indeed warm enough, each of you will come visit us and meet *our* new boy."

This little coda was unremarked upon by the congregation in the church for the balance of the proceedings as a matter of politeness. It could not be contained, though, once the parishioners had left the church itself and after they one after another wished the vicar and Mrs. Collins well and extended congratulations to them on the blessed event. Speculation was quickly rampant about just who this little child could be. Or, more precisely, *whose* this little child could be.

That he was illegitimate could not be doubted, given Mr. Collins's reference to him being "without fault." Seeing as all the women in the parish were accounted for, and only married ones had full bellies, everyone was at a loss for who the mother was. From London or the north or west were the generally accepted places where the wench was thought to have abandoned the innocent boy.

Several even suggested *very quietly* that their landlady might be her, but since she'd been seen in early December and exhibited no signs of being with child, those suggestions were quickly (and guiltily) squashed.

In the end, Charlotte put the speculation largely but not entirely to rest when on the next market day, she "mentioned" to one of the vendors that the child was from a parish close to the Channel and left it at that.

Chapter 34. Again to Rosings

As the trees began to bud, it was time for Anne to return to Rosings and for Kitty to go with her.

On a late March Friday morning, the two women's trunks were stacked at the rear of a carriage at Russell Square and soon the two women followed and sat across from one another in the coach before Anne in short order crossed to sit close to her dear friend, kept warm in part by a blanket they shared and even more by their simple and increasingly natural presence next to one another as the carriage pulled out and disappeared into London traffic and on to Kent.

And it was at the conclusion of this travel that the next act of Catherine Bennet's story began, when she alit from Anne's carriage with the help of a tall, slim footman, the moment her right boot touched the crushed stones of the drive of Rosings House.

In the foyer, she and her host were met by a line of servants. Anne formally introduced Kitty to each and bows or curtsies and smiles were exchanged. She'd met most of them but that was when she was a guest. Now she was the house's newest resident.

Dowling the butler and Mrs. Nestor the housekeeper and down the line. The next to last girl was a young one, not much older or younger than Kitty herself with amber hair and light skin that made her seem Irish, a suspicion confirmed with the heavy brogue in her, "Thank 'ee, Ma'am" to Anne.

"This is Teresa Riordan," Anne said to Kitty, "and she'll be your maid."

The girl curtsied a second time. "Pleased to meet you, miss," the Irish girl said. *A maid for me*, Kitty thought. She'd never known any such thing, at best having shared Sarah with Lydia at Longbourn.

In Anne's grand foyer with its black and white marble floor tiles and grand turning staircase bordered on one side by a series of family portraits (most prominently of Lady Catherine and Sir Lewis de Bourgh with a small one near the top of a young Anne looking very little, and very little like the woman she'd become), and after the servants dispersed, Kitty suddenly realizing that she was truly in her new home, did several revolutions as she looked up at the wrought iron chandelier, to Anne's great amusement.

* * * *

THE NEXT WEEKS WERE, however, often difficult for Kitty. She didn't see Will nearly as often as she wanted to, though her brain at least understood why. She knew, but she was helped in her occasional melancholia by feeling an increasing closeness to her maid. Though their backgrounds and positions were so different. Teresa Riordan told Kitty she was a farm girl from County Wexford who found a position in the home of an Irish gentleman and his young, English wife.

"She was, in fact," Teresa said while brushing Kitty's long hair a week after they'd met, "our mistress's cousin, Miss Georgiana Darcy as was. And things being as they were, she thought I might like being in England meself. So, I come over and Mrs. Nestor and maybe the mistress too liked me well enough, I suppose, so here I am, miss."

She said she'd never been home since—it being a long and hard and expensive journey—and hoped that someday she would cross back. It was clear to Kitty that the maid didn't wish to speak much of Ireland, so she asked no more questions of her and spoke more about her own history and her own slight dealings with Mr. Darcy himself, Georgiana's brother and guardian, and left it at that.

Kitty had only heard vague things about Darcy's sister. Anne told her that Georgiana was now Mrs. Edmund Evans and that her husband was a quite wealthy MP who came to London during sessions of the Commons.

"He has a suite of rooms near Westminster, but she will stay with us at Russell Square and maybe come here at times, his rooms not being quite appropriate for her," Anne said.

True to her word, some three weeks after Anne and Kitty arrived at Rosings, Anne said the lady herself was *en route* and would be with them in only a few days, after a brief stop in London to see her brother and her husband.

Georgiana was a year younger than Kitty, but Kitty recalled her in their one meeting when her brother married Lizzy as a tall woman, statuesque like her brother but with far softer features. She was spoken of by Anne and later by Teresa as being of the highest quality and quite in love with her far older husband, though they'd not as yet been blessed by a child. She was also said to be very shy.

"She is still quite young," the not-quite-young Anne told Kitty when their talk a day or two before she arrived turned gossipy, "and in time a child will surely arrive."

When the lady herself did arrive, Kitty liked her immediately. After the long trip from Ireland, she'd been two days in town, squeezing in with her brother's family at Mount Row. Tired as she was from the first leg of her trip, though, by mid-afternoon the day after her arrival at Rosings with a delightful breeze playing across the estate, the three women sat quite comfortably in the sitting room with its view down the drive. There they gossiped away the time till they had to prepare for dinner.

* * * *

IT WAS JUST ABOUT then that Kitty felt bolstered enough to go for walks alone even in the chilled air, in which case she made sure—and Teresa made sure—she was adequately bundled up. At first, she invariably took the path that led to the Parsonage. She passed it without stopping unless Charlotte saw her and called for her to visit.

For a change, though, she at times turned in the opposite direction, following the path to the north and into a small wood that extended she knew not for how long. As the path the other way had logs positioned for resting, including the one where Elizabeth sat when she met with Anne what seemed so long ago, so did this one and it was not long before Kitty identified her favourite.

It was a large log whose top had been shaved so as to provide a flat surface for one to sit on. More, it had a view through a slight opening in the wood that looked into the distance across the vale to the west of the estate, and beyond was a series of hills that undulated magically even in the bleakness of the winter's bare and not yet budding trees.

The log sat just to the south of a curve in the path and so avoided the winds that made other spots uncomfortable. Each time she stopped, Kitty looked forward to when spring would come and the trees around *her* log—for that is what she'd come to consider it—filled in.

She did not know what she thought while she sat but whatever it was seemed a great comfort to her. To allow her mind to wander from topic to topic, no longer obsessed with her Will. He was safe not two miles from her and so she could allow herself to think of herself and of Anne and Elizabeth. Even Teresa. She did not, pointedly, think of men, real or imagined. Her girlish obsession seemed to have vanished as Will grew inside her and when the thought did appear, the realisation that what she had done made it impossible for her to enter a favourable match caused her only slight regret but no more than that.

It was after one such walk when she got back to the house that she came upon another housemaid, she being named Molly, tending a fire in the drawing room.

"What can you tell me of the Collinses? What do they say in the village about that little boy? Did you know Mr. Collins is my cousin and that Mrs. Collins was a great friend of our family before she married Mr. Collins and came here?"

The questions flooded out as Molly was brushing ashes into a copper bin.

"Oh, I knew of Mr. Collins for quite some time, miss. He was a meek and mild man, he was. His sermons were oh so boring. Even when he suddenly appeared with his wife—I was very young then—and word was that he had expected to marry…Was it one of your sisters he expected to marry, miss?"

"Indeed it was. My sister Lizzy, who married Mr. Darcy, did not feel she could give Mr. Collins the happiness he deserved."

"That's it. I believe she's been to the Parsonage here since then, at least after Lady Catherine died."

"Yes, she has, Molly. But what of the village's view of the Collinses now and the baby?"

"Oh, the baby." Kitty made a point of watching Molly very carefully. "Everyone is so happy for Mrs. Collins. We all expected she'd have at least one child by now but seeing as she is a little on the old side it wasn't too much of a surprise that she didn't.

"Course she's so sweet especially after Lady Catherine died, and Mr. Collins was a little sweet too after that, and we all was sorry for 'er 'cause we thought she'd make a fine mother, you know? So when this little boy come and how happy she and Mr. Collins was the village was overjoyed."

"But what are they saying about where the boy comes from?"

"Some say it's a miracle, but that's more of a Catholic thing, you know? We all know, even a stupid girl like me—"

"Oh, dear, Molly. You are not 'stupid.'"

"Thank 'ee for saying so, miss. Thank 'ee. But as I says, even I know there's women who ain't married and get in the family way and has to give up their babies because they can't support 'em and the father is nowhere to be found. So, when Mr. Collins heard about this young boy in some parish down by the Channel and he and his missus took him in, we was so pleased with him and, as I says, we was overjoyed. I 'spect there'll be some sort of event for 'em in the village square once the spring comes and we can all actually see the little one.

"I'm sure you'll be more than welcome to come, Miss, though I guess you and Miss de Bourgh has already met him."

The conversation wound down and for her part Kitty slept better that night than she had in many months.

She felt more secure when, thanks to Anne, word got around of Kitty's long-time relationship with both Charlotte and Mr. Collins himself and no eyebrows were raised about the amount of time they spent together. Though it was sometimes difficult for Kitty to break herself away from Will, overall she agreed that the course designed by Elizabeth with Charlotte and Anne was the best one and was happy enough to accept the role of the boy's special "aunt."

*   *   *   *

WEEKS THREATENED TO become months and idyllic as Kent was, the ladies needed to return to town, with Georgiana returning with Mr. Evans, MP, to Ireland. The night before leaving Kent, a Sunday in late April 1816, the Collinses came to dinner. Indeed, for this last night, Kitty walked to the Parsonage to collect them, and was allowed to carry Will much of the way. The evening passed well though it was shrouded with a sense of regret, especially to Kitty, about their departing.

That morning, with Kitty and Georgiana joining Anne in the de Bourgh pew in the Hunsford Church for services, Mr. Collins's sermon reiterated the pleasure the delivery of a little child had given him and his wife, "though pleasure tempered by our realisation that we are charged with the care of one of our Lord's great creations, as we all are a great creation of our Lord."

The next morning, the three were comfortable in Anne's landau as it headed north up to London. The journey's time passed quickly as, again, the three were themselves very comfortable with each other.

When they got to Russell Square, Taylor had the front door open. When each got herself decent, they met in the drawing room. It was nearing three. Sandwiches and ales were arranged on a table not far from the windows overlooking the Square. Several servants arrived from Kent shortly thereafter, including Teresa.

"I know the others will be anxious to see us," Anne said as the little group were nibbling on their food and sipping from their glasses, "but would it be too horrid of me to put off visiting them till tomorrow?"

They were more tired than they expected. With the others' consent, Anne wrote a note to the Bingleys begging their forgiveness for not visiting but promising that she and Kitty and Georgiana should be expected late the following morning. This was promptly dispatched and the women set in for an evening of quiet, calm, and a mix of reading and needlepoint and some light improvised playing on Anne's German piano-forte by the quite accomplished Georgiana, with Kitty adding what was a delicate soprano to certain familiar songs, much as they had done in the country.

The trio did get an early start the next morning and made an unfashionably early appearance at Mount Row. Elizabeth suggested the women all head out for a turn around the upper reaches of Hyde Park, and Anne agreed and soon that is what the group—consisting of Jane, Elizabeth, Anne, Georgiana, and Kitty—was doing.

Georgiana could not stay in town very long, and on the Thursday, she was to set off early with her husband for their trip home. Her room at Anne's was next to Kitty's and when Kitty went to find if she needed help packing, she saw Georgiana and Teresa deep in conversation. Though their voices were low, they carried to where Kitty stood in the doorway. She was about to retreat to avoid being detected when she heard Georgiana say very sweetly to the servant that "you have done well. All I did was give you a second chance."

As she stepped away, Kitty saw Teresa's shoulder drop a bit and Georgiana's right hand rise so her fingers could run across the maid's check to clear away, it was obvious, a tear. Which was the last Kitty saw or heard of the encounter between the two before she herself was gone. She waited until Teresa left before retracing her steps to Georgiana's room and offering her help.

Georgiana assured Kitty that none was needed. She always had a pleasant countenance and whatever happened between her and the Irish girl left no traces on her face. Kitty saw no signs of any alterations in Teresa not ten minutes later as they assembled with Anne and several other servants. Only Anne and Kitty—and a footman who'd carried out her trunk to the Evans's carriage—went with her to the pavement and thanks and regrets and promises of a return and waves were exchanged as the carriage joined the traffic heading to Westminster to pick up her husband for the start of their long journey to Ireland.

Kitty could not make out anything about the peculiar exchange she'd witnessed. She tried delicately over the next days to learn the nature of Georgiana's relationship with Teresa, but the maid remained much as she always had, at best saying how Georgiana was kind to her when she was home in Ireland years before.

Some days later, as she and Anne were taking a turn around the Square, Kitty found the courage to raise what she'd seen.

"I did not understand it. Teresa is a...a maid yet there was something more than a servant's admiration or devotion in what I saw."

"There is nothing to be said about this," Anne said. Without altering her tone, she continued more crossly than Kitty expected, "But you, of all people, should recognise that there are secrets people may have that are of no concern of ours."

Kitty felt as if she'd been slapped.

"I did not mean to invade. I thought it touching that there was clearly something between the two, but I cannot imagine what it could be."

There was an empty bench just after the pair turned to the west and Anne directed her companion to it. Once there, they sat very close to one another. Anne lowered her voice.

"You must tell no one. Not even Georgiana or Teresa. No one must know. No one. Do you understand?"

The tone had shifted. The crossness had turned gentle as Kitty said she did.

"The fact is that Teresa found herself with child while working as a housemaid for the Evanses. The housekeeper trusted Georgiana enough to bring it to her attention with the request that if possible, something should be done for the poor girl."

"Was she married?"

"She wasn't married, and she has told no one who the father was."

"What became of the baby, if it survived?"

"Before the girl's—Teresa's—condition was discovered, she was sent to a house in Dublin. It was in the neighbourhood where the Evanses had their house and the woman was somewhat older than Georgiana. In her late twenties.

"She'd not had a child though she wanted one and Georgiana had the idea when she learned of Teresa's condition that it might work out much as what happened with you."

"She arranged for Teresa to have the child and surrender it to that family?"

"Exactly. Teresa, like you, realised it was the best thing for her child. Indeed, the *only* thing. So, she was cloistered in the house until her time came and a process for the child to be adopted was completed quickly and Teresa was sent to me."

"How did that come about."

This initial disclosure having been made, Anne stood and they resumed their turn of the Square.

"My cousin wrote to me shortly after she'd come up with this plan about the baby. 'What was to be done about the girl?' she asked. She was confident about telling me since I was so far away.

"Perhaps it was because of what happened with you, but I suggested that if the girl—Teresa—was willing, I would retain her for my household. Which is what happened."

"How could she leave her baby?"

"She was a servant. It would be impossible for her to have anything to do with it. That was the reality, I'm afraid. You are different of course so your sister and Charlotte came up with their own scheme to have you the chance to know—"

"And love—"

"Indeed, and love Will."

"So, your taking on Teresa was an act of charity."

"I suppose it was, but Georgiana assured me that she was a conscientious, good maid and that I would not regret it and I have not."

"I will treat her differently then."

"No. You must not. She can never know that her situation is known to anyone but me. And I only know because it was absolutely necessary. No. You can never disclose this part of her just as you will not have anyone disclose that part of you. I only confided in you because I trust you and do not wish you to reach perhaps the wrong conclusion about what you saw."

"Does Georgiana know about me?"

"She does not. To her and everyone but those you have told, you are simply my companion attempting to break away from your parents and your sister Lydia."

The pair were nearing the gate by the de Bourgh house and with a final "I understand" from Kitty, they went home.

Apart from this revelation, life moved onward as is its wont. The traffic was constant between the two London houses. In some ways given Anne's temperament and Darcy's financial embarrassment, that they were not invited out often did not matter. Nor, apparently, did anyone care that only a few received an invitation to Mount Row or Russell Square.

For his part, Darcy had also developed quite a fondness for the Gardiners, and they were frequent guests at the Bingleys' and all of the Bennets and their spouses visited Cheapside at least once a fortnight. Jane remained a particular favourite with the four Gardiner children (especially the two girls) as she always was and was sure to spend at least one afternoon at the Gardiners' each week.

Matters were more delicate with Caroline Brown and the Hursts but blood being what it is, they were among the few other London residents who were regulars at Mount Row, with a sort of uncomfortable truce existing between Caroline and Elizabeth (and Anne never coming on nights when Caroline was expected).

Chapter 35. A Trip to Longbourn

Kitty was content. In London, she regularly received letters from Charlotte. In truth, though, there was not much to be said about a healthy, growing boy other than that he was healthy and growing. Kitty still read each word again and again and held each letter tightly and when she was not reading it, she was often clutching it to her breast.

Shortly before Anne told Kitty they'd soon be making their longed-for return to Rosings for the summer season, Kitty, Jane, and Elizabeth took the trip to Longbourn, where they'd be seeing Lydia (and Georgie) as well as their parents.

They made all the required visits in Meryton to Lucas Lodge and the Philipses, and Lydia savoured the renewed attention due her as the widow of a war hero as she paraded about with her sisters.

This was barely tolerable to the others. Less so was Mrs. Bennet's behaviour. She would not keep quiet about a visit by the Collinses to Lucas Lodge—"though I suppose I must call her 'Mrs. Collins' now"—with that bastard of theirs. It was a word she insisted on repeating even after Jane said, "Please, mother. He is just an innocent child" and her daughters (excepting Lydia) glared silently at her, and she said, "How could you compare such a creature to our poor, sweet Georgie, and this bastard, who will I suppose have Longbourn after Mr. Bennet and that cousin of yours Mr. Collins are dead and I am thrown out on the street"— which she continued to say and believe even after Mr. Collins himself wrote not once but twice to Mr. Bennet that "in the event of your passing—which we all hope and pray will be in the far distant future—you can assure the sweet Mrs. Bennet that she will always have a place in the house and always be a member of our family."

To which Mrs. Bennet more than once said "I would rather be an old beggarwoman on the street than be considered a member of *his* family seeing what they have become."

For his part, Mr. Bennet simply said about Will, "he seems to be a fine-looking boy with the requisite number of arms and legs, eyes and ears, and just the one nose and I hope he and Georgie become the greatest of friends at Cambridge in twenty years' time."

Yet again Kitty could not get back to London too soon, a sentiment joined in by Elizabeth and even Jane. And once they were back, Kitty resumed her life as a lady's companion in a fine house on Russell Square in Bloomsbury. She could never marry. That much was certain. No decent—and few indecent—men would have her (as a *wife* at least) after what she'd done, and she was brave enough that she would have to reveal her secret to any man who might fall in love with her.

Strangely, as we have seen, that reality did not weigh on her. Things were now exciting, and Anne made an effort to integrate her into society. Unlike some, and like the Darcys and the Bingleys, Anne did not travel widely in society. Neither her mother nor her father had gone out often even when they leased a house in Mayfair, which was where they lived in town before Lady Catherine bought the house on Russell Square.

Anne de Bourgh was of sufficient standing, though, that she received many more invitations than she could accept. This was especially true because she was regarded as among the most financially attractive single women of merit in town. Over thirty years of age, though, she was getting a bit old for a match, though many subtracted a number of years from her true age since her mother, because of Anne's weak constitution, never did have her formally come out.

She would be, it was universally acknowledged, a fine catch for any gentleman or even a member of the aristocracy. Though small, her looks had become more than adequate, and her money would always be, particularly since she was an only child with no encumbrances or familial obligations (save, some whispered, by the danger that her supposedly impoverished cousin Darcy would latch onto the poor girl's money). Indeed, there were those who feared some rake might take it upon himself to kidnap her and carry her to Scotland to marry and take her money. Darcy was the one who feared this fate the most—Wickham had nearly done it to Georgiana—and he and his cousin had taken steps to protect her person in ways only the trained eye would recognise.

"Yes," more than one legitimate prospective mother-in-law told her friends, "I would allow her to set some money aside for that proud cousin of hers, but the rest would be a fine dowry for my son."

Anne de Bourgh had no formal guidance in these matters, which led society to be confident that it was only a matter of time before some lord or duke or mere baronet would take her off to some sagging estate whose roof would finally be repaired or perhaps a disused wing could again be habitable with the funds she brought with her. In this, though, they failed to appreciate that in this one regard she *had* taken after her mother. She was clever and she was stubborn. More important, Anne's parents did not entail the estate. *That* was the fate of the poor Bennet girls and their complete want of any legal interest in Longbourn. This was why it was Anne and not some male relative—Darcy himself most likely—who obtained title to Rosings Park (and why Lady Catherine had it after Sir Lewis passed on).

This did not mean Anne was free and clear. Marriage would insert some *complications* as to her money, as it had Georgiana Darcy's. In Georgiana's case, tradition was followed and, fortunately, she was fond of and even in love with her husband, as he was with her.

And perhaps Anne de Bourgh would be so fortunate. After all, except for Mr. and Mrs. Bennet themselves, all of those close to her had favourable marriages (subtracting the marriages of the Wickhams and Bingley's sisters as not being of people to whom she was close).

This will explain why Anne was the recipient of invitation after invitation, to all types of society. And were it not for Kitty, she would not have accepted nearly as many as she in the end did. Because Kitty did not have the luxury that Anne had of not caring to marry someone She Did Not Love.

Of course, there was someone that Kitty did love but for him she could only be his aunt.

Why, one might ask, did Miss Anne de Bourgh bother coming to town at all if she was not to partake in what society had to offer? There was one thing she could get nowhere else, at least in England. Music. Her mother was liberal in telling visitors to Rosings how accomplished she would have been in music had she only bothered to apply herself.

Dear Anne had a true musical ear and appreciation for a well-performed piece and was a most fair, if harsh, critic of those who played the fine piano-forte in her country house. She'd had an even newer, finer instrument and a delicately carved harp delivered to Russell Square and was known to insist upon accomplished guests playing delightful tunes on it to "pay for their supper" and was suspected of providing pounds to help some of them to eat more regularly.

Like her mother, though, Anne herself was little accomplished as a player since her education was much neglected. But she spent many of her evenings in town enjoying both the high and the low performances given throughout London.

Shortly after the Bennets were back from Longbourn, and Kitty restored in Bloomsbury, Georgiana came from Ireland to stay while her husband, the Right Hon. Edmund Evans, was sitting in the Commons. She did this at Anne's house.

Once settled, Georgiana slipped into the world that Anne was constructing around Russell Square. In ways, it reminded Kitty of Longbourn, of the wonderful, relaxed if very small world the Bennets shared there, a reminder that was particularly vivid when Lizzy and sometimes Jane came to Russell Square at whatever hour of the day they felt like coming by, disregarding, as family members may, the rules of protocol.

One night after dinner at Mount Row though, while tea was being drunk and Kitty was playing quadrille, Kitty overheard Elizabeth ask about a servant, a young maid, at Pemberley. "Yes," Jane said as she and Elizabeth sat on a couch with tea. "As I recall she was a plain but sweet girl."

"Well," Elizabeth responded, "according to a letter Darcy got from his steward, she was forced to leave because she was put in a family way with one of the stable hands. She left and I can't say what will become of her."

"I should prefer not to speak so much of such things," Jane said.

Her sister reached for her hand. "It is uncomfortable, but I think we must admit to being at least aware of it."

"Of course, I know that Lizzy. But perhaps the family there should allow her to stay?"

"They are a very conscientious family. They've only recently made their money and are deathly afraid, Darcy said, that any wrong step will forever destroy their chances of being accepted in places where they wish to be accepted. So, I understand that she is gone with no hopes and no prospects."

"Oh, Lizzy," Jane said. "I know what she did was wrong, but what is to happen to her? Perhaps Mrs. Reynolds knows. But what matters is that she's gone. She must be from nearby so unless she finds a sympathetic parson or has a strong family, things will be very hard on her."

It was at that moment that Kitty's eavesdropping was interrupted by Anne's telling her it was her turn to play, and Kitty heard no more of what her sisters had to say to one another as she tried to gather what happened with the cards while she was distracted.

It was a curious thing that lingered after an otherwise innocuous evening. Kitty didn't mention the unfortunate maid to Anne as they rode back to Russell Square. Sad as it was, she knew it was not uncommon and in the end that it was unavoidable. How could she, Catherine Bennet, not sympathize with the poor girl? One who would suffer a fate likely far worse than her own maid Teresa had.

Pemberley, though, was far, far away. Kitty had little of the attachment to the place and its aura, unlike Elizabeth or even Jane. Jane had spent the prior autumns there, before and after the financial storm altered everything. Kitty's attachment went in the opposite direction. To Kent. She was overjoyed when one afternoon Elizabeth said how much she missed Charlotte. If she went to Hunsford for, say, a week, she teased, would Kitty care to join her?

"I'm sure, Anne," who was remaining in London for another month, "will allow me to stay with you at the house," which of course she did, and in a matter of days, Elizabeth and Kitty and Little Fitz (and a nurse) were together in a de Bourgh chaise for the hours long trip to Hunsford. And what a pleasant surprise it was to the Collinses when they pulled up to the Parsonage to begin their visit!

Charlotte insisted on hosting them each evening (except one, horribly wet one) for dinner and talk and some no-stakes card playing. Will was brought out each night by his nurse.

Elizabeth especially relished exploring the spots she'd visited when she was so much younger and not yet married. She retraced her steps time and again from those walks with herself and with Colonel Fitzwilliam, and especially with her Darcy.

The three women sat in the front pew for services on Sunday, where Mr. Collins was in his best form and Elizabeth was yet again struck by the alterations in the man. At the Parsonage, Charlotte still spent time in her little room and Mr. Collins was often in his garden and Charlotte confessed that to Lizzy her surprise that she'd begun to enjoy the simple times when they were together, with or without Will.

For all that, though, Elizabeth never felt a moment's jealousy for she was right when she said those years earlier that she was the last woman in the world who would make him happy. And how pleased she was that Charlotte, perhaps with some slight assistance from Will, turned out to be the woman for him and he the man for her.

But needs must, as they say, and their all too brief visit soon came to an end, They, though, and many more would be arriving in a month's time for the season and the halls and rooms of Rosings House would be full.

While she was not gone long from town, Kitty found she missed Teresa. She and Elizabeth were tended to by Molly quite well and the housekeeper, Mrs. Nestor, was as always kind and efficient. Kitty, though, had become accustomed to her own maid, and when they were separated, she'd missed being able speak to her at each day's end.

And knowing she'd see Teresa (and Anne) when she got back to Russell Square eased some of Kitty's sadness when she and Elizabeth bade their farewells to the Collinses—all three of them—a week after their arrival and with the promise that it would not be long until their return.

Once she was back, Kitty made herself comfortable in her room with Teresa, giving free rein to the Irishwoman to ramble on about the house's (slight) goings-on in her absence. Kitty sat on her small bench facing her oval mirror while the maid ran a brush again and again through her hair and she heard perhaps half of what was being told to her while her mind floated through the memories she'd recently accumulated.

This reverie was disturbed by a knock. After a "come in" from Kitty, an unfamiliar housemaid came through and after a curtsey advised that "Miss de Bourgh" would appreciate, if you please miss, for you to join her in the sitting room as soon as convenient.

Kitty quickly made it convenient to make herself presentable and within ten or fifteen minutes was herself knocking on the sitting room door.

Chapter 36. Colonel Fitzwilliam

Kitty first saw Anne getting up but her eyes quickly were drawn to a finely dressed man who turned toward her.

"There is someone here I wish you to meet. He is a cousin. And a widower. Recently arrived from Belfast. I will say no more but I think our Elizabeth was particularly fond of him."

Anne turned to Kitty.

"Miss Catherine Bennet, may I present to you my cousin, Colonel Richard Fitzwilliam," Anne said.

Said cousin bowed and in a moment Kitty recovered sufficiently to curtsey.

"*Another* cousin of Miss de Bourgh?" Kitty asked. She recalled vaguely being introduced to him at Elizabeth's wedding.

"Indeed," he said with a smile. "Miss de Bourgh, Mr. Darcy, and I share a grandfather although unlike those two I am not the eldest in my family."

"Yes, Catherine, he was required to find his own way in the world and has done rather well for himself."

"Well, my father, an earl, bought my commission in the Army and—"

"And you have done the rest," Anne said as she stepped beside him and put her arm through his. Kitty struggled to see similarities between the two cousins (with the Colonel being much taller than her friend), and between the Colonel and Darcy, but was at a loss.

"And my sister, Elizabeth?" Kitty asked.

Anne maneuvered so the three were all seated comfortably, and Taylor came in with a tray with tea and cakes, which he placed on a small table but that they at first ignored.

"I had pleasant strolls with your sister Elizabeth at Rosings when my aunt was alive. And I have since learned that I may have said something quite impolitic that might have hastened the marriage of both of your eldest sisters, for which I now take due credit."

He smiled at this last observation, and Kitty felt an immediate fellowship with him and suggested that if he gave her but a moment to recover from the journey she'd be delighted to clear her head and accompany him to Mount Row to see those sisters again. Though she was tired, it didn't seem so to her, and it became a long and quite pleasant walk.

"Miss de Bourgh said you are a widower. I am very sorry," she said soon after they left the house.

"I was very fortunate. As a second son, I had few prospects beyond a commission. My regiment was stationed in Belfast and there I met a woman of a small fortune. She was much younger, of course, but I became very fond of her and her father was fond of me."

He smiled. "I believe she was fond of me as well, Miss Bennet. We were married. This was some time after your sisters married. My wife, Estella, was quickly with child. I was overjoyed, of course. My regiment was shipped to France during her confinement, and it was there that I received the horrible news that she and our baby girl died while she attempted giving birth. There was, they said, nothing that could be done about it. For either of them."

He was silent and she could only say how sorry she was for what happened. He nodded and resumed.

"After the war ended, my regiment returned to Ireland but became largely inactive. I stayed with her family for some time, but it was very difficult for us all. Thank God for her parents' sake she had a younger sister, who is now married to a gentleman of some means.

"I wrote, oh, a month ago, to my cousin Miss de Bourgh and asked if I might visit Rosings Park as I so often did when her father and mother were alive. She, of course, told me I would always be welcome there but that if I could, I should stop here in London before going there with her and the others for the season."

"And so you agreed, and I am glad to have met you."

They were nearing the Bingleys' and upon their arrival were admitted and directed to the familiar sitting room. After a brief time and still being fatigued from her journey from Hunsford, Kitty returned to Russell Square alone—leaving the Colonel to dine and spend the evening with his other cousin (and Kitty's sisters and Bingley)—where she and Anne had a light meal and relaxed afterwards reading and as to Kitty doing some needlepoint in the warmth of the drawing room.

The pleasantness moved south on a Thursday in August. Jane, Lizzy, and Fitz sat in the Bingleys' carriage while Darcy, Bingley, and the Colonel rode behind them on horseback to go into Kent, and many similar groups embarked to their own country houses at about the same time. Anne and Kitty had arrived some days earlier.

As they approached the estate, Darcy and Bingley rode ahead, and when they passed the Parsonage and had less than half-a-mile to the house they gradually but unmistakably spurred their horses until they were in a full gallop as they reached the drive out front, Bingley's chestnut crossing the imaginary line barely a head before his friend's did, with both men reining in their horses and quickly dismounting to help the stallions cool down, letting the steam rising from them dissipate as they congratulated each other on their little bit of fun.

The Colonel rode easily, and both the others knew neither of them would have prevailed had Darcy's cousin contested the point. When all three had dismounted and their horses collected by two grooms, they turned to await the others.

All of our travelers assembled at Rosings House and some of the servants—either already there or sent ahead—were ready to direct the visitors to their appropriate rooms and see to the storage of their clothing and other essentials.

Their first night was a blessedly cool August evening. Several tables were placed end-to-end on the patio at the rear of the house. It opened to the northwest, its view slightly down and then to a long grove of trees beyond which there was a vale and then some hills. It was through this grove of trees that the path of which they were all so fond ran, the one that passed the Parsonage as it went to the south and to Hunsford itself.

The Collinses were of course invited. Both Elizabeth and Kitty traipsed to them when Elizabeth had sufficiently recovered from her journey, and Mr. Collins himself rushed to them when they emerged through the gate in front of the Parsonage.

Charlotte soon followed her husband, carrying Will and handing him to Kitty before she had the chance to ask.

Yes, yes, Kitty knew in substantial respects it wasn't her child anymore. Yet in the brief initial moments she had with him, she could never suppress her natural connection with the boy. Charlotte, sweet Charlotte, understood, stepping slightly back and turning to ask Elizabeth how the trip down was and Mr. Collins inquiring about the health of her family.

The intensity of those initial minutes soon passed, and the group was again back to being its own little family of people who long knew and loved—however briefly—each other. They flowed into the Parsonage itself, where Kitty handed Will to his nurse and the group sat down in the familiar front parlour. And they gossiped and Mr. Collins gave news of the happenings in the little parish until Elizabeth realised they must leave promptly or would never get to dinner on time.

She and Kitty rushed out to get changed as the Collinses hurried to their rooms upstairs to do the same and they met again not an hour later at those long tables out on the patio in outfits none of them would ever wear let alone be seen in while in town.

In the days to come, it was inevitable that Colonel Fitzwilliam more often found himself with Kitty than he did with anyone else, and he joked with her about that long ago time taking walks when he and Darcy were called to visit their aunt and he had the pleasure of seeing and walking with her sister, Elizabeth.

"Oh, you should have seen Anne back then," he said with a bit of a chuckle in his voice. "You couldn't imagine she would blossom into such a woman."

"Are you particularly fond of her then?" Kitty asked.

They were on a path that afforded a fine view across to the lush vale that stretched for some miles through the eastern part of the estate, and the wheat fields in their waving golden brown created a panorama in the high sun.

He laughed at the question.

"I know my aunt—her mother—had certain intentions and desires and even expectations about Anne and Darcy. Anyone with any sense—which apparently did not include Lady

Catherine but did over time include both my cousins—knew they were like oil and vinegar."

"I have noticed that they do not seem to be in any way related."

"It was worse when Lady Catherine was alive and I've heard them laugh about the absurdity of it, of them being husband and wife."

Kitty wondered at this, but she agreed, having now seen them often enough that the thought of them *marrying* was absurd.

Darcy was but a slight (and truth be told improved) version of the haughty, proud man Kitty'd first met when she'd gone with the others to visit an ailing Jane at Netherfield so long ago (oh and meeting that insipid, unmarried sister of Bingley's, who'd gotten her just deserts as far as Kitty could tell from all the tattling).

She could not imagine Anne being happier than she plainly was in her freedom. She'd sometimes flirt with gentlemen she'd see at parties or dinners that Kitty attended with her, gentlemen who in a thousand years would not cast an eye in Kitty's direction. Anne's riches and her haughtiness and pride drew them in; frequent were the nights when she'd confessed to how enjoyable she found toying with their affections. And their mothers' expectations and aspirations. She confessed, too, that she sometimes felt some remorse for her behaviour to at least some of those gentlemen (though never for their cloying mothers).

"There was a great deal of independence my mother had with her own money," she once told Kitty when the pair had collapsed in chairs in Anne's room at Russell Square after a fete in Mayfair. They were both still in their finery and Anne's maid and Teresa waiting in the hall to be called in to help them get out of their muslin, jewelry—Anne was liberal in lending fine pieces to her "Catherine"—and such.

"Perhaps I could be tempted with the right person and hope springs eternal that I shall someday come across one, but for now and being who I am, I am happy that I can return and lie on my bed in my gown and converse with great friends such as you and Elizabeth and my cousin Georgiana after returning from being out."

And never in all the days since that night had Anne given the slightest suggestion that she was tempted by any of the men who would have been hers were she to give them the slightest serious notice. And part of Kitty was happy about that.

*　*　*　*

WHEN THEY RETURNED TO London in early October in a convoy of carriages, Kitty and Anne were again separated from the rest, including Colonel Fitzwilliam, who'd obtain rooms for himself not too far from Mount Row. Kitty and Anne were glad of it. A country house filled with guests offered none of the intimacy of a house in Bloomsbury, even a quite large house in Bloomsbury, with just the pair of them.

Chapter 37. Catherine Bennet's Idea

Alone and away from Will, Kitty's thoughts more and more wandered to that poor girl dismissed from Pemberley. The one she'd overheard her sisters speak about. Kitty knew nothing of her, of course, but like Fanny Price or some character in one of Maria Edgeworth's novels about whom she felt empathy and who were fictional, she found herself strangely touched by the struggles of the unknown yet very real maid, the misery of that poor girl. It was so much like her own and even more like Teresa Riordan's. She was upset that nothing could be done as it *had* been done for her and as it *had* been done for Teresa.

One afternoon when she was alone with Elizabeth on Mount Row, she asked about the girl. She confessed to having overheard Lizzy's speaking with Jane. *Was there anything that could be done?* Of course, there wasn't, her sister said after she was able to recollect what Kitty was referring to. Kitty asked about the next one.

"The next one?" Elizabeth asked, not understanding her sister.

"You have said, and I know it's true, that that poor one wasn't and won't be the only one. There must be dozens, hundreds like her. Can we not help *any* of them?"

This was quite unexpected to Elizabeth, and she had no response other than, "It is the way of the world. Not just us, I think, but all peoples."

Elizabeth could do nothing about it. Even if she wanted to, she could not imagine what it could be. Surely the Darcys lacked the funds to make a contribution to the charities that cared for such cases.

Kitty was not so resigned, being aware as she was of what care was taken with Teresa. Voicing the words aloud convinced her she had to speak with someone. Which meant Anne. And perhaps the two of them could approach Georgiana.

Back at Russell Square, then, when next alone with Anne, Kitty told the story of the Pemberley servant. She said how tragic it was, even though everyone knew it was inevitable.

"I," she said, "had the benefit of the kindness of others, including of those like you who were complete strangers to me. It was difficult but not *impossible* for me to get some degree of happiness after what happened."

"You were a gentleman's daughter."

"Why should that matter?" Kitty asked.

"The ways of the world, I suppose."

"Which is precisely what Lizzy said. But why? *Why* must it be so?"

"So, you wish to do something for *servants* who end up like you?"

"Exactly. Like Teresa. I don't know what it is, and I don't know how it could be done. When I spoke to Lizzy, she was completely at a loss."

"About doing it or about how it could be done?"

"Both, I think."

"Where does all of this come from, Catherine?"

"I don't know. Perhaps mostly from Teresa."

At length, they came upon yet another scheme involving a woman in the family way. It had to be modeled on what happened with Teresa and Georgiana. After some hesitancy, Anne agreed that Georgiana should be contacted about it.

My Dearest Cousin,

You have been gone far too long and we anxiously await your return. Please promise me you will accompany your husband at the House's next sitting.

There is a matter of some delicacy I wish to broach with you. Should a servant girl become with child, arrangements would be made for her to be placed somewhere where she is not known for the final months of her confinement. There is no doubt that she may not keep the child, and we would endeavour to make appropriate arrangements. As to her (the servant and mother), when she is sufficiently recovered, arrangements would be made for her to return to service at a different, perhaps far distant place where she is unknown. Whether the new mistress and housekeeper would be made aware of the circumstances, I also do not know.

These are the rough thoughts that Miss Catherine Bennet and I have had and that we share with you and only with you. Neither her sister nor your brother has any inkling of our scheme. I reach out to you because of the value I place on your opinion and in the hope that if it is something worth pursuing, we can do so with your support and even assistance.

I ask that you destroy this letter after you have read it. Similarly, be assured that any notes you dispatch to me will only be seen by me and, if you permit, Miss Bennet.

> *I remain,*
> *Your most admiring cousin,*
> *Anne de Bourgh*

With Anne's letter gone (and the shared knowledge concerning Teresa Riordan left unmentioned), she and Kitty could only wait for a response and resume their lives in their fashionable part of town.

Chapter 38. Return to Lambton

For several days beginning nearly a week after Anne's letter was dispatched to Ireland, she and Kitty did not have the pleasure of the company of Darcy and Bingley. They repeated their journey of just over a year before, when in the summer of 1815 they'd ridden like Valkyrie to Pemberley to learn for themselves the status of the estate, before all was saved by Anne de Bourgh (a fact of which only five people were aware, they being the two principals and their solicitors and his banker, and not including Bingley).

The two stayed at Lambton and did not inform the family renting the estate of their presence. Word of their appearance in the town, though, spread quickly to the house, and Mr. Quinn, the man who rented Pemberley itself, interrupted their dinner at their inn to say how honoured he would be if Mr. Darcy and Mr. Bingley would visit him the next day.

"I should not like to impose, Mr. Quinn," Darcy said as the three men stood at the table where the dinner sat.

"Mr. Darcy, Sir, it is *I* who am imposing on *you*. I will not brook dissent. You will come when you have finished your business with your, I say 'your,' steward, Mr. Darcy. I promise you that we have done nothing, I hope, to alter the beauty of your, I say 'your,' home, Sir. Indeed, I could not improve upon it."

"Very well, Mr. Quinn. We are to meet Mr. Lewis at ten o'clock and we will come to you immediately thereafter. I am sure it will be over by two, so that is when I suggest we come to see you and your family, if that suits."

"'Suits'? Goodness me, Mr. Darcy, coming at midnight would be fine enough for us Quinns. Indeed, Sir. Though, yes, two o'clock in the afternoon, I say 'afternoon,' Sir, would better suit."

With a deep bow, the tenant bid *adieu* to the landlord and his friend and was quickly gone.

When he was out on the street and Bingley and Darcy were back in their seats over their now-cold beef, Darcy said, "It is my own fault that I depend on the charity of that man."

"Oh, Darcy," Bingley said. "You are so, so hard on others. Indeed, I recall how harsh you were at first with me seeing as there were not generations behind my money."

"That is true, Charles," Bingley said, taking a final gulp from his glass of claret and holding it up so a refill could be had, "But you were an exceptional sample of your breed and warranted my respect."

Bingley laughed as he held his own glass up for the porter. "You are incorrigible, Sir. But I will admit that over time you prove to be a fine judge of a man's qualities, no matter whence he comes, and perhaps you will find some value in Michael Quinn here and will not be so dismissive of the man who," and he leaned forward and lowered his voice, "helped save your bacon, my friend."

What Fitzwilliam Darcy might have done in times past didn't signify. He was with his closest friend—at least the closest friend whose bed he did not often share—and knew Bingley was right and offering a veiled compliment and so he lifted his glass, and they toasted the fine Michael Quinn who, Darcy said somewhat loudly, "has helped save my bacon." And they drank to it. And to the king and returned to their beef.

The news from Lewis the next morning was good. The harvest in Derbyshire in general and at Pemberley in particular looked to be very fine. Prices would be strong since other counties had suffered from some mid-summer dryness. The tenants would have no problem in paying their rents. It would, should all go as it had gone, mean Anne de Bourgh would receive more than was projected when she and Darcy spoke about a schedule of repayment. The date when a Darcy would again sleep at Pemberley *might* come earlier than expected.

While Darcy and Bingley were up north, Colonel Fitzwilliam naturally visited Russell Square each day, and he found himself quite welcomed there.

Anne made no effort to discourage this. As often as not she suggested a turn around the Square and once or twice, when the weather was not conducive to a walk at all, insisted that they explore the nearby British Museum, clustered as they went 'neath several umbrellas.

And who were Kitty and the Colonel to disappoint their host?

Alas, several times found Colonel Fitzwilliam disappointed that the ladies were not at home when he called. These were after Anne received a response from Georgiana to her letter. In it, Georgiana said she was not free to disclose certain confidences, but she thought the idea of creating an opportunity to a select few women to have a life after making a horrible mistake was a capital one. She would expectantly await further information on the topic and would in any case retain the confidences that her cousin entrusted to her and expressly provided that Anne was free to fully discuss her views with Kitty.

On the very afternoon of her receiving Georgiana's letter, Anne sent a note via a footman to her family's long-time solicitor, begging that he be available for a conference the next morning at eleven, at his chambers. He immediately sent word back that he most certainly would be available "for my dear Miss Anne."

At the designated hour, he sat with Anne and Kitty in his very large office with a young solicitor in his chambers taking notes. The general terms of the formation of a private corporation to be known as the Islington Charity for the Protection of Female Servants were worked out but the older solicitor pointed out that a man was required by law to be the entity's president. Anne assured him that she had "just the man" for the job.

Immediately upon leaving, Kitty asked who that might be.

"My cousin Richard Fitzwilliam, of course. He would be ideal, if we can get him to agree."

They were quickly in the privacy of Anne's carriage. The moment it pulled into traffic, Anne smiled at Kitty. "And what, my dear Catherine, do you think of our Colonel Fitzwilliam?" she asked.

"He is surely not a handsome man and I think he loved his wife quite well and would have loved their child even more."

"Aye. A love like that will not soon be forgotten or gotten over. I do not know if a man can ever recover from such a devotion of the heart to such a woman, though I never met his wife. My knowledge comes only from the Colonel himself, who spoke of her virtues when I saw him while she was still alive and especially when the child was expected."

"I'm sure you will learn love yourself."

"But what of *him*? The Colonel?" Anne asked.

"I think he is very fond of you. I think he enjoys being with you quite much, now that he needn't worry that people will think him an adventurer after your money."

"'Adventurer'?" Anne laughed. "I've never known anyone less a corsair than him. Do not prove yourself such a fool, Catherine. This cousin is no more suited for me than the other was."

"Mr. Darcy?"

"The very one," Anne replied with a smile. "You know what I mean and stop avoiding it. Do you love Colonel Fitzwilliam?"

"'Love'? Me? Now who is the fool?"

Anne would not respond, and Kitty could not abide the silence.

"He is civil enough, I suppose. With his small fortune."

"Do you need anything more than a 'small fortune'?"

Kitty laughed. "I am not my sister Lydia. Though she may have to survive on something less than a fortune of any size."

"She has her brothers-in-law."

"Who are not quite what they were in the way of money. And, of course, there's Mr. Collins swooping in when my father dies." It was the type of thing she would never dare say in the presence of her mother or her younger sister, but neither was with them and her favourite woman was.

"You have again, my dear Catherine, avoided my direct question. Do you or could you love the Colonel."

"You quite astonish me," Kitty said truthfully. The thought had never occurred to her before. But its appearance had a profound effect on her. Her countenance changed markedly.

"Do you think it is something I *should* consider?"

"I think it something you *must* consider. I believe he is in danger of becoming very much in love with you."

This was absurd to Kitty. She'd not had a hint of any such nonsense.

She said, to correct the illusions Anne obviously had, "Do you not see how he hovers around *you*? How often he comes to visit me but mostly sits with *you*? Talks with *you*?" This was ignored, and Anne fought to keep her expression blank with a hint of disapproval.

"Do not forget, Catherine, that he is a soldier, trained to use a bit of stealth to achieve his objective."

"Oh, you are just too absurd."

In this new silence, Kitty was without the words to fill it. Could she love Richard Fitzwilliam? Another soldier like Wickham, that dangerous obsession she'd had as a girl.

Alas, they were soon back at Russell Square, and Taylor had the carriage door open, holding an umbrella that gave both women cover as they hurried up the steps to the foyer and no more was *said* about the widower.

Seeing as he was a frequent visitor already, and apart from what either woman might have thought ephemerally about him, his involvement with the charity would not cause any alarm or concern.

That he was a military man with a fine sense of organization and preparation was an added factor in Colonel Fitzwilliam's favour. When the broad outlines were explained to him by Anne, his enthusiasm could not be hidden. Of course, he would do whatever was asked of him by his cousin. Most immediately, he agreed to act as president of the charity, though acknowledging that it was a titular title accepted because of Anne's disability, that of being a woman.

The Colonel would prove particularly useful in the acquisition of a building that would house the girls. No place but London could leave them so well concealed. It had to be in a good neighbourhood but one to which no fashionable woman would venture. It would provide such medical help as was needed and gave the greatest chance of a successful birth. The girls would be together, and something would be found to occupy them. Some type of piecework. As maids, they'd all be adept at many things. They would not be isolated and abandoned in some dank cottage in the Scottish highlands or in the west of Ireland.

Chapter 39. Darcy Meets with Anne

Early on the Monday afternoon after he returned from Pemberley (and after the Colonel's position at the charity was formalized), Darcy made a quite formal appearance at Russell Square. "Taylor," he said, "I should like to have a word of a sensitive nature with my cousin, if you please."

After a bow, the butler suggested that he head up to his mistress's study on the first floor, "where you shan't be disturbed while I see if she is in."

He was pacing in the room, but not for long when there was a rapping on the door, and Anne was through it. He gave her a stiff bow and she gave him a similarly stiff curtsey.

"My dear cousin, I assume you are here about the...about the debt."

They had not spoken of it since the papers were signed months earlier. Anne was never tempted to contact the Pemberley steward directly for information. Fitzwilliam Darcy would tell her what she needed to be told and when, good or bad. And the news was good. Very good. He could not guarantee it, but Darcy said he was confident that a significant portion of his debt would be taken care of once the harvest was in and sold.

"It will not be nearly enough to extinguish my obligation to you," he said as they sat on either end of a leather sofa that was along one wall of the paneled room. "But it will go a ways to it. Perhaps next year will do it."

"You have a fine steward, good land, and happy tenants. That's always the secret, isn't it?"

"My father was a good man and took care of them and I like to think I am the same."

She knew it was true. And while there was Elizabeth beyond everything and Anne de Bourgh was quite fond of her (though fonder of Catherine), there had always been a special bond between her and her cousin Darcy. Her mother never understood it.

"I hope we shall all be together again at Pemberley in the not-too-distant future," she told him.

"God willing, and another fine harvest and I verily believe we will be. Bingley and I did meet the current man who has the house. A tradesman by the name of Quinn. He was a good and clever man so far as we could tell. Invited us to dinner. Insisted we come and insisted that I sit at the head of the table for dinner at the house. I asked the butler about them, and he said they had none of the airs he expected them to have and did so much for themselves that he and the others were sometimes at a loss for what they were to do.

"I will confess that after I was told this, I took Mr. Quinn aside. I explained to him that the servants were quite uncomfortable and confused by not being permitted to do their jobs. 'They are unhappy,' I said, and he was truly astonished but promised that he would see to it that his family begin acting appropriately and I hope he is good as his word. For everyone's sake."

"For how long does he have it?" Anne asked.

"The lease is for two years, and I am glad of it, to have him there. I could not afford to keep it up yet anyway, as you well know. Our hope is to be there again in early 1818. And you shall of course come. You will at last begin to appreciate that it is the most wonderful house in England, excepting Rosings Hall."

She laughed. "Oh Fitzwilliam. Don't patronise me. I know full well that Rosings Hall pales in comparison. Elizabeth sometimes goes on and on about your Pemberley and how it affected her judgment of you."

"She has mentioned that once or twice," he said. Speaking of his wife was always a pleasure.

Anne resumed. "My father and mother never had the eye that yours did and your father's father. Though you will admit that I have made some improvements. And Kent is, you will agree, quite a bit closer to town than is Derbyshire."

"Well, cousin," Darcy said, the mood much lightened with her reaction to his financial report, "I cannot debate the geography with you."

There *was* a great affection between the two, but, as Anne understood, it was not the type her mother hoped for. And Fitzwilliam Darcy and Anne de Bourgh were much the better for it.

*   *   *   *

NEITHER ANNE NOR DARCY was foolish enough to share the news about how things were faring. They were too aware of the foibles of nature and would not feel comfortable till the harvest was paid for. At least it appeared that the diplomats had come to terms with matters on the continent—for longer this time—and would stabilize the peace and perhaps expand the market for England's, and Pemberley's, wheat. Darcy's news, however fragile, eased both their minds and those of the others, who were told that the hopes kindled when Darcy announced his salvation from an anonymous benefactor—he credited James Drain for engineering the resolution—was moving apace.

The hints of good fortune lifted the mood at Mount Row.

Chapter 40. The Colonel Finds A House

A mere week after he'd been brought into the ladies' confidence, the Colonel arrived in the late morning at Russell Square and leapt to the door and rang the bell, it being his turn to rush past Taylor into the foyer the moment the door was opened with his news.

"I must see Miss de Bourgh at once, Taylor."

Taylor was quite familiar with the Colonel but had never witnessed such a display of youthful enthusiasm in him.

"Oh, hurry, Taylor. You must get her at once. Surely, she is up by now."

Somewhat hurt that the visitor would think he would not do his duty in the way his duty was to be done, the butler nodded and began the climb to his mistress's room on the second floor. She and Miss Bennet had already breakfasted and were up. He found a chambermaid polishing the furniture in the drawing room and instructed her to advise Miss de Bourgh that Colonel Fitzwilliam seemed in urgent need of an audience with her.

The Colonel's wait was brief as his cousin sent word that he come to her study, where she and Kitty were already cloistered. When they were together, Colonel Fitzwilliam explained his news. He'd found a location that met all of Anne's criteria even if it needed updating and repair.

"It can be ready by new year's," he said.

The Colonel had been as good as his word. The house was No. 42, Theberton Street. It was one in a row of almost identical four-storey houses. Each had its kitchen in the basement, and a sitting room, dining parlour, and small den in the right rear on the ground floor. Going up the non-descript wooden staircase that ran along the right wall in the front hall, one reached a landing and hallway off of which was a small parlour looking out onto Theberton Street. More bedrooms were on the second floor and several and a small, tiled room with a tub were on the top floor, as was a large storage room.

He agreed to accompany the ladies there the very next day after announcing his find, which was a fine day. The three shared a cab, which quickly covered the under two miles from Russell Square. They wandered carefully (and with the Colonel's aid) through its rooms and Anne pronounced it "perfect" when they were back on the pavement.

Their presence naturally attracted attention from neighbours, mostly poor women out running errands, and three or four of them were gathered on that pavement when the three gentlefolk emerged. One, a not unattractive and tall woman who was neither young nor old but whose outfit while well-worn had once been stylish and who was carrying a bag with groceries stepped to the Colonel as he was opening the cab door for the ladies.

"'xcuse me, Sir, what ye be doin' if I mights be so bold to ask?"

The Colonel stepped back and looked to his cousin.

Anne smiled and said, "we are looking to establish a sort of charity for needy women, my dear."

"Ah, m' lady. And when might that be and what might it be for?"

"First, I am not a lady just someone with a desire to provide a brief place for servants who need some help."

A second woman spoke. "You mean for a maid in a family way, don't yer?"

Anne de Bourgh had a smile that could not fail to disarm in part because there was not the least bit of falsity in it.

"That is it quite. And who are you?"

The first woman said she was called Edwina Jaggers and the second was Martha Doltering.

"I am pleased to meet you. I assume you're of the neighbourhood."

"Indeed we are, Ma'am," Mrs. Jaggers said.

"And I am Anne de Bourgh and here is my great friend Miss Catherine Bennet and my dear cousin, Colonel Richard Fitzwilliam."

"Be you a real colonel?" asked Mrs. Doltering, to which Anne said that indeed he was.

"He is retired now and is helping us establish our space here. We will be needing some help from the neighbourhood to support what we're doing, and I wonder if either of you or of these others might be willing."

The group of women, now swelled to six or seven, looked to one another and Mrs. Doltering said she was sure that some would try to be helpful.

"Whoever works here will of course be compensated for her time," Anne said. "But now we must get back."

The Colonel stepped forward. "It will be some time for us to be ready but as the work is being done, one of us will likely be here often so you can approach us should you like to work with us."

With that and after hearing a general murmur of acknowledgement, he again opened the door to the cab and after Anne thanked the women and Kitty nodded to them, they were all three in the cab and shortly heading back to Russell Square.

After the lease was signed, work began on converting the building to its new use. The rooms on the ground floor were left as they were. On the first, the parlour was made into an office. A partners' desk was made to fit, and it dominated the room. A series of wooden filing cabinets ran along the wall opposite the window where the door was, and two wooden chairs were along one of the other walls. Two leather chairs fit into the slots at the desk.

After some debate, Anne bowed to Kitty's insistence that she live at the house and Kitty's bedroom was opposite the office and Teresa's was beside it, both facing the rear garden and similar houses on Moon Street. Given the closeness of the house and the nature of what was to go on there, it was decided that the second floor would be given up to the girls. There were four small bedrooms as well as that storage room so the capacity was set at six or seven. It was unlikely that any of those staying for their confinement would ever have had their own room before, but not only did it comport with what the ladies (and Teresa) said would benefit the girls, it was dictated by how the house was built.

Chapter 41. Catherine Gets A Home

Winter was nearing, but "Miss Bennet" was a familiar sight along and around Theberton Street. It was not a large house in a not particularly fashionable portion of Islington—Islington itself having no fashionable portions—truth be told—but it was her home. She could walk the under two miles to Russell Square in less than an hour and often did when she could, usually with her maid. They were accustomed to the unusual looks a lady and her servant got as they neared Russell Square, but Catherine Bennet was not quite a lady and Teresa Riordan not quite a maid.

A small orphan named Jo—he couldn't have been more than fifteen or sixteen but he didn't know himself—was brought to Kitty by Mrs. Jaggers from the neighbourhood shortly before the house opened. He was hired to live in the house to run errands and help, and he was given a small room off the kitchen in the basement, which had a small eyebrow window that opened to the small back.

Anne took advantage of the knowledge of the servants at Russell Square and a cook who Anne's own cook knew years before but who'd left service and lived not half-a-mile from the house came in to prepare lunch and dinner, with the others required to arrange for their own breakfast, another obligation that Anne and Kitty thought important for the girls' states of mind, including as a means to lessen the boredom that would inevitably descend on the place.

And the woman brought in as the cook put Kitty in touch with a former soldier who'd lost his left arm at Waterloo and was serious and conscientious and had dwellings not too far from Islington. Beaten up as he was from the regulars, he was a good man with whom Kitty immediately knew was proper for the position of a general male servant at the house notwithstanding his physical limitations since there were girls and women in the house who could be of use carrying this and carrying that as needed.

While Kitty was seeing to the arrangements for the house, with the Colonel's assistance, Anne undertook the far more delicate task of arranging for the house's occupants. She and Kitty had taken Teresa aside about a week after receiving Georgiana's agreement to participate, however distantly. They made no reference to their knowledge about her or about Georgiana and the maid didn't volunteer any. Instead, they said that Kitty wanted to do something to aid servants such as that one at Pemberley Mrs. Darcy mentioned. They also knew that only Teresa had any understanding about such women in service and they would need her help.

Teresa was all questions about it and what her role would be in it and what her role with Kitty would be in the future. This, too, was awkward all around, but Anne left them alone to speak about it. And they resolved that while Kitty would still require Teresa's assistance in certain respects (since her time would be devoted to pursuits that likely did not require the meticulousness in clothing and hair and accessories that were normal for a lady in a fashionable house), Kitty's demands would be lessened. Anne agreed to the modifications of Teresa's duties, with the approval of her housekeeper, and that when the time came, as we said, Teresa joined Kitty in Islington.

As to chores at the house, Kitty agreed with Teresa, who knew far, far more about this than the Bennet did.

"They must be told that they are expected to bear the bulk of the lighter work in the house," she said, getting more adamant as she went. "Life is going to be harsh for them, very harsh. They cannot feel like they need not do work that they can do. Until they can't do it, they will perform maid-like tasks and they'll spend the evenings together with a roof over their heads and food in their bellies."

The most important task, the one without which it would all be for naught, fell to Anne de Bourgh. She was not integrated into London society. She'd never formally come out. What's more, her natural inclinations were not conducive to the activities of society women her age. Even less than country girls Jane and Elizabeth.

Anne did have a select few friends who were about her age with established households. They with their new and growing families were the ones more likely in need of another servant.

In Teresa's case, it was sheer luck that Georgiana knew a woman—Anne de Bourgh—who would never turn away a servant who Georgiana said, "was in particular need of a position." Who would never ask whence such a need arose though Georgiana (as we know) recited the story to Anne in confidence before Teresa appeared at Rosings. Anne's goal, then was to find women like herself to whom one of *her* girls—she was beginning to think of them in those terms even though they did not as yet exist—would be accepted without reservation.

By Christmas, Anne had met with five women and their housekeepers who said they *might* be interested depending on the girl. They were somewhat mollified when Anne assured them that she would be very careful in assessing what girls were brought into the scheme and into what houses they might fit. It would be made clear that there was to be no insolence or disobedience, as it would not be tolerated in any other servant.

"It does none of us any good," she said several times, "if someone is not suitable so all depends on my ability to look at the background and skills of the girl before even broaching the subject with a house like yours. And it will likely be from the north or from Ireland that they will come once we get established."

She brought Kitty with her to a number of houses when she went for a second visit, and Kitty proved capable even if her Darcy connection did not prove as useful as it might have done before that family's great loss.

* * * *

FINALLY, THERE WERE the girls themselves. This is where Teresa came in. Though she was Irish and only recently arrived in London, she knew where maids congregated on their rare free nights. There was not a single spot. For each neighbourhood, there were one or two taverns. The one closest to Russell Square, for instance, was somewhat clean and bright. The type of place a young woman working at a respectable house would find others like her.

Of course, there were less respectable places, and everyone understood that those were the more likely to get a girl in the family way. But they also understood that the type of girl who went to such a place would not be the type who the scheme would have any hope of placing in a house. Shipped off to a country estate, maybe, but even then, chances were that they'd simply flee back to London at the first opportunity.

This was discussed time and time again, but in the end all three agreed to narrow their approach to the better establishments. Those and the Catholic Churches. Perhaps the most badly affected by a child were the Catholic maids. Their priests would do all they could to snare the poor girl and take a child (should she survive to have it) for a proper Catholic home and the girl herself would be left to toil for all eternity, on earth and beyond, for what she had done.

Girls would vanish from London rather than risk being discovered at a Sunday Mass. The scheme hoped to catch two or three of those beforehand and cloister them away from the prying eye of Mother Church and the fate that would be inflicted upon them if they were found out. As with servants she spoke to at several taverns, then, Teresa let it be known that there was a place where there might be salvation in this world even if their priest said there would not be in the next.

In all these cases, the others were depending on Teresa's judgment in who she told and what she said.

Anne and Kitty were concerned about the effect the scheme would have on their own families. They decided to discuss it openly with Jane and Elizabeth. Kitty's sisters were invited to Russell Square on a Thursday in late November.

"I knew you were up to something," Elizabeth said. "I think this is a fine idea." Jane nodded, though she wasn't sure just how "fine" an idea it was.

"I think you must not be afraid," Elizabeth said. "You are doing a good thing, though many, perhaps most, will condemn you for it. For tending to these fallen women. We must proclaim that it is the Christian thing to do. To bring the sinners, for these women will surely be branded as that, back into the fold. Like Mary Magdalene."

Elizabeth had not forgotten how she and Charlotte used the Gospels in the cause of finding Will a home and was not above quoting scripture again for a similar purpose for the hypocrites she encountered every day in town.

"You should name it for your mother," she said.

Anne was stunned by this suggestion. "For my mother?" she asked, quite beside herself.

"The Lady Catherine de Bourgh House. Something like that," Mrs. Darcy said. "Not only will that give legitimacy to it, but it will gather the support of her family, most tellingly my Darcy and Colonel Fitzwilliam's family, especially the earl. Even Georgiana and I expect Mr. Collins too. All would not think of despoiling a home with her name on it."

Jane said, "Lizzy, you have quite lost your head. Lady Catherine, from what I have been led to believe, would never have tolerated such a thing."

"What she would or wouldn't have done does not signify," Elizabeth observed. She was rising to the conversation. "Yes. That is what you should name it." The universal but unspoken thought *and what can she do about it* encircled the room and then vanished and no one of the four cared a whit about what that woman would have thought of *anything*.

"And as we have the Colonel's agreement," Elizabeth said, "I promise you that my Darcy will not stand in the way of this," which would prove to be the case.

As to the venture's actual operation, it was to be made clear to each girl that was considered after Teresa found them—though they were hardly "girls" anymore—that at the house they would have to be careful. Their mere presence, were it discovered, would tarnish them in the eyes of many, so they were told to expect to remain largely out of sight throughout their confinements.

By mid-January, all of the rooms were full. Some of the residents were closer to term than others. Over time, it was hoped that this would be the case. Those there the longest and thus the closest to leaving would act as mentors to some extent to the new arrivals.

An Islington physician and two midwifes were retained to be available, the type of service normally reserved for women in a fashionable house who would give birth at home. The Lady Catherine House had a room on the second floor set aside for the birthing process. It was the largest of the bedrooms and allowed more to be there than in the others.

Teresa eventually was able to convince Kitty that the House would survive her absence for an evening and Anne was then able to convince her that she would benefit from several days in Kent.

That fine country was never far from Kitty's mind, and she regularly received somewhat veiled letters from Charlotte on Will's progress, now that his first birthday came and went. *A fine lad*, Charlotte said more than once, and in each letter she said how much she was looking forward to Kitty coming for a visit.

Charlotte was fully aware of the House and what Kitty (and Anne) were doing, and she and Mr. Collins approved, particularly after the House was named for his former patroness.

In late March of 1817, when things at the House were established and Kitty was convinced that Teresa with the help of the Colonel and the others were well able to care for it for a week, Kitty and Anne traveled to Rosings. Kitty spent each day strolling with Charlotte and Will, excepting the one day when a spring rain drenched the place, and on that day, they sat with Mr. Collins in the Parsonage's little parlour of which Kitty had become so fond.

When the week expired, Anne and Kitty returned to town. They'd head back in a fortnight or so, bringing the Bingleys and the Darcys with them so they could all enjoy the calm and quiet of the Kentish countryside.

Chapter 42. Discovery

It was a fine spring evening, and the large windows were open wide to get the air flowing in from across Russell Square. The group of Londoners were joined by those from Longbourn and the Collinses from Hunsford. They'd be continuing on to Meryton the next morning. It was the first chance in quite a while for all of the families to be together.

This night, the one before those who'd be going north would be going north, was a sort of farewell dinner. Anne arranged for some light entertainment in the form of a quartet playing some Mozart after dinner for the group.

The presence of Colonel Fitzwilliam, at times cloistered with Anne and Kitty and Elizabeth, did not go unnoticed, particularly by Mrs. Bennet. *Oh*, she thought, *how fine it would be to have another officer in the family. And a colonel, no less.* Much as she adored George Wickham, he was a dead hero and would forever be simply *Captain* George Wickham.

Colonel Richard Fitzwilliam though was a (live if retired) colonel. The son of an earl, too. And Mrs. Bennet lavished praise on the newly met officer to her sister-in-law, who had more sense than to pay particular attention to Mrs. Bennet's insistence that the Colonel would surely catch her final eligible daughter, Kitty.

"She is not getting younger," Mrs. Bennet said as she and Mrs. Gardiner sat on a small love seat along one wall while there was mingling among the others. "And he is a well-off widower with, I hear, some property in Ireland that must be worth a pretty penny, I'm sure. I predicted that Jane would marry Mr. Bingley and I was right there, wasn't I?"

In this, Mrs. Gardiner merely nodded now and then as there appeared to be a lull in what was being said.

"I always knew my Kitty," Mrs. Bennet resumed, "had something that would attract the finest of men. And a widower, poor thing. I am sure Kitty will do her best to fill his life with joy and happiness and lots of little colonels. I do think his countenance may actually exceed that of poor Wickham. Indeed, I do."

Mrs. Gardiner saw the butler come in to announce dinner, which would rescue her from her sister-in-law, but not soon enough.

"Oh, how nice it would be," Mrs. Bennet continued rapidly in light of the lurking interruption and in a voice getting louder from the excitement of the image, "to have a live colonel in the family. So much better than a dead captain, don't you think, sister?"

Mrs. Gardiner was saved from responding by the call for dinner, though she did set her eye on the colonel and did find him a curious specimen who she was sure had his charms but seeing as she'd never exchanged a word beyond an introduction with the widower it was not for her to have or express an opinion.

Mrs. Bennet rose quickly and raced to Colonel Fitzwilliam and claimed him as her escort down to the dining room and how pleasant she found him in performing that duty. A colonel, after all!

When all were settled in their places, Anne de Bourgh welcomed her guests. A hearty soup was served, and the chattering was interrupted by the slurping and noise from the spoons hitting the bowls. When they were cleared, Lydia slightly raised her voice to the woman sitting across from her, but her words cut through all the other conversations at the table.

"Tell me, dear mamma, what do you think about your grandson?"

Mrs. Bennet was at a loss for what her youngest child was going on about.

"Georgie? I've known him practically his whole life, Lydia, and you know how much I love him."

Lydia, who'd chanced to overhear her mother say to Mrs. Gardiner, "better a live Colonel than a dead Captain" and had not recovered from it, moved her fork lightly around the linen tablecloth but the pause was brief.

"No, mamma. I mean Little Will. What do you think of *him*?"

Anne, Lizzy, Charlotte, and even Mr. Collins quickly looked to Kitty. What they saw was a woman suddenly panicked.

It was Lydia's turn to stare at Kitty.

"How *stupid* do you think I am?" She punctuated this with the flinging of her napkin on the table in front of her. "With your disappearing here and disappearing there. Your sudden affection for this stranger whose mother is that awful Lady Catherine.

"And then to see *him*. Oh, it is clear that he is a Bennet alright. A *bastard* Bennet. You have some nerve bringing any of us, especially Georgie, into contact with him."

Lydia looked around the table, one after the other.

"No one has anything to say to that?" Her eyes burnt into Mrs. Darcy. "Lizzy? Struck dumb for a change?"

She glared back at Kitty.

"Me, Kitty, your longest and best friend and you couldn't come *to me* about it. I'm sure you went to the venerable Mrs. Fitzwilliam Darcy who arranged this charade. Enlisting the support of the so-innocent, so-desperate, so-barren Mrs. Collins and her stupid husband.

"How you got this horrible Miss de Bourgh involved I cannot say. Oh, I was never fooled by you becoming her 'companion.'"

The words were flowing from Lydia so dramatically and so quickly that no one could have interjected anything even if they had anything they wished to interject.

"Only Jane and Mary I think are innocent."

Jane tried to say something to try to restore some peace, but Lydia would have none of it. And Mary? One could be sure she'd be shocked by this, but she was not there.

"You can't defend yourselves can you. *Miss Bennet* and *Mrs. Darcy*. You both always wanted my Wickham." She was spitting almost all of her words out. She seethed as she turned to Kitty. "I saw how you looked at him. I can guess what officer lay with you to give you your bastard, but I promise whoever he is he will be happy never to see you ever again even if he ever gave you the slightest thought beyond—fathering the bastard."

She looked at the Colonel and back to Kitty. "And now you only have your ancient 'colonel' for all your efforts," this accusation being news to both of them.

The violence of the speech had to cool, and Lydia sat back in her chair waiting to see who would have the nerve to say a word against her indictment. It was her mother.

"Oh, my sweet Lydia. I am sure you are mistaken in this. I'm sure—"

"Mother, have you not looked at the bastard? Do you not see he is, I'm ashamed to say, a Bennet? The moment I saw him, the very moment, I understood what was going on with Kitty and I knew that Lizzy was a part of it."

Her voice again rose. Her stare went back-and-forth between Elizabeth and Kitty. "You both wanted him but *I* got him. *I* loved him and he loved *me*. He was *my* husband and I am *his* widow. He will never be anything to any of you but your poor, dead brother-in-law. And *I* was the one who bore his child."

Had there been a moment's pause things might have gone in a different direction for each of those who were at the table that night. Or if Lydia had not displayed a triumphant scowl at the others there might have been a recovery in time.

Without thinking, however, Kitty pushed back in her chair with such force that a footman only just caught it before it clattered to the floor.

"So did I," she said, flinging her own napkin to the table—the salad course having been delayed until this storm cleared. Before anyone could move, Catherine Bennet was gone.

PART II

Chapter 1. My Flight

I raced across the Square, leaving *everything* behind and not knowing what was ahead. I vaguely traveled the miles to Islington and when I arrived at the Lady Catherine House, I saw a de Bourgh carriage in front, the coachman sitting on top and a footman standing stiffly beside it, looking up at the front door.

I could not let myself be seen and turned down a side street until an idea formed of where I might go so I wouldn't be wandering the streets or sleeping in some park.

Mrs. Jaggers did not live so far away, though I did not know her precise address. After the charity was established, she'd regularly come by to offer whatever help we could use but as she was far older than me, I was awkward with her.

But who else was there? Where else was there?

It was dark as I found the area and after stopping two or three passersby, one told me where her flat was, which turned out to be less than a block away.

It was a brick three-storey building neatly kept along a row of similarly pleasant-looking homes. Her flat, I was told, was on the top floor in the rear and it was at that door that I stood, pausing a moment before knocking.

"Miss Bennet!" she said in quite a surprise when she saw her visitor. "What's the matter?"

As I stood there, a voice, a woman's voice, called out, "Who is it at this time?" but Mrs. Jaggers ignored this and stepped out to collect me, as I stood like a fool and had begun to shed the tears that had been building since I left Anne's house on Russell Square I could not say how long before.

Mrs. Jaggers led me in. There, in her small parlour where three or four candles were sprinkled about, sat a woman perhaps a few years older than her, looking up from some type of garment that she was sewing some ribbons on.

"Now, now," Mrs. Jaggers said. "Collect yoursel' Miss Bennet. This here is me sister Abigail Johnson, a widow too"—and Mrs. Johnson looked up.

"This is Miss Bennet. She's one of the ones at the House they have near the park for girls that are in the family way and got no place to go or no one to go to."

"She be quite nicely dressed for such a girl."

"Nah. She's one who ran the place. I knows her from before it opened, I do."

"Ah, but she do look quite young to be doing that. And quite the lady too."

I didn't know how to respond to this even if I might have been able, which I wasn't. Mrs. Jaggers pulled me off to a chair near the window, the only chair with any cushion and that cushioning was quite worn in spots. But I was very grateful for being allowed to sit and being allowed to sit off to the side. She told me they'd let me recover from whatever I needed recovering from—she left me to decide whether I wanted to say—and I was greatly relieved when they resumed their sewing and their talking as if I weren't in the room at all.

At some point, comforted by the rhythm of their simple conversation, the words I couldn't pick up, I must have fallen asleep because it was very dark and quiet when I awoke from some sound in the street and a blanket had been spread across me.

I heard Mrs. Jaggers but could only see her shape in the light of a single candle on a table off to the side.

"Ah, you be awake, love." She lifted the candle and stepped closer. "Abigail's off to bed but I didn't want to leave you alone and we didn't want to move you, you was so peaceful like." There was a clean chamber pot off to the side and she nodded to it. When I nodded to her, she lit a second candle and took it with her to, she said, check on her sister and left me to do my business, which I was suddenly desperate to do.

That done, she was back. She handed me a bit of bread that was not too stale and some ale that was in a chipped mug on the counter and I relished that too before she held out her hand and when I grasped it, she pulled me toward the other room, where I could hear her sister snoring. There was just enough light to see that the bed was quite wide and there was more than enough room for one and perhaps even for two to join the sleeping, snoring woman. Mrs. Jaggers, keeping her voice very low, insisted that I lie down.

"Yer be needing your rest, love. In the morning, we can all talk about what's to be done with you but we is all tired and I can sleep right enough in that chair in the parlour, that's fer sure, and so you lie down here and you be a different person in the morning, I bet you, and we can talk about what...what's to be done with you."

*   *   *   *

FOR ALL OF THE deficiencies in my upbringing thanks to the lackadaisical view that both of my parents had to any of their daughters becoming decently educated and adequately accomplished, I was always the one most capable of wielding a needle. I think Mary thought it was beneath her and Jane and Lizzy learned enough needlepoint to pass the time during evening hours with visitors (and, of course, Lydia had even less skill than any of us, at least skills of the type a gentleman's daughter ought rightly—I now realise—to know).

This proved an incredible blessing in my current situation. I'd have no particular use for speaking French or playing the piano-forte or knowing where Zanzibar (if there even was such a place) could be found on a map in the life I was entering in Islington. But I could, Mrs. Jaggers assured me, make my own living, however slight, by sewing.

It was a godsend for people like Mrs. Jaggers and her sister. It was hardly lucrative, and it was sometimes a battle to be paid for the work that was done (as I would quickly learn) but it was enough to keep body and soul together and it was, as I say, a godsend for me. That I would not end up like that poor Lady Hamilton, destitute and dead in Parisian squalor.

In the next days, a second- (or third-) hand settee was found, and it slipped well enough into the bedroom for me to use it. Mrs. Jaggers was able to get an increase in the work from the jobber who used her and her sister. Soon, the three of us sat contentedly in the parlour doing our work from dawn till dusk, with the others tacitly agreeing not to inquire as to the cause of my downfall (though I'm sure they speculated between themselves that there must have been a child involved).

I, of course, remained indoors except for sometimes taking early morning or early evening walks alone or with the sisters in the neighbourhood, always walking away from Theberton Street.

Mrs. Jaggers did continue her visits there, though, but avoided saying anything about the conditions beyond the most desultory "Everything is still lovely there, Miss Bennet." Except for one day about a week or two after I arrived. That morning, she said, "Miss de Bourgh came by."

This immediately got my full attention, and her sister and I both glared at her.

"She went and spoke to the Colonel"—Mrs. Johnson by then knew most of the particulars of the House and had ventured to walk past it a few times out of curiosity—"and I don't know exactly what they was saying but I think you was mentioned."

Perhaps it was wrong of me, but I truly wished she knew some of the particulars.

"The Miss said she'd had no success and that the only thing to be done was a lot of prayer and I knew you didn't want me to say nothing so I didn't. But it is good that they are looking, ain't it?"

"Or at least that they care," Mrs. Johnson said. "At least it don't sound like they're trying to arrest you or somethin'."

I had to agree with this, though I already was sentenced to suffering more harshly than any of the inmates of Newgate Prison, maybe even worse than the noose, though I didn't add this later point.

And, yes, the pair of them insisted on calling me "Miss Bennet" and never Catherine often as I asked them not to and insisted that I call them by their Christian names and so we got along quite well.

Indeed, there was little tension until the subject of rent came up as we were reaching the new month.

"Yer cannot stay here forever, Miss Bennet," Mrs. Jaggers said when I asked what my portion of the rent was.

"Aye," Mrs. Johnson said in what was plainly a conspiracy, "Whatever brung you here must be painful for yer. And you never going out 'xcepting real early and real late and not even going to Sunday services. You think it's too dangerous hereabout. Mrs. Jaggers and I figure it got something to do with that charity of yours, or that was yours, but we ain't interested in you telling us unless you're of a mind to be telling us..."

"Aye," her co-conspirator continued, "so we wants you to put away what you can to pay for you to get wherever it is you's got to go. You pay us for food and drink and little things about the flat but you put something aside so you get to go to where it is you's got to go."

I had, of course, given much thought to what alternatives there were for me. I could set out maybe to a big city in the north, even back to Newcastle where Lydia and I, sometimes with Wickham, visited. I imagined that if I could find work in London, I was sure to be able to find something in Newcastle. And if not there, there were other places to the north and west, where I'd never chance to encounter any memories of my past life, most painfully my Will and (increasingly) my Miss de Bourgh.

I came to realise, though, that my best chance would be to return to Exeter and perhaps even to Mrs. Elster, who I'd come to like a great deal in my confinement and in the months after giving birth to Will. She knew most, though not all, of my secret and yet she treated me as a person of value, not as a woman who had fallen.

I could trust her, I knew. It would take me far and far away from Kent and my Will, but I knew that however close I was to him, I could *never* see him. I could *never* be seen near him as it would ruin it for everyone, especially for him.

And I knew Mrs. Elster would not betray me, especially to Anne de Bourgh. I loved Anne quite deeply and would have enjoyed spending my days as her true companion but the weight I would press upon her was far too great for me to inflict it. For, as I say, fond as I may have become of Colonel Fitzwilliam, I loved her quite deeply as perhaps my greatest friend.

But she was gone. My family was gone. The Collinses and the Colonel. Gone. And William Collins, Jr., forever removed from me.

I could not dwell on it. I was a plague and to protect those I loved, I must be exiled.

I even thought of going to America. And perhaps ultimately I would, if I managed to scrape together money for the passage to the new world. But what would I do there that I could not do in isolation in Devon?

So with each day and especially after I conceded the wisdom of the sisters' decision about me not paying rent—a decision I agreed I would atone for financially if I was ever in my life able to—and I plotted my escape from London and I struggled with how I would present myself to Mrs. Arnold Elster.

Chapter 2. Traveling West

It had turned cold though not yet winter by the time I had made enough to afford to travel by post from London to Exeter, with some money to buy things I'd need to bring with me. But at last God smiled down on me for the long trip. That morning, after a painful and tearful parting from the two sisters who had truly saved me, it was cold but not too cold for me, though I managed to have enough to sit inside for the trip. Nor had the frozen ground thawed, making for a bumpy but largely uninterrupted journey.

I had, of course, taken this trip before, in the autumn two years earlier. But how things had changed! As then, the trees were bare. One could look out across a wasteland of uncultivated fields with the occasional flock of sheep or herd of cows grazing on what was left of grass. In the towns and cities where the coach stopped, there was little coming and going, and I was able to walk a bit when the horses were changed, and we stopped at an inn along the way each night where I shared rooms with other women who were my traveling companions.

But at last, I reached Exeter itself. It, too, was calm, but still busy.

We arrived at the station at around midday and though the day itself would not be long, there was more than enough time for me to hire a carriage for the short trip to Mrs. Elster, praying that she still lived on Grove Road. I hadn't dared write to her. I was afraid she'd tell me stay away. But I was sure she wouldn't turn me away were I to appear at her door.

I needn't have been worried. She welcomed me as I should have known she would, much as Mrs. Jaggers had done on that first night months before.

But she didn't seem nearly as surprised at my sudden appearance as I expected. It was just getting dark and there was warm bread, and she was just tending to a chicken dish, of the sort I found such a comfort when I was last there. She added some stock to the soup and let it warm and my first taste of it was beyond even what I imagined it would be as I sat in the post as it rocked its way west.

Once I was somewhat, if slightly, settled after finishing the soup with the bread and the bits of chicken she'd made into a stew as we sat by her fine fire, she confessed that she was not entirely surprised at my coming to her door. She wasn't expecting me. Yet she wasn't surprised either. She got up and pulled out a letter from a chest of drawers in her front parlour.

"This came some months ago. I think you should see it."

She stepped from the room and left me to read by the light of a single candle on the mantel.

Russell Square
March 31, 1817

My Dear Cousin Frances,

I have some very distressing, but I pray not tragic, news for you about our mutual friend Miss Wilson.

—this being the name I was known to her—

For reasons that I am not at liberty to disclose, she has exiled herself from her family and her friends, even those—such as I count myself among—to whom she is most close and intimate.

I will tell you that she believes her shame in relation to the child she bore when you so carefully tended to her would exceed anything that could be considered appropriate in decent society and has (I believe) resigned herself to removing her existence from all the world.

I hold out the hope that she will venture in your direction, though it is far from London, where she was last seen. I know I will not need to ask you this, but I hope you will have no difficulty in extending to this poor creature the care you gave when you first met her.

I ask only one thing of you. That if she does appear at your doorstep you beg of her that you be allowed to communicate that fact to me. You can assure her that I will abide completely by her wishes with respect to having any contact with her until she expresses the desire that I do so and that I will not tell anyone of her whereabouts unless she specifically authorizes me to.

You may assure my dearest ƐNancy

—and I saw the slight correction—

that I forgive her for all she has done in her life, especially what she did with respect to the child. You can assure her, too, that I will do what I can to remain an angel to the little boy whose absence from her is perhaps the greatest price any woman can ever pay.

I will not compromise you by asking that you tell me if she is not in Exeter. I know that if she were to appear and did not wish me to know that, you would be compromised by lying to me that she was not. I will not do that to either of you, who I love most dearly.

So, I will wait. It is all I can do other than doing what I can for the boy. I will wait and pray that I will hear from you and that she is healthy and well insofar as that is possible given the turmoil in which I know she has found herself, and which I truly understand.

Your cousin,
Miss Anne de Bourgh

It took me some time to read through this between my tears and my emotions and especially with how she described myself to her, my own dear Anne.

I will admit that in the ensuing days, I was in a fair way of knowing it by heart. But then, I held the letter in my lap as I looked into the fire. How warm it was and how violent its crackling sounded, the flames spitting out from the wood. I was shaken from its mesmerizing by a stage-cough by Mrs. Elster.

"May I come in dear?"

I turned to her and gave some sort of smile, enough for her to see that I wanted to speak to her and to have her near me.

She explained that the letter arrived some months before and that, as directed, she made no response other than a brief note saying simply that she had received Anne's letter. She said she'd heard no more from Miss de Bourgh. Given the circumstances of my appearance the first time, she said she was not entirely surprised that I had befallen some grand inconvenience in the society of which I was so clearly a part when I came to Exeter.

"But," she said, "I expected that if, as my cousin suspected you might, you sought refuge here, you would have done so straight away, some months ago and surely not as winter was closing in on us."

I explained how I could not do so, even if I had wanted to and formulated the idea of finding a refuge in her small house (as I had those many months before). I knew she wanted me to say something more, to indicate whether I wanted her cousin to know where I was and how I was, but I was not ready to decide that question and she allowed me the time to make that decision.

So, as happened with my friends in Islington, I fell into a routine with Mrs. Elster. I could not live off her, of course, so I spoke to her about what opportunities there might be for getting work sewing.

"I confess," she told me, "that it is good to hear a girl like you speak of working. You always struck me as a woman who'd be quite restless in a life of leisure and would have found something to be done even if you'd marry."

"As you were forced to do."

She'd told me only generally what her background was in my first visit to her but now she explained in far more detail, seeing as we were much more equals than we had been that first time.

She was, of course, a cousin to Anne de Bourgh, being the daughter of Sir Lewis's youngest sister. In that, she told me over time, she had few options to marriage and all, herself included, thought she'd done quite well by marrying the son of a tradesman who had a business of bringing things into the country through Plymouth, which was on the Channel, not too far from Exeter.

"I was past twenty when we married," she said near the fire in her front parlour. Her husband, one Mr. Thomas Elster, was nearly thirty. "It was considered a good match all around, including for the not insignificant amount of cash he received from me as part of my family's settlement.

"We were soon living in a fine townhouse in a booming section of Plymouth sufficiently away from the docks,"

But it was not long before Mrs. Elster—that had been Frances Powers—came to a different conclusion as to the worth of her husband. Suffice it to say, he fell victim to several vices, "though gluttony was not one of them."

Once he put his wife in the family way, he abandoned her. Oh, he remained living with her and periodically socialized with her solely to keep up appearances.

"I was sure lonely," she told me on a night when she was being particularly relaxed and forthcoming, "but at least had my child in me. He never touched me again, saying it'd hurt the baby.

"I knew he was getting satisfaction elsewhere, of course. Whores, mostly, but he sometimes seduced the wife of someone he happened to do business with. It was a dangerous game, in the end, made worse by the gambling."

"Gambling?" I asked.

"Oh, he was not foolish enough to bet for high stakes and sometimes he did win, which he made a point of telling me when he came home. But I think he did it because he was bored. He imagined how high up he'd been, 'higher than Nelson,' he'd say sometimes, if his father had put him up for a midshipman when he was a lad."

She got up and added a log to the fire and move things around with a poker before resuming.

"This was when Nelson was still alive, so it was in the year four or the year five. Then he apparently said something about the wife of someone he was at whisk with and things got out of everyone's control.

"I just heard this from some of the people he said were his friends, though I never met a one of them until after he died and they came to give their condolence calls, me being very pregnant by then.

"So what happened was that words were exchanged in which my husband tried to defend the honour of the other's wife. Can you imagine that?" she said in true amazement about it. "He was defending the honour of another man's wife to that wife's husband. Course, neither he nor the wife had any honour, as the husband made clear, and before anyone knew it a knife appeared from no one ever admitted where and it was sticking out of my dear Mr. Elster as he fell back on the floor of the tavern where the game was going on."

She paused. I was about to say something, though I did not know what, when she laughed darkly.

"And they tried to save him and the one who killed him fled and got away and apparently sailed for America a day or two later before he could be got and the wife...I never found out what happened to the wife, but I can't imagine it was anything good.

"So I was a widow getting heavier and heavier and it must have been the anxiousness but I started having pains and more pains and then the midwife told me the baby was dead inside me and they got it out and I was left on my own, there being no real money in the business, at least the way my husband ran it."

She smacked her hands on her thighs and rose. "And that, my dear, is how I came to be a bitter widow with no child and no prospects. I fled Plymouth with all its memories, but my family wanted nothing to do with me. They said what happened to my husband was beyond the pale and would bring dishonour on anyone who had anything to do with me.

"So, I got some money from my parents and was told to set myself up somehow and find myself 'a proper husband this time.'"

She laughed that dark tone again.

She said that not long after, her parents died of consumption and left a fair estate to her eldest brother but he was of the view that any money that went to one of his siblings was food taken from the mouth of his own spoiled son (and heir and namesake) so he closed the family coffers after he sent the token amount.

"He said it fell to my husband—who was by then already dead—to care for me and that if he hadn't provided for me before his tragic death, that was my fault for having married a fool and myself being a fool and this was complete justification for the small amount that I received from the family.

"'After all,' he said more than once. 'You did get a rather generous settlement when you married him so it would be unfair to provide you with any more than that.'

"And, so, I've not seen or heard from my brother or any of my siblings in over five years, and I have no expectation of ever hearing from or seeing any of them ever again and I'm all the better for it."

Chapter 3. My Letter to Anne

Once Mrs. Elster showed me Anne's letter, I thought long and hard about how, and even if, I would respond. Some weeks later, I decided I must, and this was the result.

Grove-road, Exeter
November 15, 1817

My Dear Cousin,

I am acting as a scrivener with regard to this as Miss Wilson is concerned about whether a quick glance at this might reveal its author. So, I have been dragooned into doing this. Without further ado, I undertake my task of writing her words.

Miss de Bourgh,

I cannot adequately express how surprised and pleased I was when Mrs. Elster, who is the kindest soul (and who I have forced to write that observation much against her will), showed it to me. I only arrived in Exeter recently and she took me in without notice and without hesitation, as if I appeared at a Bethlehem manger. I did not leave London for many months after I fled your house. You see, I had to earn enough money to pay for my travel here. Someday I will tell you the kindness that was provided to me in those very dark days from someone we both know. For now, it must be enough to say that thanks to yet other kind souls I was able to transport myself far from London and other places where my shame would be most felt by those innocent of my misbehaviour.

You, of course, now know my great secret, far worse than you or anyone else could have imagined. I assure you that I have told Mrs. Elster all of the circumstances of my shame and this saint—again I am forcing her to write this—has redoubled her support of me.

I will say to your great question, however, that if your feelings are still what they were when you wrote your letter, I will be most pleased to have such intercourse with you as you deem fit and appropriate. Do not trouble yourself with schemes and such as to how I might return to London or Rosings or Longbourn or even Pemberley. They are treasured locations, but they must remain treasured locations for a life that I can no longer live.

I ask that you refrain from revealing anything about me at least for now to anyone. Even my Elizabeth as I cannot place her in a position of having knowledge that would harm her family's efforts to continue in society.

Be not discouraged by this. I have come to like the newness and anonymity of Devon and the areas around Exeter. With Mrs. Elster's help, I have been able to continue with the trade that I developed in my final months in London and that then and now allow me to support myself in the simple tastes and desires to which I have become accustomed. Be comforted that in my anonymity I will not starve and will not find myself destitute and in the streets or a workhouse.

I go on far too long. You must know that your expressions of concern and, I hope, affection for me under the circumstances have proven, with the kindness of which I have written, to be the saving of me. I will rely on your discretion in determining what you wish me to know and about whom. Especially the one who is the only soul to whom my heart goes more than it goes to my dearest Anne.

As I dictated this to Mrs. Elster—who you must know by now had become her Christian name to me—dictated to my dear Frances I realised how true a friend she had become to me. By the time I'd finished and was certain I had sufficiently embarrassed her, I did think that we could be grand friends for quite a while though she was a widow over ten years my elder.

So, it was true that our life had taken on the simplicity of simplicity. We were known in the town as the "gentlewomen-who'd-fallen-on-hard-times" but were sufficiently of the neighbourhood that we had the respect of all we passed on the street. We were invited to some of the finer homes nearby for tea and though our, by which I mean Frances's, house was small, it was large enough to accommodate visitors as well.

Of course, as befitted our financial circumstances and the kindness of our friends, those who visited kept their visits short so she and I could get back to what needed to be done to make a living for ourselves. And we socialized well on Sundays after services, which I was glad to be able to attend again in the grand Cathedral not too distant from the house.

But as winter crested and we were approaching the blossoming of spring, our attention was diverted by a visit from Wilbur Johnson. He was introduced to me by Frances when he appeared unannounced on a Thursday afternoon some three or four weeks after my letter had been dispatched to Anne.

Frances introduced him as the banker through whom she received regular payments from an unknown benefactor, which enabled her to maintain her tidy home and take me in when I was in need of a refuge.

As I put our work to the side and arranged the chairs, with Frances insisting that I remain, she went to make some tea for our guest. Mr. Johnson was a short man of perhaps forty and he wore a beard and clothing of a style that was out-of-fashion in London but not in the provinces. When the three of us were settled, he removed a document from an inner pocket and handed it to Frances.

"I can tell you nothing, Mrs. Elster, except that I have received an order for £50 to be deposited in your account."

Frances looked at and then up from the paper.

"I don't understand," she said.

"Nor do I, I'm afraid," the banker said. "I received the slightest of instructions, that you were to be given the money—a princely sum indeed—to do with however you please. Those are my only instructions."

With a quick sip of his tea, he stood. He'd left his coat on a rack near the door and stepped to collect it. He turned at the door.

"As I say, Mrs. Elster, those are my only instructions."

Frances was up close to him, still not understanding what had just transpired. In her silence, I spoke.

"Thank you, Mr. Johnson, for this...this news."

"Well, Miss Wilson, you may thank me for conveying this news to you, but all thanks should be given to whomever it is who has sent the money to Mrs. Elster. As none of us know who that fine person is, I will accept your thanks on his behalf."

With that he buttoned his coat and put on his hat and with a nod was gone and into the carriage that would convey him back to his office, leaving two rather stunned but happy women. Of course, the money was most welcome. We could not hope to make so much in a year, and Frances was at first reluctant to accept it.

"You have been so abused," I told her when she was talking nonsense about not taking this small fortune. "Your husband and his family. Your brother and the rest of your family. I cannot say from whom it comes, but it is meant kindly, and we can surely use it and it would be an insult for us not to take advantage."

I was not sure why I used the word "we" there, but it was natural to do so, and she did not object.

"I do not like to take charity," she said.

"It is not charity. It is coming from someone who believes that you deserve to have this money."

She explained how back in 1813 she suddenly received a significant amount, also from an anonymous benefactor. It provided the means for her to acquire a lease on the house and acquire the old furniture we now shared and where she cared for me. In addition, a sum arrived each month at Mr. Johnson's bank, and it was used to pay her expenses.

Now we could easily afford to purchase some pieces to replace the ancient ones that were well past their being comfortable. We could do all manner of things to the rooms to make them more presentable and show us as being gentlewomen who'd recovered some of their financial dignity and no longer needed to work well into each night to do the sewing that did little more than provide us with the basics for our existence.

Though we never spoke of it, I think we both began to understand that our benefactor was not a benefactor at all. She was a benefactress and we both knew who she was, but it was some time before we shared our suspicions (which proved to be correct), even to each other.

Shortly after the visit by Mr. Johnson, I received a letter from Anne. Though I have committed it to memory, I shall only say three things about it, beyond that it was quite short.

First, she assured me that her feelings were unaltered from what they were when she wrote her letter.

Second, and equally important, she said that she regularly visited the Parsonage when she was at Rosings and that at other times she engaged in a regular correspondence with Charlotte and that all news about Will, apart from a bout of illness that lasted a week around Christmas time but that had passed by the new year, was positive.

Finally, she begged me to consider allowing her to tell at least my sisters that I was safe. They, she said, were at times nearly beyond anguish—they being Jane and Lizzy—about what had become of me.

I did promptly respond. I thanked her for the news of Will. As for the others, I told her that she could delicately and privately assure Lizzy and ask her to tell Jane as well as Darcy and Bingley and Lydia and my parents—much as I feared my mother would find it difficult to keep the news close I felt I had no choice in having her know with the hope that embarrassment and perhaps shame would suffice to not tell another soul—that I was doing well though far from London and that it was my great wish that they not be tarnished with me so that I could tell them no more.

And Lydia? She was entitled to at least and I could only pray that she would find something of value in the news.

In the next letter I received from Anne some weeks later, in addition to being told that Will continued to be fine and healthy, she told me that Jane and Lizzy were overwhelmed by what I had allowed her to say about me and that they would breathe easier and hoped that someday we could be reunited. They each told their husbands the slight news, and Elizabeth had written to our papa, who was asked to tell our mamma and Lydia as he thought best.

Frances and I fell into another pleasant pattern (though to be clear we never made mention of the windfall or of our suspicions as to the identity of our benefactress) in which we wrote regularly to Anne, and she responded in kind.

It took many days for a letter to cross from us to her and many more for her response to arrive, so we were content in our waiting, and the reality of the time removed the anxiousness about when a letter would come or why we'd not received a response to our last.

For me, more than anything I needed word about my Will. Just news, anything, and Anne accommodated. There was still not much to say, of course, about what was happening with a small boy, and she spent some time at Russell Square, so she didn't know as much as I perhaps wished she did know. Each report, though, was welcomed and read and re-read and eventually shared with Frances. Each report said he was growing and even running and was able to make himself understood even if no one understood the sorts of "words" he used.

News was sprinkled in about the other members of my family, but I knew I could not concern myself with them beyond hearing about them, at least for some time. And Anne referred several times to the progress that was being made in the Lady Catherine House charity and I regretted, perhaps more than anything (except not being able to see Will of course) that I was no longer part of that effort.

Lest you think I'd forgotten one of my obligations, I will say that I included the following in of one my first letters.

There is a separate task I charge you to undertake on my behalf. I expect that you have spoken with Mrs. Jaggers and perhaps my name has appeared. I confess that she (and her sister Mrs. Johnson) were additional angels without whom I could not have survived. For several months after I fled Russell Square, I lived with them not far from the Lady Catherine House. They taught me how to sell my skills at sewing and with that I was able to earn some of my keep— they would not allow me to pay them rent—and enough beyond to pay for what I needed to come to Exeter.

I regret that I have not told Mrs. Jaggers what has become of me. My request, then, is that you advise her of my current situation and happiness in the west. I know neither she nor her sister can read particularly well so I entrust this message to you and only you.

I took her and her sister into my confidence about all of my particulars as I felt it was my obligation to do in exchange for their kindness. I expect they have kept my secret well and I ask that they continue to do so.

Tell them I hope to be able one day to repay them for what they provided me, or I should say for a portion of what they provided me since I could never repay them for the entirety of it.

Their address is No. 81, Packington Street. Islington.

And that is how I tried to fulfill, although only in part, that promise.

Chapter 4. A Visit

There is contentment and there is joy. Much as I was pleased by the former, I was overwhelmed by the latter. For on a rather dismal April day, Frances called to me. A very handsome but dust-encrusted carriage had rolled up to and stopped at the front of our house late in the afternoon. As I reached the window, there she was and in no time, Anne de Bourgh was sitting in our little parlour, with our work hastily put aside by this most pleasant of interruptions.

I blurted out that it was "your cousin Anne," though I think Frances probably guessed that though she'd never before set her eyes on Miss de Bourgh. She rushed to get some refreshments—Anne had sent the coach and her men into town to recover and dine, at the better of the taverns in town for the men and the best stable for the horses and carriage—I held her as I don't know I'd ever held anyone before and I felt like a baby in her arms, blubbering and unable to speak for several minutes until she pushed herself away.

"I so wanted to be here sooner, and you must forgive me for my tardiness," she said.

"Forgive you? You will never do anything to me that will warrant my forgiveness. It is I who—"

"Now, there, there. Let us put that behind us. That I am here tells you all you need to know about my view of what has sadly happened to you. We must be practical, I suppose, to the world. But for you and me, and Mrs. Elster"—who'd just been noticed waiting in the doorway holding a tray—"we will only speak of the future."

"But—"

"Except for that one thing."

She waved Frances in and looked at her. "I understand that Nancy has advised you of the circumstances, all of the circumstances, of her exile."

"Indeed she has, cousin. And I've told her that it was a mistake for which she has more than adequately atoned, and we have spoken no more of it."

"Except," Anne said, "for that which is most important to her."

She turned to me. We were sitting on a pair of new chairs that had become the favourites of Frances and me when we were sewing or doing needlepoint, especially when a roaring fire was on the other side of the screen. "He is very well." She reached across to me, and I could not shield the sudden smile that shot across me.

"I saw him on the day I left Rosings to begin my journey to you. Charlotte and Mr. Collins are so good with him but as you'd expect they are very nervous about you. Mr. Collins is quite adamant, and I cannot say how he would react were he to see you again, though over time and as the child grows, that may change.

"Mrs. Collins, though, is torn. She will not admit it, but I think she has come to understand your needs as the boy's mother to at least see him now and again. She does not confide in me, but I have made it a point to spend time at the Parsonage, stopping regularly for tea when I am returning from Hunsford and sitting with them in the church while Mr. Collins gives his sermons."

Frances had made herself comfortable on one of our old, worn chairs placed close to our pair, after providing us with our teas and cakes, which she'd placed on the small round table between Anne and myself.

"I will admit that his sermons did take a turn to the fire-and-brimstone shortly after you were gone but, especially after Christmas, he has begun to revert to speaking of the virtues of Christ's care for children."

"And," I began.

"And your family. I am informed that your parents are both healthy, but I will get to them in a moment. I'm afraid things are not so pleasant there. Whatever any of them might have done were they free, as I am, they understand what would likely happen were they to be seen associating with you. My cousin Darcy is hopeful of largely extinguishing his debts within the year so he can return a chastened but full member of society, or at least the society he wishes to be a part of.

"Of course, Elizabeth I am sure would come to you except for what it would do to her Little Fitzwilliam. And I believe that what

Elizabeth and Darcy do will be followed by your sister Jane and her husband."

I had sufficiently informed Frances of the members of my family, or at least of members of what was once my family, to allow her to keep somewhat up with what Anne was telling me.

Frankly, I did not know what to think about Mary and Lydia, both of whom I knew would never forgive me. Especially Lydia, for what I'd done to and with her husband. Though nearly from the moment I uttered the fateful words about Will's father I regretted the hurt I knew I'd placed on her *for no earthly purpose* and would regret it to my dying day even if (as seemed unlikely) no other consequences were visited on me.

But, of course, those consequences were. In any case, Anne knew little of those sisters, Mary ensconced somewhere in the northeast and Lydia at Longbourn, or of my parents, who were also there, never having returned to town since that night that seemed a lifetime ago.

I did, of course, desperately care for my parents, especially for my dear papa. I'd seen how he blamed himself for what happened with Lydia when she'd run off with Wickham. Yes, Anne said, she'd asked Lizzy about them. Lizzy regularly corresponded with my father and said that that he was content to let my mother and Lydia alone while he sat in his library with his books and his letters. He was healthy, as was my mamma.

Anne rose and stepped to a valise that her footman brought into the house before he, the coachman, and the carriage left his mistress. She opened it and removed a small paper. I saw it was a sealed envelope when she came back to me. "I did receive a note some weeks after you left from your aunt Gardiner. I think she understood that I had a particular fondness for you. She enclosed a note for you, she said, in case I were ever to see you again, though I did not tell her that was my intention. This was well before I heard from you but not long after I sent my letter to dear Mrs. Elster," who nodded at the mention.

"I've not read it and I thought I should hand it to you," which she did after which she said, "As it is near time when we must find a place to dine—I insist that we do so—I leave you to read it while Mrs. Elster and I get ourselves ready."

When the pair was out the door, I opened the note.

Gracechurch-street,
London
April 20, 1817

My Dear Niece,

I cannot know whether you will ever read this, but I pray that you do. I am heartbroken at what you must be going through. I visited Miss de Bourgh on Russell Square unannounced, and she was kind enough to devote a significant part of an afternoon speaking with me.

I did not know the extent of what you have done since you returned from the north after the tragedy of Mr. Wickham's death, both in terms of the child and in terms of becoming your own woman. From what I have seen and what I have heard, it is clear that you bear little resemblance to the child I felt too ready to traipse in the footsteps of Lydia, though please do not take me to mean I do not highly regard my other niece.

It is that my regard for <u>you</u> is heightened.

As I now know that Miss de Bourgh is behind you, a great weight has been lifted from me. I write to assure you of my and your uncle's continued love in what I know are and will always be trying times.

You are of course free to write to me and I assure you of my discretion in all matters. I ask that if you do communicate with Miss de Bourgh, you allow her to advise me of your condition and your situation.

With fondest regards,
M. Gardiner

I was overwhelmed by the kindness of my aunt and uncle. I regretted never knowing them other than as sometimes interlopers in the playful life I had with Lydia. They were much attached to Jane, as were their children, and always seemed to look down on me and on Lydia as being mere children even when we plainly were no longer that.

Then I saw them when Lydia and I came up to London after poor George Wickham's death, but again I was so engaged with my own concerns that I paid little mind to them.

Now, even knowing what I had done *and what I was*, they were reaching out for me. I hoped there would be a time when I could repay this affection towards me. I did not know whether that chance would appear.

Once I'd read my aunt's letter and Anne told what she knew of my family, she settled in for a week. She simply would not agree to stay in one of the finer inns in town. The house had a room that neither Frances nor I made use of and once we'd rid it of the potpourri of things that were piled there, including a fair share of the old furniture that the gift from our benefactress made obsolete, we set up an old bed for her.

Both Frances and I, of course, offered to have her sleep in our rooms in our beds but she would not hear of it.

She also insisted that we stroll into town with her. She walked very briskly, I imagine from her being accustomed to navigating the pavements of London. On King Street, we had a grand time poking into the shops one after the other, with her making each of us choose what single item we would like to have her purchase for us as a gift.

She would not allow us to deny her this small pleasure, she said, and I chose a beautiful coloured silken scarf that the merchant said was from Paris itself, and Frances found a similarly fine hat—a "chapeau" she insisted it was—in the same shop. And during dinner that evening in a fine inn, Anne told us that it was nearly time for her to leave us and that she hoped she would not be forgotten.

There was little chance of that, surely, but the news of her departure, though expected, was still difficult for Frances and me.

And after one final shopping trip she insisted we accompany her on, she had her men load up her goods and place them on the rear of her carriage and with a wave she was gone back to her life and left us to our own lives, immeasurably enhanced by her visit, neither of us knowing when we might set eyes on Miss Anne de Bourg again.

Chapter 5. My Spring

As the spring opened, I became happier for being in Exeter itself. It was worlds larger than Meryton and worlds smaller than London. Frances and I could, and often did, walk down to the River Exe as it was becoming increasingly lined with mills and warehouses. And with the £50 windfall, not only did we have more time not to be working but we could eat at one of the taverns not far from Grove Road, although in truth we only did that once or twice as I had painfully learned the value of a sixpence since I'd left Longbourn.

But there was no cost for our turning about the neighbourhood and venturing to the Cathedral. Even better, the sum allowed us to get a subscription to the DEI, the Devon and Exeter Institution. This was a lending library across from the Cathedral, and our subscription allowed us to borrow books. It was a luxury we didn't have at Longbourn—my father had his extensive library but only Lizzy was given free rein with it though I suppose I might have been allowed had I shown the slightest interest. Which I didn't.

That was yet another thing that was far different from what I'd become and now I regretted each wasted afternoon spent doing nothing. Usually doing nothing with Lydia, except pining for some known or unknown red-coated officer who might take us away, which, of course, turned out not to be as pleasant as a girl's dream postured it as.

*   *   *   *

IN THE LATE SPRING, Anne included a request in a letter. Might she, she wondered, inform Colonel Fitzwilliam and Teresa Riordan (in confidence) about my condition and my whereabouts?

"I ask this, my dearest, because I am considering undertaking a venture not unlike the one you and I (and they) created in Islington."

She said she expected that they would very much like to know this information and join me in Exeter but that in fairness they would have to speak for themselves on the topic of having anything whatsoever to do with me. She was more diplomatic, but that is what she meant.

I cannot now say how enthused I was about all of this. Not only to be (I hoped) reconnected with these two dear friends but to continue in Devon to do the work of the sort I so enjoyed in London!

I of course consented to Anne's proposition after speaking to Frances about it. But with the prospect of the impending arrival, I became most anxious. *When would Teresa and the Colonel come? Would they come? Would they forgive me my sins?* Then Anne's next letter said that they were indeed not only agreeable to coming but enthusiastic about it (and about learning my fate). More, she told me she went to see that building where Mrs. Jaggers and her sister lived and told them what I had asked her to tell them and that they refused to take anything for the kind acts they'd performed (but I knew that there soon would be more comfortable furniture in that flat of theirs).

And then the pair of them—the Colonel and Teresa—were on Grove Road, standing on the pavement looking up at our little entryway when I answered their knock.

I tossed decorum to the wind as I stepped down to them, Teresa first and then the Colonel.

I was all aflush and aflutter till Frances had the good sense to direct us from the public and into our little parlour. It was, of course, quite improved since when I first arrived at the house for my second extended visit with its new chairs and other new and comfortable pieces of furniture and even slight landscape paintings that were spaced along the walls.

"Miss Bennet," the Colonel spoke when we'd all arranged ourselves, still standing mind you, inside and I'd made the appropriate introductions.

Frances looked at me with a smile and I sheepishly confessed that I was not in fact "Nancy Wilson" but "Catherine Bennet."

"I doubted you were 'Miss Wilson' but it was not for me to contradict what my cousin told me."

I was touched to be freely known as Catherine Bennet by my dear friend.

"As to that cousin," the Colonel resumed, though he was interrupted when Frances insisted that we all get ourselves seated while she went to see about preparing some refreshments for us. When the three of us were seated, he resumed.

He lowered his voice. "As I am on Lady Catherine's side of the family and I've been told that Mrs. Elster is on Sir Lewis de Bourgh's side, I did not know of that good woman's existence until Miss de Bourgh prepared me for my mission here."

With that he sat back and raised his voice enough that the aforementioned Mrs. Elster could hear what he had to say.

"Miss Riordan and I have, as you by now expect, come on a mission of my dear cousin. 'Your good works,' she told us, 'need not be limited to London.' She explained your presence here, Miss Bennet, and confided in us at least some of the circumstances."

"Those I think she thought we needed to know," Teresa interrupted.

"Aye," the Colonel interrupted in turn. "And you can see by our presence that for all that has befallen you, we—and we spoke of it on our journey here—do cherish and admire you and always shall."

Such validation I could not have imagined, but the proof of it sat with me in our little parlour.

"So we must," the Colonel said, "discuss our plan. I can only give it to you in general terms. For the details, we all have an appointment with—" he removed a small paper from an inner pocket—"a Mr. Wilbur Johnson, who I understand you and Mrs. Elster have met, at ten on the clock in the morning at his office, who will explain the details."

"Yes, Miss Bennet. We are to set about creating a Lady Catherine House like the one we did in London, you remember," Teresa said.

"That is the plan and Miss Riordan and I hope you and Mrs. Elster—"

"Me?" the referred-to woman said in quite a great surprise.

"Miss de Bourgh was quite insistent, subject, she said to what you wish to do," Colonel Fitzwilliam said and before speaking she was out of the parlour and moving about the kitchen to get us the refreshments she'd promised but forgotten.

We other three waited for her. When she was back, the Colonel resumed. "We cannot say how this will go, but Miss de Bourgh said she has every confidence that you, Mrs. Elster, will show the care and competence that she saw in Miss Bennet when we first did this in Islington."

"What about the Lady Catherine House there?" I asked.

"Indeed, that was part of the delay in our venturing here. We had to be satisfied that those we brought in were capable of continuing the work."

"Miss de Bourgh said," Teresa added, "that we had done the hard work of getting it established and seeing as Mrs. Jaggers would be helping out—"

"You have been dealing with Mrs. Jaggers?" I of course wanted to know. "Has she said anything about me?"

"About you?" The Colonel looked puzzled. "Only that she was very sorry that you had disappeared and hoped that you would find yourself safely established if you didn't come back. But that was long ago, just into the New Year."

I was pleased that that very good woman had kept my confidence even after Anne told her about me having arrived in Exeter long before, as she confirmed she had.

I was further pleased on a more practical level too. Teresa of course comfortably moved into the house, in the room that Anne used when she visited. And in no time the three of us became quite comfortable with one another on Grove Road.

Chapter 6. The Exeter Charity

Once the details had been explained to us by Mr. Johnson in his little office on the Exeter High Street, I understood why it had taken so long to create the charity. To try to match what had been done in Islington, Anne had arranged for Mr. Johnson to survey available properties that might be suitable. The Islington house was the model for his search in terms of size and accommodations.

In the end, and accepting that the locations on offer might not be up to London or even specifically Islington standards, he did quite well. At the conclusion of our meeting him, the four of us—Frances making clear her interest in participating in the venture—accompanied him several blocks away to a quiet street on which there were small shops on the ground floor facing the street and three floors of flats above them.

The particular location had a store which was recently vacated and with it the flats above had become vacant. Anne had, we were told, purchased the building on Mr. Johnson's recommendation and when especially the Colonel, Teresa, and I surveyed each room on each floor, we assured him that he had done quite well in his search and that with his help in finding laborers who could do the necessary alterations, it would be fit for our use and our purposes in under two months.

I rushed to write to Anne as the Colonel did as well, and we dispatched our letters together.

Chapter 7. Anne's Letter to Me

In all my life I do not know if I was as shocked as I was when I received a letter, a very long letter, from Anne late in the year. We exchanged correspondence regularly, no longer waiting on the schedule we'd established before the charity was opened since there was business to attend to. Her correspondence with the Colonel had become somewhat regular as well.

But the letter to which I refer, well, it overwhelmed me and set me into such despair as I had not known for many, many months. I am not able to speak much about it. Here are its full contents.

Russell Square
October 15, 1818

Dearest Catherine,

There is no way for me to delay telling you that your sister Lydia is dead. I of course did not know her but I must prepare you for the vilest of tellings.

As you know, when I spoke to your sisters Elizabeth and Jane about you, it was very slight, amounting only to the fact that you were safe and settled but did not wish to do anything that could compromise them in society.

I of course had regular dealings with them, and especially with Elizabeth. Jane and I were not, I would say, "friends," but under all the circumstances (some of which I will relay to you when I next see you) and especially because of my relationship with my cousin Darcy and my (secret) relationship with you, I was always eager to at least know of the goings-on of the Bennets.

Through that time, as to Lydia, it seemed that everyone wished to say "she has gone to live at Longbourn" and nothing more and under all the circumstances I did not find this suspicious.

How wrong I was. Just this morning, Elizabeth came to me at Russell Square. It was well out-of-time for a visit and I saw immediately how distressed she was. When we were in my sitting-room, secure in the knowledge that we would be neither disturbed nor heard, she told me the following story. I am certain she would not deceive me about it so we must both take it as true.

It seems that Lydia was very bitter upon learning what she learnt from you about Will. She vanished to Longbourn with her parents and was sufficiently distraught that your parents feared she would do something drastic and conclusive to herself were it not for her son.

By some act of the devil, one of Wickham's colleagues, a something Denny, appeared (it was at the time thought) uninvited in Meryton and Lydia happened to run into him when she was walking through town with Mrs. Collins's sister Maria. She and Denny professed confusion and excitement at the "fortuitous" encounter—though I am to understand why Denny would be in Meryton otherwise than to see your sister is a mystery.

I delay too long. Denny put up some weeks at the inn in Meryton and then began a series of liaisons with Lydia. Some months later, after your father wrote to Elizabeth reciting these events and expressing concern about Lydia as, Elizabeth tells me, he had not those years before, Elizabeth ventured to Longbourn alone. She confronted Lydia about the news her father had given her, and Lydia denied that anything improper or inappropriate had occurred between she (the hero's widow) and him (the hero's best friend).

As Denny was not in Meryton at the time, Elizabeth could not speak to him, but she did with Maria Lucas, who confessed that Lydia had confessed to her that the "rendezvous," as she called it, was not unplanned.

Elizabeth understandably flew into a rage, she later told me with some regret, and several days after Elizabeth's arrival and some uncomfortable days with your parents, Lydia was gone. There was nothing to be done, apparently, as Elizabeth and your father rightly suspected that the pair had absconded to Scotland, which was confirmed a week later, after Jane joined Elizabeth at Longbourn, when Lydia wrote another (Elizabeth said) childish letter saying how surprised the family would be when they learned that Lydia had in fact become Mrs. Denny and expected the appropriate welcome when she and her "new husband" returned.

This was, of course, too much for all of your family. Apparently even Mary was applied to, and she came (alone) to Longbourn to be in attendance at Lydia's return.

Now to the even more dreadful news. Not six months after the wedding and well after it was clear that Lydia was in a family way and had already been when she and Denny set off for Gretna Green, the birthing hour arrived. There was difficulty in extracting the child, but it was managed but in doing so, Lydia suffered terribly and lost much blood. There was nothing the midwife could do and by the time the doctor arrived, Lydia was sadly dead.

When she came to my house, Elizabeth had just returned to London with Jane and their husbands the prior day, having attended to your parents with your other sisters until Lydia was in the ground, sadly not with her (Elizabeth believes till the end) beloved George Wickham at Pemberley but in the Bennet gravesite at Longbourn.

As to little George, he came to London and is living at the Bingleys' house with the understanding that he will be taken into the care of Jane. The fate of the little girl is uncertain. Denny did appear at Lydia's funeral but showed no signs of wishing to have anything to do with the little girl (who of course was named Lydia). That may change, but for now a nursemaid is being sought in London—it should not be difficult to find a bereaved mother to fulfill that task—and she will remain also with Jane and Elizabeth until final arrangements may be made. Though Elizabeth very much doubts that Jane will ever release the poor child from her loving arms and all will be the better for it.

There is a final point I must make in this connection. I am certain that Elizabeth wished me to be the tool of transmitting this information to you.

On this, she told me that the circumstances regarding Lydia were completely unknown outside of she and Jane and your parents and Maria Lucas (and thus, perhaps, to Mrs. and thus Mr. Collins, though they would have the sense not to allow the news to flow freely). What Denny will say about it cannot be controlled.

I say this because I believe that Elizabeth thinks that should this information become common knowledge, it will forever tarnish the Bennet name without regard to anything that you have done. It is a way, I think, for her to attempt some sort of reconciliation with you, at least on her part.

I cannot say more on this as I must get this well too long— you will understand its length by its contents—missive to you.

Please, my sweet, respond to me as you think best. I have never seen Elizabeth so distraught, not even in those hours and days after you yourself fled my home. How your parents are faring, I cannot say given how raw the news is. I think we must agree that they are in the best of hands in Jane and Elizabeth.

> *Your most dear friend,*
> *Anne*

It took me some time to complete my reading as I had to return over several sections again and again before I could move on with it. Fortunately, I was alone in our house because Frances was off running errands, but I still had to prepare what I would say to her upon her return, which would not be long after I was finally through the complete letter a second time.

Since returning to Exeter, I'd kept no secrets from her. She was like an older sister, as if I'd allowed myself to confide in Jane (or Elizabeth after our first truly intimate moments when I'd arrived in London from the north) when I still lived with them. Or as I did allow myself with Anne when we'd become close.

So, when Frances did come back, I told the story in an abbreviated form of what had happened to the vivacious younger sister with whom I'd spent my youth. And my new—yet is some ways old—friend, who'd of course suffered the loss of her own baby, held me tightly for what was a very long time.

In the end, I wrote back to Anne. I told her how regretful I was about what had befallen my family, and especially my dear, sweet Lydia. I expressed the guilt I felt for the large role I played in the tragedy of her life and her death. I did not know how I could forgive myself for that brief time of intimacy I had with *her* Wickham and that the events surrounding the clear unhappiness of Lydia after I stupidly revealed the truth—for it had not set any of us "free"—about Will and her sainted, hero husband.

I still bear the scars of what I did and what I caused those years earlier but in the end, I must continue to suffer them alone and in my heart and soul and I can only hope that I have redeemed myself in some small way since. And that is all that I can say of it in this narrative, but you must trust me that I suffer greatly for it.

At the time, though, I had to complete a separate letter to Lizzy. It was included in the letter to Anne with the request that she personally deliver it to my sister.

It was a short note, amounting to little beyond some type of re-introduction of myself to her and (at that point) to her alone. Mostly I assured her that I was succeeding, even flourishing in the place I had found myself far from London. I owed much to Anne de Bourgh but said I left it for Anne to confide what she had done to me before and after I fled. I expressed my regrets about my role regarding Lydia. And I ended by expressing the hope and indeed expectation that we try to rekindle the sisterly relationship we developed when I had returned with Lydia from the north a lifetime before. This, I said, would be best accomplished with some secrecy by again using Anne as an intermediary. Then the letter was gone, and I spent many hours in the Cathedral and in its graveyard missing my Lydia, truly the sweetest and most innocent of God's creatures and wondering what, if anything, I would ever have to do with her namesake.

Chapter 8. The Colonel's Proposal

Mere moments after Frances went out to run some errands and Teresa was off for the day at some event at the Catholic church she frequented on a Saturday afternoon some weeks later, there was a knock and who should it be but Colonel Fitzwilliam? The call was entirely unexpected, and after I recovered my wits, I directed him into the parlour.

"Frances is out," I told him.

"Yes, I know," he said as he stood looking out down to the street. Without turning, he continued. "It is you with whom I would like to speak."

I had never been so flummoxed about a private meeting in my life and the moment I imagined what it could be about my mind became a muddle and I am not sure what I *did* say to this. We were soon, though, sitting in the pair of chairs that had long been the favourite for holding conversations of some intimacy.

"You know, Miss Bennet, that I have only slight prospects, and those largely derive from my late wife's family."

"I do indeed, Sir," I said, trying to maintain some unemotional tone.

"So, there is little I can offer a wife."

"Well, Colonel, you can surely offer yourself and that would be quite sufficient for any woman worth her salt." Perhaps I'd gone too far in this, but it was immediately what came to mind and was spoken perhaps too hastily.

"Thank you for saying so, Miss Bennet. I am much in your debt for doing so."

He stood in a single motion and was again looking out the window, with his hands behind him, wrestling with each other, and his shoulders hunched. I took advantage of this interlude to try to decide how I would gently respond to what he was about to say. As I was still constructing that and had not yet reached my destination, he turned.

"Do you think Mrs. Elster would think so?"

I sat back, my eyes large.

"Mrs. Elster?"

"Aye. The sweet Frances. I do not dare speak to her of this matter lest I be rejected. I fear no man's sword, but I cannot bear the thought of being slain by that fine woman's 'no.'"

I felt a strange but immense relief in hearing this. He'd spent an inordinate number of his leisure hours at our little house and, frankly, I thought he'd developed inclinations and perhaps even ambitions to me of the sort—how ironically—that precipitated my mother's awful yammering at Russell Square so long ago and the sort Anne teased me about a lifetime ago. I realised that I'd failed to recognise what was suddenly so obvious, the growing attachment of the widower to the widow.

Now, though, the Colonel proved that while he surely liked me, he surely loved her and that it was not the other way round.

I jumped up to him and grabbed his hands, now dangling down very unofficer-like in front of him.

"Oh, Colonel, she has not *said* anything to me, but I have little doubt she will be von Blücher to your Wellington," and I saw how the entirety of his existence changed when he heard me and understood that it was the truth.

And when Frances did return not half-an-hour later, thirty minutes during which he nearly wore a hole in the fine new carpet we'd gotten thanks to our windfall and I watched him do it with pleasure and admiration for my two dear friends—and relief at not having to pierce his heart should he have sent an ill-aimed proposal my way. When she was back, I excused myself to run some "forgotten errand," and passed by the house several times until I saw the door left open as a sign for my return. And it was not long before Colonel Richard Fitzwilliam, retired from the Second Regiment of Horse Guards, announced to me as the first person to know that he had asked Mrs. Frances Elster to be his wife and that said Mrs. Frances Elster had agreed to become Mrs. Richard Fitzwilliam, a name she knew was infinitely superior to the one she had long been forced to carry.

Pleasant as this news was all around, it became more so when the Colonel received the blessings of his first wife's family and their regrets for being unable to attend the ceremony since it was such a long trip.

I became concerned about my own attendance, however, when the Colonel announced that in response to a letter he'd sent to Georgiana, he'd received a reply from his cousin saying that as she was intending to head to London for over a month to be with her husband while the House sat, she could easily divert her travel from Wexford so she could be in Exeter for the wedding, if it were at all possible to arrange the ceremony to complement her trip.

This, of course, the Colonel said he would gladly do, not having seen her since she was last in London—which was after I'd already flown to Exeter.

Teresa saw how quiet I became when this news was shared. She took me aside. We walked.

"You know," said she, "how Mrs. Evans was an angel to me." She had long ago confirmed what Anne had confided in me about how she came to be Miss de Bourgh's and my maid and how it was Mrs. Evans who'd rescued her from destitution and was the model for what we were doing at the charity.

"I am sufficiently intimate with Mrs. Evans," Teresa said, "that I can write to her about it. As you have confided your truth to me and I have confided mine to you, I believe we can rely on her if not approval—though I am hopeful of that—at least of her discretion."

It was, after all, not in anyone's interest for her to announce to the world my presence or even existence in Exeter. It would do nothing but reopen wounds that had been healed by the passage of time.

But it was not for Teresa to write. It was my obligation and I told her that I would do no more, should she permit it, than refer to the relationship I had with the former housemaid to explain why I was contacting her directly.

I wrote the letter. Georgiana, I was certain, had long since learnt what I had done with my brother-in-law. I told her that she needn't have any sympathy for me, that I suffered because of what *I* had done, not what was done by anyone else. That I understood how vile she must feel towards me. I said that I would understand if she conditioned her appearance at the wedding ceremony on my being absent from it. I ended by referring to the forgiveness she extended to Teresa—I had my friend read this portion of the letter, and she approved of my saying what I said—and begged that she forgive me if only in some small part for my sin.

I'd told Frances what I said about not appearing if Mrs. Evans objected. She and the Colonel agreed that since Mrs. Evans was his cousin and was making a significant effort in coming, it was best that I accede to Georgiana's decision.

Of course, it did not matter in the end. A week before the ceremony was to take place, I received a letter from Mrs. Evans, in a beautiful leaning script.

My Dearest Catherine,

You can, I am sure, understand my shock upon hearing from you. You wish to know my view about you and the ceremony between my cousin and your great friend.

It is that not only would I have no objection to your appearance but that I would be most offended should you not appear in the (mistaken) view that I did not wish to see you.

There are certain things I cannot speak to you about in a letter but will tell you when I have the joyous opportunity to sit with you. Suffice it to say that you do have my great sympathy and understanding about what you have suffered. I will not tolerate your insistence that what was done was entirely of your doing and I will tell you so when I see you.

I hope that that will occur not long after you read this as I am anxious to cross over to England and travel to Exeter to visit my cousin—I regret that my cousin Anne and my brother Fitzwilliam are unlikely to be in attendance given the distances involved—and share some small piece of his joy, which will suffice for an old, long-married woman such as myself.

With unbounded affection,
G

Once again Frances (the friend and not the bride-to-be) found me in tears in the parlour but she knew me quite well enough to understand they were tears of joy, and I did not have to show the letter to her. She stepped behind the chair, the chair I liked to sit in for reading since it was close to the window, which afforded good afternoon light and a fine view of those passing by on the street, and wrapped her arms around me and shared my happiness.

And of course when I told Teresa, she teased me for thinking for even a moment that Mrs. Evans would do anything other than the wonderful thing that she did.

And Georgiana appeared three days before the wedding and insisted that I accompany her on a long walk down along the Exe, where she told me the shocking tale—yet another shock to me!—of how George Wickham had sought to elope with her when she was fifteen, and that it was only by her brother's timely intervention that that tragedy was avoided.

"So, you see, my dear, I know where the true blame for what happened lies. I will not say you are completely without fault. You would think me a liar if I did. I will say that your sin is worthy of forgiveness, and I have no hesitancy in extending it to you."

And with that, although still with her expressed agreement not to share my story with anyone or to reveal where I was (though I told her that her cousin Anne knew the truth of where I was), I had taken one more step towards becoming again alive.

Chapter 9. Other Happenings

Do not allow the various personal issues I've recited since I returned to Exeter make you think that there were no other goings-on goings on there. Indeed, the center of all of these events was our attempt to build the charity as I have already suggested. It was to be along the lines of what was done in Islington and, as Anne said, there was far too much need even in a town so much smaller than London for us not to attempt to create a refuge for ill-served women. Or, too often, ill-served girls.

There were not nearly the many fine homes that had large household staffs in which a new housemaid with a sympathetic mistress—as Anne was with Teresa—could find a position little noticed. But with the increase in business in Exeter came an increase in the smaller houses that required housemaids.

The charity's headquarters was to be furnished much as the Islington one was. That task was assigned to me and to Teresa.

As to soliciting either donations or the more precious potential positions, that was for the Colonel and Frances. Although Miss Anne de Bourgh was unknown in Devon, the name of Sir Lewis and Lady Catherine de Bourgh had resonance and thus usefulness there. So, Mr. Johnson was imposed upon to introduce the Colonel and Mrs. Elster to bank customers who were "moving up in the world." Some might be wanting servants. The Colonel and Frances arranged to visit these houses. They would sit with the wife and a housekeeper if there was one and sometimes the husband, the Colonel, I must say, being quite resplendent even though he no longer wore his red coat and decorations. There was, and always will be, something about a true military man that will shine even without the benefit of a uniform, and Colonel Fitzwilliam was a military man through and through.

He carried with him a letter of introduction from his cousin, which was particular in making reference to his father (the earl) and his late aunt and uncle. This and references to Frances's father with an explanation about the death of her poor husband was generally enough to allow them to pass a fine hour or so at the house to discuss whether there might be a need for a new maid.

In this way, the charity had a clear sense of where we might place a girl.

It was for Teresa and me to see that we had a girl worthy of being placed. But given Exeter's size, we could not rely on maids put in the family way in one of its households since the connections between an old and a new house would be too easily made. For this piece of the puzzle, the Colonel, Teresa, and I traveled to Plymouth to spend several days there. Our task, as it had been in London, was to identify places where maids and other servants met during their few leisure hours. The Colonel was there for our protection, and I was there to give Teresa support. She was the one who interacted with servants, again as she'd done in London. Over several trips, she was able to establish a group of confidants who could communicate news of an affected maid to us.

When Exeter's Lady Catherine House was ready, the three of us made the trip to the southwest and arranged to meet with maids early with child (and in confidence) and ask if they were willing to begin the process of having them transported to Exeter when they could no longer work in their house.

This sounds unduly dry, I know, but I found that I had developed a certain expertise in making this system work and within three months of beginning the charity, we had our first patients (or residents) who were seen by a midwife upon arrival and throughout their confinement. And by the time that the Colonel and Frances were married, several were close to having their babies. Indeed, when she came to town for the wedding, Georgiana Evans toured the charity and, I will say, she quite impressed the girls with her kindness, particularly seeing as she was married to an Irish MP.

Chapter 10. Getting the House

Over time, Mr. Johnson's appearance at the door became a good omen, and so it was while the Colonel and Frances were away in Plymouth as husband and wife. He sat with Teresa and me and as always wasted no time.

"In light of Mrs., well now Mrs. Fitzwilliam's moving in with her husband," he said, a fact we regretted in some ways, "her benefactor has written to me promptly upon hearing word of their impending nuptials. I was instructed that the lease should be transferred to you, Miss Bennet, which I assume will be shared by you, Miss Riordan."

Somehow my friend's hands had become entangled with mine and a wave of relief crested over us. We attempted to thank the dear banker for this news.

"Thank me not," he said in his normal, ubiquitous flat tone, "for it was your benefactor, as I say, who is responsible for this. I am merely the bearer of what I see are very glad tidings to you worthy ladies."

He stood, declining our offers of at least some refreshment, pleading urgent business elsewhere in town, and like a breeze (and with a bow) he was gone almost as soon as he'd arrived, leaving nothing but happy thoughts in his wake.

In relief, then, we sat as we usually did before the fire—it being a chilled evening—in those two pleasantest chairs and spoke idly as we did our needlepoint until it was time to adjourn to our rooms and wish each other good night and I will admit to sleeping quite well that night, and for many more to come in the security of the little house—*our* little house—on Grove Road.

*　*　*　*

EVERY FEW WEEKS, TERESA and I each received a letter from Anne. These letters were mostly bits and pieces of gossip that were, frankly, not of particular interest to either of us, excepting of course what tidbits Anne had about my family.

My secret remained tightly held, she said, even after Mrs. Evans had come and gone, validating our faith in Georgiana's discretion. Included as often as not was a letter from Lizzy, where she went on in loving detail about the excitements of Little Fitz and the further news that Jane was again in the family way and begging that I pray for her.

But far far greater than everything was news of my Will. Anne continued to report that she saw the boy as often as she could when she was at Rosings and made a point of visiting the Bingleys' in London when the Collinses spent the night on a trip to Meryton (where, Anne thought, things remained unchanged).

"I suspect," Anne wrote, "that they will be spending far more time at Lucas Lodge than they will anywhere near Longbourn." And as to what did actually occur during that visit, Anne reported that it was as uncomfortable as everyone expected it would be and that my mother had no time to say a word about William Collins, Jr. and was quite satisfied to see the back of the whole Collins clan.

It was not aided by the fact that my mother expected (and no one could convince her otherwise, though several tried) that Mr. Collins was again assessing the quality of Longbourn and its furniture in the expectation of soon taking over the place.

Much as I liked Teresa, I truly missed Frances when she was gone and things became worse when she and the Colonel spoke of moving to London, where he could resume the friendships he'd developed over the years, including with his cousin Mr. Darcy. I admit to being somewhat jealous of these aspirations, though I was never part of any sort of society outside the small one of Meryton and the temporary one in the Newcastle barracks.

I was jealous too of their ability if they were there for trips to Rosings (and of course exposure to Will) and the mere comradery of being in a city so much larger than Exeter.

I also felt I was losing a connection with Teresa as well. She'd met several fine men during visits she and I made to our favourite tavern or among those who attended mass or other events at her church and was spending Sunday afternoons going on strolls with them about the town and along the river. It wasn't long before she'd caught the eye of a nice-looking Catholic lad from somewhere along the Cornish coast who'd moved for a job in one of the new factories.

And as it happened, he caught her eye as well and before I knew it, he was sitting uncomfortably in our parlour sipping tea and eating cakes on a Sunday afternoon so that I could assess and hopefully approve of him. And he was a good, hard-working, and, it seemed to me, honest man and I realised that my loss would very much be his gain and I could not deny that I quite admired him and her choice and in what seemed like an instant since Frances was gone so was Teresa Riordan, married and happy and soon enough to be with child living only a few blocks but a veritable world from me.

Teresa sat with me in that little parlour before her wedding. She assured me that she had told her Thomas—that was his name—about events that seemed so long ago in Ireland. That she always thought of what had become of the child she gave birth to and that she told him that she always would. "He promised me," she said, "that he'd love me the more for that but that'd we'd be making our own baby or two or three,"—she broke into a laugh as she recited these numbers—"and they'd help me be happy."

And she was happy and I was happy and, as I say, soon the first of their babies was (God willing) beginning its own journey.

I hired a local girl from a good family to work at the charity. She couldn't do some of the things Teresa did with regard to connecting to the maids who we helped. But by then we had developed a group of the more senior servants in Plymouth that we did not need to search out such maids. They came to us and soon came to us in numbers that we could not handle, though a letter from Anne gave me directions to work with the Colonel and Mr. Johnson to make inquiries about additional and larger locations for Exeter's Lady Catherine House.

Being alone compelled me to find ways to keep myself entertained. I was a regular visitor to the library and fell into friendships with several of the ladies I met there. But I also found myself...inspired is the word, to put down my thoughts, and this narrative is in fact the product of that inspiration.

I began writing my memories of things that occurred to me. I recalled little of my early life except that it was spent largely with Lydia rushing around foolishly and the pair of us being very much the silliest creatures in England, as our father was wont to say. I sadly remember little of the details of my father or my mother. It is only in the broadest strokes that I do, and I now understand how I thought only of myself in those days. Until reality interrupted and I had my Will.

It will not do to dwell on the inadequacies of my memory but my thoughts here are as clear to me as if they happened yesterday and I think I can vouch for the accuracy of what I have written.

I say this here by way of explaining how it was that I came to write this story in the first place. Or any story for that matter. It was a spring day some months after Teresa had moved from the house. I was passing by my regular row of stores and stopped as I often did at a small paper shop. In times past we could only buy paper enough for letters, scribbling our words on every bit of space. And, of course, we had to pay what we had to pay for the letters that were sent to us.

For reasons I did not understand, that day I decided to act recklessly and bought a small package of stationery and a group of pens and bottles of ink such that when I returned to the empty house and placed my purchases on a table in the parlour, I stared at them for some time and wondered why I had done this foolish thing and advised myself that it would be even more foolish not to *use* these implements and mend my own pens to write a story, which grew, as you see, into my story.

I interrupt the tale here to introduce yet another character. It is not a person *per se*. It is me for as I discovered the life-saving value of having some slight talent for sewing, I came by accident to appreciate the value of writing. And, well, I leave it to my readers to decide how that has turned out.

Chapter 11. Anne's Letter

Russell Square
April 1, 1819

My Dearest Catherine,

I will not beat about the bush. I wish you to return to London. I have corresponded in confidence with my cousin (the Colonel), and he is sure that the Exeter Charity has been sufficiently well established that he and those you have chosen to take on the work left over by the (truly happy) departures of both Mrs. Fitzwilliam (as she now is) and my sweet Teresa Reilly (as was Riordan) can continue quite well without you.

I mean no disrespect to you, my dear, but you have I fear rendered yourself replaceable in Exeter and it is my intent to make those parts of you that are irreplaceable closer at hand, including so we can expand the work you and I began some years ago.

I believe circumstances can be such that if not welcomed—though you never fear the extent of my welcoming you—you will at least be "tolerated" should you come back to town. With your permission, I will speak to Elizabeth and see if we can agree upon a means to prepare my cousin (that would be your brother-in-law) and Mr. and Mrs. Bingley for your return.

Please consider this and respond to me. I wish you were closer than Devon, but I promise you that if you do not feel it is time yet to come east, I will endeavour to have an extended trip so I can again see you.

With the warmest of regards,
Anne

I knew that I would do whatever I could to return to London and to again spend time at Rosings and Russell Square. Those were the places where, I realised, the two people most important to me were and so I quickly wrote back, assuring Anne that I was pleased to place my fate in her beautiful and delicate hands, figuratively and otherwise.

A day or two later, the Colonel pulled me aside and asked if we could take a turn down to the Exe. I of course agreed, and once we were alone, he told me that he too had received a letter from Anne.

"I had an earlier correspondence with my cousin about the charity and, frankly, about you. I was concerned when she inquired whether I was confident that the charity could continue without you, which I told her it surely could. When I understood that she asked because she wanted you to return to town to help her with her work there, I was overjoyed for you to be able to settle there."

"What of you and Frances?" I asked.

"We will miss you greatly, of course. But we have given off thoughts of moving to London. We will settle here. While I think you could be quite content here, you pine for something else. You've made no effort—I do not mean to chastise you for this— no effort to socialize as Teresa did. And she found herself a wonderful husband."

"I don't know if that is what I want."

"Precisely. If you wanted it, I believe you would have tried harder to find it."

"Or tried at all."

"Do not be so hard on yourself," he said as we turned to head back. "You have always, since I've known you, done what you wanted to do, and I admire that about you."

He paused.

"And it may not be for me to say," he resumed, "but I believe from how she speaks of you that my cousin very much...desires that you be near her."

It was a fine conversation and I understood that while he and I'm sure Frances wanted me to stay, in their hearts they knew I must leave. As did Anne.

Chapter 12. London

My protest about being well able to pay for the trip via the post was ignored as I knew it would be. Instead, Anne made arrangements for a carriage to take me and all of the things I'd accumulated over the prior two years from the house on Grove Road in Exeter to Russell Square in Bloomsbury. I asked the Colonel and Frances if they would like to join me for the trip, but they declined, seeing as they were only newly married.

That was too bad, as I would have enjoyed the company, but I understood. As to the Exeter house itself, it became a wedding gift to Teresa, now Mrs. Thomas Reilly, where there'd be room enough for however many little Reillys might be brought into the world.

My ride to London began after a sleepless night and, indeed, I fell asleep not long after we'd left Exeter behind for what I hoped was not the last time. Anne made sure that fine rooms were made ready for me each time we stopped for the night, and hour after hour I sat in the comfort of the coach as we headed east. There was one dismal day with an at-times harsh rain, and I felt for the horses and the men up top but otherwise the weather was quite good for such a trip. I had bought some books to read along the way and regretted that I could no longer borrow any from the Devon and Exeter Institution library, where I'd been a frequent visitor and was told when I returned my final stack of books that my presence would be missed when I was gone.

It was a fine gesture and I resolved that the charity should expand its literary offerings for the girls and women who stayed in our homes. We could instruct on reading and writing too, so someone like Teresa would not be at such a disadvantage (though she learned while we were together and had begun to teach her sweet Thomas by the time we parted).

Our schedule for arrival was not precise but we more or less reached Russell Square just about when we were expected.

In all my life except when I first held Will I was never so pleased to see someone as I was when the door to the house opened, and a perfectly prepared Anne de Bourgh emerged and was down the steps and upon me just as my foot hit the pavement.

Before I knew it, I was in a tub filled with warm water carried up by a pair of young footmen and Anne asked if she could remain with me while I cleaned myself and of course I said she could.

"I've been like a schoolgirl awaiting Christmas," she confessed when all but my head was safely under water. She was on a stool by the tub.

I don't know when I'd last had a proper bath and we were both silent as I luxuriated in it until the water began to chill. She, acting like some servant girl, held a large towel for me to wrap around myself and use to get dry. That done, she pulled a soft robe from a hook on a stand near the door and held it, again acting like some sort of maid, till I was covered. When I turned, she smiled in a way that I did not know I had seen in I knew not how long, if ever.

I did not see her again for the evening. She had a tray brought to my room—it was the one I'd last occupied so long before and had been freshly painted and the draperies and other coverings updated for me—for my dinner and I fell into the comfortable bed shortly after I was done and awoke, discovering my first London morning when I opened the drapes and leaned close to the window.

And it was a beautiful morning, my room looking out over the rear but still allowing me to hear, and smell, activity in and around the Square.

I rang and a housemaid appeared promptly.

She entered when I bade her to and curtsied in her very smart frock and cap.

"Good morning, Miss Bennet. Miss de Bourgh has asked me to see to whatever it is you need seeing to. Miss de Bourgh also instructed me to request that she be allowed to visit you as soon as it is convenient to you and that I am to wait either here or in the hall until you send me to fetch her."

She was a charming young woman from the north, of the perhaps naïve sort I often saw at the charity, both here and in

Exeter, and I would later learn that she was older than her apparent years—in looks and experience—and that she had come through the charity not a year earlier from Liverpool and was now assigned to care for me and her name was Margaret Sullivan and she would become a great friend to me in the years to come.

But that morning was not the time for me to learn such. My hostess was waiting so I made quick work of getting ready and found a wonderful, well-fitted wrap dress in the wardrobe with matching slippers. With Margaret's help, I was soon presentable and ready to be presented to Anne.

"Oh, you do look rested," she said after we exchanged curtsies in her familiar room. She promised at once that we would soon be heading to Kent. And soon we were!

"The roads are in fine condition," she said as we rolled out of town. As I began to recognise the landmarks approaching Hunsford, Anne's hand tightened its grip on mine.

"I have met with them and while your cousin Mr. Collins is somewhat wary, he has agreed to sit with you. You must thank Mrs. Collins for getting him that far. She, I think, is far more forgiving. But I will be beside you through it all."

All I could do was nod and pray that Mr. Collins would see me as reformed or redeemed and that the Christian kindness that allowed him to welcome Will into his life and into his heart would extend to me, at least in some ways.

"He thinks that how he acts towards you may have practical consequences regarding a future living that I might control but I would never make things any more difficult for Charlotte or for Will than they already are. His thinking it might be otherwise, though, might be the 'vision' he needs to do what we all know is best for all of us."

Then, as we rolled up to the front of the Parsonage, Mr. Collins and Mrs. Collins stood together and Will was standing beside his mother wearing his Sunday best. Anne tapped me twice and it calmed me as we stepped onto the drive as they reached their gate. There we exchanged curtsies and bows. My eyes barely strayed from Will as the adults exchanged greetings. Finally.

Finally, Charlotte took a step towards me and said to a very severe-looking boy.

"And this, Will, is your aunt, who is a sister of my friend Mrs. Darcy. She met you when you were very young and has been doing some good works in the west for some years before returning here."

Will's eyes got large as he stared. "You were in America?" he asked, and I could barely contain my smile.

"No, Master Will," I said. "Your...mamma means I was in the west of England. I should never have thought of going to America."

"If you had," he said, again with the utmost seriousness, "I should ask you if you knew Lord Nelson, but you seem much too young for that to have happened anyway."

"Indeed, Sir," said I. "I was a wee girl when that great sailor was killed by the French."

"But he did win the battle, did Lord Nelson" and he would have continued about Nelson and Wellington and all of our recent heroes had not his mother—I can call her that seeing the two together—tugged his arm slightly and told him that I and his other Aunt (Anne) were tired from our journey but that he was going to visit us in the big house later and could tell us then all he knew about England.

And with that we had a round of farewells, me particularly reaching for Mr. Collins's hand and him, after a moment's hesitancy, shaking it pleasantly, and our group of visitors were soon finishing the trip to the big house.

How I did not wail in that final stretch I still do not know. Perhaps it was the presence of Margaret and Anne's housemaid (neither of whom knew of my relationship to the boy). In any case, when I was in my room, which again was the one I'd long occupied in days long past but also made to look quite fresh, I asked Margaret to leave me be so I could lie down and I took the chance in my solitude to wail and wail in some strange combination of sadness and joy at again seeing my son, so grown and so clever.

Indeed, as Anne and I later sat in the front sitting room awaiting the arrival of our three guests, she told me that Mr.

Collins had fallen into teaching in a way that in the end was not a surprise.

"He is so proud of the boy. His happiness seems complete with him. His sermons are far more New Testament than Old and he can be seen every day, even on the wettest and coldest, walking the paths in the neighbourhood when he is not called away to tend to a member of his flock.

"Any concern about where Will came from have long since disappeared as he and Charlotte have established that the child was in his way a gift from our Lord."

Just then we heard the front bell ring, and we were up to await our visitors in the foyer, where the greeting ritual was repeated, and we adjourned so we could relax in the sitting room.

I cannot say much about what happened there or at dinner as my mind was fixed on Will. I do recall that he sat quietly in a corner with some type of child's book until his father allowed him to leave for his playroom with his nurse.

* * * *

ANNE AND I HAD LITTLE time alone in all of this and I think she wanted to see what would happen when I saw Will before she gave me information about my family. Or should I say the rest of my family.

I'd not given her leave to reveal my whereabouts but, as I have said, I did allow her to use her discretion. And we walked the Collinses back to the Parsonage, it being a wonderful evening in more ways that I could have imagined. After we'd dismissed our maids for the night, we sat alone in her study.

It was nothing like my father's library. It was painted in a lively colour and in addition to the requisite pre-Revolutionary French-style desk and chairs, it had an intimate area in the corner with a pair of fabricked chairs set at an angle to one another, separated by a small table. She put a pair of Irish crystal glasses that she'd slightly filled with port on the table. It took little time for us both to feel comfortable. When we were, each of us lifted our glass.

"Elizabeth was always the key," she began after taking a slow sip of the drink and then shushed me when I said, "she always has been."

"That does not surprise me of course," she resumed. "As you know, she is my second favourite of the Bennets though," and her voice lowered and she leaned slightly to me, "I confess I have never brightened in my view of Jane and have yet to meet Mary.

"Elizabeth was always in your camp. I can tell you that. You, of course, trusted her with your great secret and no one else—" and I began to apologize not knowing whether she understood my not telling her and she again put up her hand to silence me.

She took another sip and for something to do I did the same. "As you allowed me to do, I sent her a note and asked her to come to Russell Square, which she did.

"I told her only that I had located you and that you as a person were in England but in a place far removed from anyone who would have any knowledge of Darcy or the Bennets or of the Bingleys. She may well have suspected, given your first visit to Mrs. Elster, I should say, to Mrs. Fitzwilliam. But geography was such that her guesses did not matter.

"That is neither here nor there because she promised me that now that she knew you were safe and if not thriving were at least not destitute—" which caused me to yet again interrupt that there was a time when I feared I would be but she said, "my dearest, if you continue to interrupt I shall never finish telling you what I need to tell you and what you need to have me tell you."

Chastened, I pouted like the child I too long was, which drew a smile from her. She resumed.

"As I was trying to say, she promised she would not try to find you and that she was pleased tremendously by the news about you. At that point, it was not clear whether she would ever see you again, but at least she knew you were safe. And as you allowed, she told Jane and Darcy and Bingley and wrote to your parents and Lydia, saying only that you were safe but that she knew no more than that, which was the truth.

"Things were very hard for Darcy especially. I met with him several times, with and without Elizabeth, in the dark months after you left us. You know how proud he is and how harmed he was by what happened to him financially, though you did not witness the worst of it."

"Only," I was allowed to say, "that the money, and much of Bingley's, was lost and he nearly lost Pemberley and was forced to give up the lease in London."

"Precisely. So, he was the source of some pity and much gloating in many circles, though as he is a most singular, and I would say admirable, man, that did not harm him as it would have most men. He stopped going to his clubs, which was a good thing, since he hadn't the money to anyway. And let Pemberley out.

"I will tell you, but you mustn't tell another soul, that I arranged for his debts to be consolidated so that I am his creditor. Only he and our solicitors and our banker knows this."

"And Bingley or Lizzy?"

"Neither of them knows. Telling no one is more for his benefit than it is mine, though it was I who insisted on it. So, as you do, I too have my secrets from Elizabeth." We both took sips as I processed this news.

"In fact, it has proven a very good investment for me. The harvests have been very fine, and he has been able to pay down the debt more quickly than anyone expected. It may not be long until he can terminate the tenancy at Pemberley.

"You will learn this as you become reacquainted with him and the rest."

"So, I am to be reacquainted?"

"Yes, but on your terms more than anyone's. As you likely expected, news of you and Wickham did get about fairly quickly. As I said, it was fortunate that Darcy did not particularly care what others thought of him, but the scandal was quite a blow to him. Remember, Captain George Wickham died a hero at Waterloo."

She stood and brought a decanter with the port in it and refilled my glass, though I'd taken only a few, diversionary sips. Before sitting, she found a comfortable spot standing behind my chair but where I could easily hear what she had to say.

"Any hopes of any Bennet returning to society were gone forever when news about what happened with Lydia exploded everywhere. He and Bingley could not go for a ride in Hyde Park without getting jeered at and as he no longer had Pemberley as a refuge, I granted him leave to come to Rosings with Elizabeth and your nephew for as long as he wished. 'You can ride to your heart's content,' I told him and as far as I know, he did."

"Your mother must have been restless in her grave."

She stepped around and to my side. "Well, she is above ground in the chapel and perhaps on a quiet evening while they were there one might have heard some rocking back-and-forth."

I doubt she would have said something like this to anyone but to me and she smiled what just in my time back I recognised as *our* smile when I told her to continue with her story.

"Of course, the Darcys did have to return to town and, as I said, things were sometimes uncomfortable and mostly they stayed in and did very little visiting."

There was a loveseat slightly apart from our chairs, and she sat there, waving for me to come join her, which I did, and I felt remarkably comfortable sitting with her like that as our legs more and more rubbed against each other.

She resumed. "In fact, I don't know of anyone they did actually visit, and I doubt any visited them."

"And you?"

"You know how little I did of that sort, but I did make it a point of going to them for dinner fairly regularly and I will say, and I expect you will meet him soon enough, that that Little Fitz is becoming quite the handsome boy and with your sister in charge he is well behaved. At least for now."

The thought about my nephew was quickly gone as Anne abruptly ended her recital.

"That's enough for now."

To my anxious look, she said. "I have told you how difficult it had become for the Darcys, and though they had less to lose than did Darcy, the Bingleys wanted you to know that whatever difficulties you created have largely been overcome by more recent, however tragic, news.

"But I also stop because I cannot do justice to the true story. Only Elizabeth can."

This was right, of course, as in the end Elizabeth remained the core of all things Bennet. But it was disconcerting to have been fed tidbits and nothing more nourishing.

"Oh, don't look so," she again said to my expression. "I would not have done what I did had I not known of the surprise for you tomorrow but seeing as you will scarce sleep anyway, I will tell you that Elizabeth will be leaving town soon after the dawn and will arrive here herself with all dispatch.

"She knew of your impending arrival—again I exercised the discretion you granted to me regarding her—and when you did come, I sent her a note begging that she join us here tomorrow and she sent an immediate return that she, and she alone, would make the journey. I think you must see her before we address your seeing her husband and the Bingleys.

"So, my dear, you are to go up to bed and sleep well again and tomorrow you will finally begin your return if not to society at least to your family."

Chapter 13. Elizabeth's Arrival

Although I did not believe I would sleep at all, in the event I was dreaming shortly after I had made myself comfortable in the fine—*my fine*—bed. I was dreaming of being again in the bosom of those I'd so disappointed and who rightly shunned me. When I awoke, though, I was taken by the fear that what was to happen to me could not match the joy I'd felt in what memories I retained from what I dreamt.

I lay in bed longer than usual as if that would hasten the moment of Elizabeth's arrival. When I did ring, Margaret was soon in my room with a tray prepared by Anne's fine cook and as I prepared myself for the day with the coffee and toast on a tray on the desk in my room, the maid—*my* maid—opened the drapes and tidied the room while I looked out across the garden that led to the opening that brought one to the Parsonage.

It was a fine Saturday and I wondered as I sipped my drink what the Collinses, and especially Little William Collins, Jr., were doing. I hoped to learn their daily routine, but for now I could only guess that Charlotte and Will were taking a walk along the road I was so familiar with or perhaps along the paths that crisscrossed the property and at times offered a fine view across the glen.

I did not have long with my thoughts as there was a knock on my door and Anne was in my room without waiting for a response.

"Oh," she said, "you are a lazy, slothful woman and I am afraid you will never wish to leave this room. I fear I have spoiled you in just the one day since your return."

By the time she'd finished this, she was upon me and leaned down to hug me deeply in greeting.

She stepped back from me, and I saw Margaret somewhat taken aback by the display, but I knew that she would not be long in understanding the casual (and many, many would say improper) manner in which Miss Anne de Bourgh conducted herself.

Anne turned to the maid and wished her too a fine morning, which received an awkward curtsey and a "same to you, m' lady," which in turn received a kind "Oh, Margaret. My mother was a 'lady.' I certainly am not," which somehow made Margaret less comfortable, though I expected that too would fade in due course.

But my host's intervention did spur me to get myself presentable for a turn outside and of course she, her arm through mine, directed me to that opening in the pale I'd thought of less than an hour before. As we approached the small gate that led to the Parsonage, I saw Mr. Collins toiling happily in the fine garden he'd created to the right of the house. Charlotte was sitting on a small bench in the front yard to the left, with Will on the ground beneath her playing with some sort of a contraption that I took to be a toy.

She jumped up when she saw us and reached down to pull Will to his feet. When Anne and I were close enough, we exchanged curtseys and Will gave us a formal bow before plopping himself down again. As there was room enough, just, on the bench, we sat on either side of her, and Will resumed amusing himself with his contraption.

I looked at Charlotte and she ran her fingers across my cheek. It was as if she'd pulled a trigger and hard as I tried, I began to blubber till she pulled my head to her shoulder and ran her hand along my upper back, rubbing it gently. I could not see, but I sensed that Anne had risen and reached for Will's hand to take him for a bit of exploring.

The five of us, with Mr. Collins, walked to Rosings after I'd recovered and had the briefest but most rewarding conversation with Charlotte. I, as his newest aunt, held Will's left hand while Charlotte grasped his right, mixing walking and swinging on the way up the slight hill to the rear of the house. There, several blankets were spread about, and a series of tables were covered with all manner of sandwiches and fruits and Margaret and Molly from those years ago and Meadows—he was still Anne's trusted servant in Kent—catered to whatever we wanted to eat or drink as we organised ourselves.

As it happened, Mr. Collins found his way between me and Anne, with Charlotte on the other side of me. For his part, Will was grabbing things and running with them and even Mr. Collins resisted the temptation of correcting the boy on his...being a boy.

The sun was quite high by then and just as I began to wonder about Elizabeth, there she was!, standing at the doors that opened out to the small patio that was slightly above the lawn.

I could not have prepared for this either as when I saw her how awkwardly I got up to run to her and again I held a true friend. The mere touching triggered my tears, though I had not so many given how many I'd spent earlier doing much the same in Charlotte's embrace.

The others made as if they didn't see us, but I didn't care. It had been so long and I so loved Elizabeth and I so missed her and...

It wasn't long before she'd gently gotten me to calm, and we joined the others but only briefly as Elizabeth said she needed to recover from the trip.

"I must tell you, dear Anne," she said, "that your coach and your horses and your men are quite efficient and rapid in their transporting or I should still be miles away from you and I wouldn't have that for the world."

"Nor would I. Or Catherine. Which is why they were sent to collect you. But now please compose yourself and take a nap if you wish and we will not disturb you until you are fully refreshed."

She directed the housekeeper and her maid to show Elizabeth to her room and where she might recover. The rest of us resumed our conversation and thoughts insofar as we could after the delightful interruption.

I may seem calm in reciting these events, but I assure you that I was anything but. It all happened so very, very quickly yet I had thought about each of these meetings a thousand, thousand times.

While I know there were long periods when none of the others gave the slightest thought to Catherine Bennet or Kitty Bennet or whatever I was to them, over time one after the other remembered me. Maybe even thought my absence was somehow a wrong that needed to be corrected. I cannot say but while with each of these reunions our emotions were deep, our ideas were well thought out.

So, having spent some time alone with Elizabeth after we'd eaten dinner that first night, I retired to my room. The Collinses were gone, and Anne had vanished to attend to some Estate business. And I could savour another night of the sort of rest that I long doubted I would ever again enjoy.

Chapter 14. Finally with Elizabeth

"Things were very difficult after Lydia's death."

Lizzy and I were sitting in the gazebo off to the side of the house where the two of us, plus Anne, had conversed years before.

"Anne told me. What became of the child?"

"We thought there might be a chance that Jane would be able to care for Baby Lydia, but Denny insisted that as he was the father, and no one doubted that he was," which cut me in a way I don't think Lizzy anticipated, "he took her away and we've heard nothing about her since."

"Is anything known about Denny?" I asked.

"Only that he was the one who brought Wickham into the militia, as you remember."

"Indeed. Well, if he is taking responsibility for the girl, I suppose we must be grateful. I've had more than enough in dealing with fathers who will have nothing to do with their child."

"Anne has told me. And something about Georgiana?"

"On that, I believe I may tell you somewhat in confidence, I saw her when I was in Exeter. She has proven a superior woman and has been the source of much inspiration for the development of the charity. How has she been affected by all this?"

"I've seen her only occasionally, when she is in town while Parliament sits."

"She was going there when she stopped in Devon for the wedding of Colonel Fitzwilliam to in fact a cousin of Anne's of whom I was very fond."

"Oh, I long to see the Colonel again. But I suppose he is committed now to living in Devon with his bride."

"He thought of coming to town but decided he enjoyed what he was doing and with whom, so he remained to take charge of the charity there, which allowed me to come back. But what of Georgiana? Surely, she was the most exposed to…scandal."

"Indeed, though you must accept that as with me, much of her concerns about having any communications with you derived from her interest in protecting her husband, as mine was."

"Lizzy. I always understood that."

"I did suffer from my distance, I promise you."

"Lizzy." Her façade was softening, and her eyes misted slightly, which I had never before witnessed. "You must always know that I always knew why you did—"

"Or did *not* do."

"Let us leave it, please. I knew why and none of it was your fault. As with everyone, I must move forward, and think forward and I must know where we are going. You. Me. Darcy and Bingley. Jane. Mamma and papa."

"Are you satisfied with Charlotte then?"

"I spent a difficult morning with her but I'm more satisfied with her than I have any right to be. And I must tell you that I feel more satisfied with you than I have any right to be."

But details, details, I told her. I must know what has been happening for good or bad with my family. I don't know when I'd last said it, though I'd long thought it. *My family.*

We rose to take a walk along one of the paths that we'd both come to enjoy. She and Darcy as well as Jane and Bingley had adjusted well to their changed financial circumstances. Apart from the sense that he had disappointed Little Fitz, Darcy was doing well, and their little boy was doing even better.

"He expects that we will be able to return to Pemberley in the not-too-distant future and even that Bingley will buy his own estate not so far away," she said.

We were holding hands at this point, though I cannot say when we began or who grabbed whose, and our arms were swinging in the clean air.

"And our mamma and papa?" I asked.

"I somewhat regret," she said, "that all of this, with you and with Lydia and with Georgie, has caused them each to be more like themselves than they had been."

"I don't understand."

We had come upon one of those benches that had been conveniently placed around Rosings Park and Elizabeth had me sit with her.

"Our mother is I understand much cloistered with her sister, and I believe they feed on each other's weaknesses. She is, according to our father, much as she always was, very happy at times for Jane and her husband and perhaps less so for me and my husband"—this was said with her particular smile—"but so misses Lydia that she sometimes keeps to her room for one or two days at a time."

That I had been in part responsible for this all must have appeared on my face because Lizzy put her hand across my cheek and that, I think, was the only reason I did not burst into tears at the thought of it.

"Our father," she said to brighten things, "was for a time also cloistered in his study but, and this will shock you, he found the existence of my husband a most revitalizing event."

This was something I could not possibly have imagined. She explained that on one of the Darcys' visits to Longbourn after Lydia died, our father mentioned a tract that he had read about in a paper. Low and behold, not a week later that tract itself appeared and with it was a letter from Darcy himself.

"As our father tells it, he was much surprised and pleased by what Darcy said, much as he disagreed with certain parts. There ensued a regular correspondence between the two on matters far outside our little worlds.

"We are sure to have a number of volumes with us when we visit, and we never leave without three or four that our father recommends to my Fitzwilliam. Plus one or two he sets aside for the education of Little Fitz as well."

Lizzy's thoughts on this delighted me, though I was not the least part of it. But she'd only told me about them. We resumed our walk, and after a pause I got the courage to ask, "And what about me? What is their view about me?"

Her hand tightened its grip.

"I'm afraid we don't speak of you often when we are with them. We do not know what its effect will be, especially with our mother and what happened with Lydia."

I pulled my hand away and looked down.

"Our father has told me," she said, "when I've been with him and in some of our own correspondence, that he is more happy about what you have become—as I and Jane have told him—than what you may have done. 'I should not have allowed her to go with Lydia up to Newcastle as I should not have allowed Lydia herself to go to Brighton,' he has said. I think he realises that there is nothing more to be done about it. 'What's done is done' he has said."

This reminded me that he relented (after Lizzy and Jane were gone) to the pleas I made, with the help of my mother, that I be allowed to go to my younger sister. More than anything, I think he was tired of being hounded and was resigned that I was beyond the point of redemption and so I was allowed to go. I again hated the many moments of torment he felt yet again for bending to the will of what was then a silly daughter and an overindulgent mother.

Lizzy took a deep breath and directed me again to the sort of bench that appeared along the path, and we sat.

"It is a horrible thing to say, I know," she began after a long pause, "but I think what happened to Lydia has softened them both as to you. Particularly after they learnt that Jane and I were somewhat reconciled with you."

"How did they learn that?"

"It could not be avoided, and I think that neither Jane nor I wanted to do so. It was at our first visit to Longbourn after Anne told us that you were safe, though we did not know where you were."

She said that when she gave them this news, "they came to realise that you did something in your youth that was very stupid and that you had paid dearly for it." And after they lost Lydia, they did not wish to lose another daughter.

With that, she was again up. I followed. Just as we were reaching the house, she stopped and turned herself and me so we faced each other.

"I cannot promise what they will say when they see you, as I know they will. Our father actually comes to London now, and Darcy sits with him, and they sometimes go to a lecture given by one Royal Society or another. It is quite an amazing thing and for you I say this because if you wish, we can wait for his next visit to have you meet him, although our mother does not come in so often, not being as favoured by her brother as by her sister in Meryton."

I thought. This later point resolved the matter. I told her that it was for me to venture north to Longbourn, to their home, to meet with them both. And she agreed that she thought that was best. When I would take that journey, though, remained to be seen.

I did not have long to appreciate what Lizzy said about me returning to my family since it was plainly brought to my attention in a most round-about way, and very soon after we'd had our walk.

Lizzy—who I took to calling "Elizabeth" more and more as I was influenced by Anne—and who at some point I did not immediately recognise took to calling me "Catherine," went with us the next morning as we walked to the church to hear the much-anticipated sermon of the Rev. William Collins, Sr.

Some in the parish stood when Anne entered, though she'd made it clear that it was something of an embarrassment to her. We—Anne, Elizabeth, Charlotte, and me, with Will between his "newest" aunt and his mother—sat in the front pew and stood when Mr. Collins appeared.

"My friends in Christ," he began his sermon after a reading from Luke, Chapter 15. The "Prodigal Son." He lifted a piece of paper and placed his spectacles on his nose and read.

> *"[W]hen this son of yours came, who has devoured your property with prostitutes, you killed the fattened calf for him!" And he said to him, "Son, you are always with me, and all that is mine is yours. It was fitting to celebrate and be glad, for this your brother* was *dead, and* is *alive; he was lost, and is found."*

Mr. Collins put his glasses and the paper on the lectern. "My friends in Christ," he repeated. "Are any of us not at times the whoring brother"—the word got the attention of those whose thoughts were wandering to what they would have for their dinner—"thinking or even *doing* things for which we must beg forgiveness. In the prodigal's case, to his father and, I hope, his brother. And to God."

I'd not heard Mr. Collins sermonise for many years and he seemed energized by his words. About love and sin and forgiveness and I wondered the extent to which he himself would be able to live by this principle on which so much of my own happiness depended.

On that day, at least, he welcomed me as he stood watch over his flock as they left his church, genuinely pleased, I thought, to greet each one and add a word of comfort to those of them who needed it and, most important, introducing me as "a great friend to my dear wife and to Will" who was standing beside Charlotte, rocking side-to-side and doing some sort of dance one does when forced to stand on a line with one's doting parents.

And in celebration, some time after we'd left them, the Collinses appeared in the backyard of the Hall, though this time chairs and a table for sitting and eating were set up. It was a fine meal marred only by the sudden approach of a storm that saw us flee with an abundance of laughter into the house itself, where we found an array of sweets and cakes.

Chapter 15. Return to Russell Square

Much as I wished to remain at Rosings, not only was I all in turmoil but I understood—though Charlotte said not a word—that my extended presence would become uncomfortable and could upset the world in which she and Mr. Collins were raising Will.

More, though, was that I had not left Exeter to lounge in a country house. Even exploring my writing there could take only so much time. Had I only known Meryton, it might have been tolerable. But I knew Exeter and even more I'd had a taste of London.

There was also work. Actual, valuable work, to be done with the charity. Though I offered to take up residence again in Islington, Anne insisted that I stay with her. I do not know if she was being polite in that insistence but, frankly, over the short period of my return after the long period of my absence, I realised how much I'd come to enjoy simply being with her and while it may have been very inappropriate and perhaps very wrong I believed she felt much the same about me.

Whether our sentiments were the same and whether they in any case would stand the test of time remained to be seen (though I can tell you now that they were and that they have). At the time, though, it was agreed that I was to return to my room with Margaret as my maid on Russell Square with its comforts and view out over our rear garden and that of the house one block to the east.

So after two de Bourgh carriages were loaded, the first of them carrying Anne, Elizabeth, and me, rolled up to the Parsonage where we exchanged farewells with the Collinses and I gave Will an extra tight aunt's hug and after too few minutes we were headed to Hunsford with the other carriage carrying Margaret and several other servants following us to London, which we reached in the early afternoon.

As we rode back to town, I realised I'd not asked about Mary, and no one had volunteered about her. But Elizabeth told me that there were only sporadic communications from her and that she had in fact had a child, a baby boy, while I was away. As we rode, Anne sat close to the side and looked out the window to afford us such privacy as could be possible in such close conditions.

"I think she felt compelled to share that bit of news with us but otherwise she did not write at all after a flurry of Biblical tracts on the lot of us being cast out for having tolerated what happened between you and Wickham."

"I imagine her view, and that of her parson of a husband, of the Bible varies markedly from that Mr. Collins."

"Thank God for that," she said with a slight squeeze of my hand. And I echoed, "Indeed, thank God for that."

I was left with sadness. Not only about how Mary had further separated herself from her old family as she built her new one. She would have sent letters to our mother that would by design or otherwise have deepened the hurt felt about the loss of poor, naïve Lydia and the loss of the baby.

"We had some hopes," Elizabeth said, "that Lydia's little girl would remain with us—particularly with Jane—with Denny living not too far away. But his mother was quite adamant. She insisted that Lydia go with her and that Denny go as well to somewhere in Yorkshire."

"So I shan't meet her?"

"I'm afraid unless they come to town, you will not."

"And what of Georgie?"

"On that, at least, we are secure. He is with us—again mostly with Jane, bless her—and I hope he does not overwhelm you as to Will."

I thought that but only for a moment. No one could ever replace or be a substitute for Will to me and instead I was excited at the prospect of seeing the two of them meet now and then and becoming the greatest of friends.

I had so wanted to become acquainted with baby Lydia, and I did not know whether that would now ever come to pass. But Georgie. To Elizabeth's news, I said, "I remember how we thought Little Georgie and Will would grow to be the best of friends."

"Like Darcy and Bingley?"

"Well," I quickly said, "I did not at the time think of them as being quite so old. But in the end, yes, like Darcy and Bingley. They will meet, and I hope Will learns of his aunt and his, I guess, some kind of brother—now that the secret is out, and we will have to decide when he is to be told it. But I think he will have to be told someday. I hope they have enough common blood to be true friends and not so much as to make them like Cain and Abel."

At this point, we were approaching the outskirts of town and our carriage had joined any number of others heading in our direction and I was reacquainting myself with the view. Elizabeth reached for my hand, and I gave it to her.

"I assure you from what I have seen in my visits to the Parsonage that Will has the temperament of Abel and I think that with the care Jane will provide, so will Georgie."

"We must hope that."

"Only time will tell, my dear," Elizabeth finished as we neared Russell Square. "Only time will tell."

* * * *

TO BE DONE WITH IT, the Darcys and the Bingleys came to the house for dinner that evening. I was most surprised by my reception with Jane, of all people. Darcy was his usual stiff self but I'm certain that Elizabeth had spoken to him about how he comported himself with me, however at variance it was with how he felt. I appreciated it. I knew him to be a man who often carried what he felt on every inch of his body, and I wondered whether I could ever recover—as I had with his wife—such opinion of me as he thought was good.

Charles Bingley was, as expected, Charles Bingley. I knew him more by reputation than anything beyond our slight encounters at Longbourn, but his showed himself to be a sweet, well-tempered sort of man and the perfect husband to Jane.

It was as if everything was diverted, though, as to my sisters. Elizabeth, as we have seen, was my greatest support from the moment Lydia and I rode up to town after Wickham's death. Even when she could not have any connection with me, I *knew* she felt for me.

Jane, on the other hand, remained distant. I cannot say whether it was me or caused by her anxiousness about her soon becoming a mother, and she knew that I, too, was one. But she could not get her disapproval from herself, the way Darcy had. Her greeting, after all these years, was cordial and no more. She drifted from me at the slightest opportunity, and I caught her glancing over at me once or twice when she was across the room before we sat down to eat.

Chapter 16. To Longbourn

Anne was a famous walker. I assume it began as a way for her to strengthen herself as part of the changes that were upon her with Lady Catherine's death. So from my first stays at Rosings, she often went for long walks while I remained comfortable in my bed and as often as not was already returned by the time I ventured from my room.

This habit continued in London, and she would often tease me when I did come down after I'd breakfasted in my room, though in truth it was not very late at all.

One morning just over a week after we'd settled into Russell Square at a time I did not know with precision but was very very early, she was in my bedchamber. The sun was barely up—this I knew because my windows were open to get some air in the night—and she was sitting on my bed.

She accused me (not for the first time) of being a lazy wench and that it was time for her to do something about it.

"You will be ready within the hour, my dear. We are off on an adventure!" She leaned closer to me. "I will tell you that it has nothing to do with Will I'm afraid and I will tell you no more," and while this calmed some of my excitement it left me further in a mystery.

When she stood and stepped away from my bed, Margaret was immediately in carrying a tray with my normal breakfast things and when that was placed on a table by the windows, the two left and closed the door behind them.

When Margaret returned not fifteen minutes later, she told me as she helped me dress that she had no idea what Miss de Bourgh was about.

"I was told very early by Mrs. Hall"—Mrs. Hall being the housekeeper—"that you was to get up for a trip with the mistress and that I was to know no more than that and I do know no more than that, miss."

I was able to get myself presentable and just as the large clock in the front foyer struck the hour—Eight!—I was there.

There I met Anne, who was pacing back and forth and calling me a slothful creature as I went down the stairs to her. Taylor stood at the door, and when Anne gave him a nod, he opened it.

"I will tell you when I will tell you," she said as we walked to the waiting chaise, her arm through mine. It looked to be a pleasant day, and the top was down. We sat beside each other and soon we were off. It was not long before we pulled up to No. 19, Mount Row. We remained in the chaise but not for long as even before Anne's footman had reached the door to announce our appearance, Jane (a very large Jane it must be said) and Lizzy were through it and in a moment sitting across from Anne and me—as hostess Anne made sure she and I were facing the rear— and in barely another moment the four of us were on our way.

There was some initial traffic, chiefly of various carriages and wagons doing their work and the occasional horseman. We were soon clear of it, and I saw we were heading north.

"I spoke to Elizabeth about it," Anne said as we entered the country, and I began to see where we might be headed. "It is time, we agree, that you see if you can become reacquainted with your dear parents. It may come to nothing, but we must at least try."

I had long thought of this since that long walk I'd had with Lizzy at Rosings. And now the three conspirators had decided for me. I was to be reunited with my parents.

It was nearing midday as the very familiar outskirts of Meryton were reached. At some point, I think I dozed off, leaning as I was against Anne with her arm around me and my head on her shoulder. She was some inches shorter than me, but we'd become accustomed to being like this and we easily melded together in a carriage, and I cannot say whether Jane or Lizzy thought anything about it.

Finally, we rolled down the drive to the house itself.

Shortly after we were seating in the front parlour, my aunt— Mrs. Philips—came rushing through the door and was in the room without being announced.

"I heard of the chaise..." she began before seeing the stranger—to her—who had been sitting beside me—a virtual stranger after all these years—on the sofa but now stood with me.

"Aunt," I began, but she quickly interrupted me and before I knew she was upon me, pleasantly surprised I think that I was again at Longbourn and throwing any distaste she might have had for what I had done to the side in her enthusiasm.

Once she was recovered and had taken a step or two from us, I resumed. "Aunt Philips, may I present Miss Anne de Bourgh," I said, and the two women curtseyed to one another stiffly. My aunt looked to my mother, who nodded, and we all sat at my father's direction, while we spent some awkward minutes in which Anne was introduced as Darcy's cousin and Lady Catherine's daughter. Both of these tidbits drew my aunt's attention, though the latter perhaps more so as she turned to my mother and began asking "Wasn't she—?" before my mamma's glare stopped her, though I was sure an answer would be forthcoming when they were alone.

That was not long in coming, in fact, as my dear papa said he had some objects that might be of interest to Anne, and with that she and I followed him into his library while Jane and Lizzy said they'd like to take some air in our garden after the strangling atmosphere in London.

"We can have peace and quiet here," he said as he arranged his chairs in a manner that would allow Anne and I to sit beside each other with a view out to the small wood to the east while he sat across from us.

"I must say Kit...Catherine that your appearance takes me quite by surprise but, my dear, I am glad of it." He reached towards me, and I took his hand.

"And Miss de Bourgh, of whom I have heard so many pleasant things you would think Lizzy was of a mind to have me adopt you," and he gave a wink, "I am honoured to make your acquaintance."

"Mr. Bennet, Sir, it is quite my pleasure to meet *you* and I will tell you that as between Catherine and Elizabeth and Jane I do feel that I am already a member of the Bennet family!"

I don't know that I'd ever heard her speak so but I was gratified most extremely by the respect she was clearly, and I thought honestly, displaying and I do believe that my father was in part taken aback by it.

"Well, Miss de Bourgh, we can forego further such accolades to one another I think and become friends. Though I cannot resist advising you that I am well aware thanks to my Lizzy in particular of how important your efforts on Catherine's behalf have been for her."

And he stood but held his hand to us to have us remain sitting.

"I have come to like your cousin quite well, Miss de Bourgh." He stepped to his desk and lifted a stack of letters. "You see, Mr. Darcy and I have entered into a chain of correspondence."

He proceeded to tell Anne what Lizzy told me and seemed quite pleased with himself and his son-in-law. And to me, he too seemed much changed for the better and far, far less bitter and...lonely than he was when I'd last seen him.

"Well," he said to Anne when we all began to leave after seeing Jane and Lizzy returning from their turn about Longbourn's garden, "my opinion as to politics is very often quite at variance with your cousin's but I doubt I could long survive within the four walls of this library, much as I enjoy it, without his letters and the Whig pamphlets he seems to believe, quite mistakenly I assure you, will improve my understanding of the true state of the world's affairs."

He smiled. "In this, I must say that he takes on certain characteristics of my Lizzy, but you must never tell either of them that I said such a thing."

And we promised that we would never breach his confidence and he appeared to accept us at our word.

We did not wish to impose so were determined to return to town that very afternoon. We also did not wish to aggravate the situation and the thoughts of the neighbours too much so with fond goodbyes and assurances that we would return and, most importantly, a heart-felt wish from both my parents that we do, we were off and arrived back at Russell Square after dropping our guests on Mount Row shortly before night fell. Though I leant against Anne as I had on the way down to Longbourn, this time I was awake the entire way, alone with my thoughts and with my friends.

* * * *

YOU WILL, I AM CERTAIN, wonder about Mary beyond what Lizzy told me. I found myself thinking of her often. Far more than I ever had, now that I'd discovered that she had a baby boy. I knew her attitude about what I had done from what she'd said about Lydia—who of course had done far less than I did. Mary had, after all, said something like the "loss of virtue in a female is irretrievable" and that a reputation lost could never be reclaimed. But though my virtue I was ready to admit was lost, I felt that in some ways I could again retrieve it, if only Mary read the Gospels as Mr. Collins had.

So, I wrote a letter seeking to renew our sisterly acquaintance. I had little hope but I will tell you that while it took quite a lot of time and perhaps parts of her heart opening with her own baby boy that she wrote a similarly brief note to me praying that I had reformed myself and that I would in the future be more guarded in my behaviour towards the undeserving of the other sex.

It was hardly the reaction I got from my other sisters—save, of course, from my dearest Lydia who was forever beyond me— but it was far more satisfactory than I had reason to expect. This was a sentiment that Jane and Elizabeth agreed with when I showed them Mary's letter.

Chapter 17. Home

For most of my life, while I well knew the Philipses in nearby Meryton, I barely knew my mother's brother and his wife, the Gardiners. Jane was closest to them since she spent time with them in London and she was the particular favourite "aunt"—though truly a cousin—to the four Gardiner children (and especially the two oldest, the girls).

And Elizabeth spent much time with them on that fateful trip where she happened to stop at Pemberley confident that Darcy was not there, a scheme ruined when he suddenly (and perhaps magically) appeared. While Darcy quite charmed the Gardiners on that trip and I believe since, I had few dealings with them when I was, well, "Kitty."

Yet the letter sent to me by my dear aunt while I was in Exeter was one of the great treasures from my exile. Indeed, in several of my letters to Anne, I included something short to be forwarded to the Gardiners and I sometimes received a similarly short note from Mrs. Gardiner. She did not know where I was, but the communications with her in light of the want of communication otherwise with my family were of immeasurable value to me.

So, I was quite pleased when, a day or two after we returned from our trip to Longbourn, my aunt and uncle were announced at Anne's. Of course, I rushed to see them, and Anne and I sat with them as we enjoyed early afternoon refreshments in the sitting room.

It was a very pleasant conversation and afterward I fulfilled my promise to visit their very tidy house in Cheapside and found myself pleased to be reintroduced to their children, who were quite taller than when I'd last seen them years before.

It was made clear on both occasions that I was always welcome to visit them as I reciprocated with my desire that they visit me, an extension of hospitality that Anne readily endorsed.

So, there we were. The group of us, Darcys and Bingleys and Gardiners and Anne de Bourgh and Catherine Bennet, exchanging visits in London and, in due course, spending weeks at Rosings.

Most importantly, only a month after I returned, the next Bingley—Lydia Jane Bingley—entered the world, pink and healthy and very loud. Jane in particular thought it an appropriate tribute to our youngest sister, however flawed she was.

And for a period, her Bingley aunts Louisa and Caroline shared her early days with the rest of us. Sadly, those aunts soon tired of the attention bestowed on the infant and recovered themselves at the Hurst house on Grosvenor Square.

For Darcy, he was perhaps too optimistic about being able to pay off his (financial) debt to Anne. The crops faltered for one year. It would be several more before he was out from under what had been done to him by that Stewart fellow. He still took the long journey up to Derbyshire with Bingley several times a year, while they left their wives and children at the Mount Row house. And the four of us—my sisters and Anne with me—got along as if we were five years younger and still at Longbourn though I will say for myself that I was quite a different woman than I had been a girl.

What's more, Darcy himself began to appreciate the convenience of Rosings, without the strains he could not escape whenever he was at Pemberley. Yes, he always hid it. That was part of who he was. But for all his protests about anticipating when he could finally return to his estate and not rely on the substantial rent he received for it—the original tenant having remained there on a year-to-year basis with, as Bingley sometimes teased Darcy, "the most amazing obsequiousness to my friend here."

While I of course rarely missed the opportunity to go to Rosings, in my time away I became, as I have said, uncomfortable living the life of leisure. To be sure, I never truly had. I was just a girl at Longbourn and Meryton and when I got to Newcastle, I was merely an appendage of Lydia in a small part on the very outskirts of the city with none of the comforts I would come to enjoy after tragedy led us to London.

Yet even in the brief period when Lydia and I were in Mayfair with the Bingleys, I could not then enjoy the comforts of their house given the weight of what would become my Will. It was not until he was settled with the Collinses that I could. Indeed, I enjoyed my time with Anne at Rosings and on Russell Square.

Then my long period of exile. But it was then, building on what I did for the charity in Islington, that gave me the strength and ultimately the desire to do something of use to someone other than myself (or Will).

Of my sisters (who remain), I think Elizabeth is the most like that, but she is well married and has a child to whom she is devoted. Jane is content being Mrs. Charles Bingley in the house in London, cramped as it may be for the time, and delightfully busy with her own Lydia Jane as well as Georgie Wickham, and the arrival of her own child I think freed her from some of the uncharacteristic animosity I felt from her when I first came from Exeter.

Bingley himself has waffled on his desire to have his own estate. After giving up the lease on Netherfield, he planned on acquiring something in Derbyshire, not too distant from Pemberley. That idea, however, waned when he and Jane could spend the season as friends, never quite guests, of the Darcys and he sometimes thought, Elizabeth told me, of leaving the honour of establishing a family seat to his son (or perhaps to Lydia Jane's husband, whoever that might turn out to be).

"I am quite pleased with living off the generosity of my finest friend," Elizabeth said he told her in half-seriousness more than once. Which of course all changed with Darcy's financial catastrophe. But now, as he was already liquid and Darcy had the realistic expectation that he too would be in some years, and having enjoyed the hospitality of Kent with its nearness to town may have given thought to obtaining some realty not so far from Rosings.

And we were proud of our creation, the Lady Catherine House in Exeter. That was now in the most capable hands of Colonel and Mrs. Fitzwilliam and my dear Teresa. That success begat a decision to expand the charity, and Anne and I decided that Derby was the place to do it. With the happy assistance of Darcy and Bingley, though I am led to understand that while they were up north, they found time and the leave of Pemberley's tenant to ride and hunt and fish on the trails and skies and ponds so loved and familiar to my brothers-in-law.

All this real estate was in the end of little interest to me excepting to the extent it would affect my ability to see my sisters and their children (perhaps someday including Mary and her family) for I was tethered to Rosings and with it to the opportunity to see and spoil Will, as is his aunt's prerogative, and as I'd become even more firmly tethered to my dearest Anne de Bourgh.

THE END

The Omen at Rosings Park

After completing this, I decided to take a stab at a purer "variation." In The Omen at Rosings Park: How Elizabeth Became Mrs. Darcy, I began with the premise that Elizabeth did, in fact, accept Mr. Collins's offer, a decision she in time comes to regret. As Darcy comes to regret his own failure to offer Elizabeth Bennet any encouragement.

The novella's ebook is available exclusively on Amazon and is enrolled in Kindle Unlimited. By coincidence, Thomas Sully, the American artist of the cover of *Becoming*, is also the artist for the cover of *The Omen*.

Acknowledgments

Melissa Anne Barbato, who contacted me on Facebook and read a draft, came up with some very good suggestions and pointed out a hole in the latter stages that I hope I fixed.

Three folks with whom I work on the monthly *A Muse Bouche Review*, Louise Sorensen, Marian L Thorpe, and Renée Gendron, gave me excellent comments. As did the ever-helpful Newfie Cassandra Filice.

Lacy Phillips took a look at the first chapters in a very rough form and endorsed my idea of building it into a *Pride and Prejudice* sequel. That was thanks to a workshop arranged by editor and literary-journal publisher Jamie Dill.

Also, I made some changes in this in light of some criticisms of the original version, in particular concerning the fate of Georgie Wickham.

The Author

Joseph P. Garland has written numerous stories and several novels. This is his first venture into the world of Jane Austen. He has published three novels set in the early years of the Gilded Age in New York and a contemporary novel set chiefly in New York. He is a New York lawyer.

His books can be found at:

DermodyHouse.com/books

Jane Austen Fan Fiction

The Omen at Rosings Park: How Elizabeth Became Mrs. Darcy
The Diary of Elizabeth Elliot: A Persuasion Sequel

Gilded Age

Róisín Campbell: An Irishwoman in New York
A Studio on Bleecker Street
A Maid's Life

Contemporary

I Am Alex Locus: My Search for the Truth